THE SHAPE OF
DREAD

For Pam and Terry —
McCone's latest
case —

Marcia Muller
4/26/90

THE SHAPE OF

DREAD

MARCIA MULLER

THE MYSTERIOUS PRESS

New York • London
Tokyo • Sweden • Milan

The Mysterious Press, 129 West 56th Street, New York, N.Y. 10019

Printed in the United States of America
First Printing: December 1989
10 9 8 7 6 5 4 3 2 1

Library of Congress Cataloging in Publication Data

Muller, Marcia.
  The shape of dread / Marcia Muller.
    p. cm.
  ISBN 0-89296-271-2
  I. Title.
  PS3563.U397S54   1989   89-42606
  813'.54—dc20   CIP

For Bill

1

San Quentin Prison stands on a windswept headland on San Francisco Bay. At first sight it does not look like such a bad place: its sandstone-colored walls and red roof are architecturally imposing. The cypress-fringed hill that abuts them and the row of sturdy palms along the shoreline lend the natural setting a certain charm. The waters of the bay are azure or green or steel gray, depending on the weather, dotted with sailboats and the sleek ferries that ply their way from Marin County's Larkspur Landing to San Francisco. Not such a bad place at all.

But as you approach the prison's iron gates down a narrow lane lined mostly with ramshackle houses, you hear the rumble of loudspeakers in the yard and the monotonous hum of the generators that keep the huge physical plant functioning. You see the guard tower and floodlights and warning signs, and the weary hopelessness in the eyes of the people who trickle through the visitors' entrance. The wind feels colder; it carries the stench of stagnant water and an indefinable decay.

Then you notice that elsewhere on the promontory no healthy vegetation grows, as if even trees and shrubs are wary of venturing too near the grim ediface. You realize how far removed Point San Quentin is from the posh newness of Larkspur Landing, the million-dollar homes of nearby Tiburon and Belvedere, the majesty of the redwoods and Mount Tamalpais. In spirit, this place shares more with Richmond, the city that lies across a graceless span of bridge to the northeast—a troubled community blighted by slums, populated largely by struggling blacks from whose ranks many of those housed behind the prison walls have come.

And on a darkly overcast winter morning, such as the one in late December when I first visited there, you are almost certain to

1

remind yourself that this is a place of misery, where human beings are often sent to die.

I'd left the city early that Thursday morning, hoping to be at the prison at eight-thirty, but traffic was slowed by an accident in one of the northbound lanes on the Golden Gate Bridge, and it was nine-fifteen when I presented my identification and signed the east gate log. I passed through the metal detector at the security checkpoint, where an officer inspected the contents of my briefcase and shoulder bag. Then I sat down as directed on a bench in the visiting area.

It was early enough that there were few people in the area; most of them I judged to be either attorneys or investigators like myself, there to confer with inmates in private. I waited for close to an hour before approval came down, even though my name had supposedly been added to the list of visitors authorized by the prisoner's attorney. The desk officer entered my tape recorder in his log of recording and photographic equipment, and then I was led to one of the segregated visiting rooms for inmates of the adjustment center and death row.

After the guard locked me in, I looked around the room for a moment. It was institutional tan, divided down the center by a wall-to-wall table. A heavy grille extended from the table to the ceiling. Had I possessed tendencies to claustrophobia, my surroundings would probably have prompted me to pound on the door and demand to be let out. As it was, I felt curiously suspended, as if time had stopped and wasn't going to start up again until some distant and unknown power said it could. Finally I crossed to the table, set my briefcase on it, and sat in one of three wooden chairs.

It was another ten minutes before the door on the other side of the grille opened and a young black man in blue prison work clothes was admitted. He was slender, of medium height, with a complexion the shade of cinnamon. In spite of his age, which I knew to be twenty, his hairline was receding; the short black curls formed an M on his high forehead. Beneath it, his eyes were heavy lidded and unreadable, his nose long and broad, his mouth set tight. When the door locked behind him, he glanced back at it and balled his fists reflexively.

I'd viewed a videotape of his confession the night before, but in person he looked different. Smaller and more vulnerable. And somehow incapable of perpetrating the vicious crime he'd admitted to on the tape.

As I studied him, I thought—not for the first time—that it was possible he'd been railroaded by a criminal justice system that is not exactly blind when a poorly educated young black with a juvenile record is brought to trial on sensational charges. A victim of that system, or a cold-blooded killer? For the moment I preferred to reserve judgment.

"Mr. Foster," I said, "I'm Sharon McCone from All Souls Legal Cooperative. Jack Stuart told you I'd be visiting."

Bobby Foster nodded but didn't move.

"It would be better if you sat down." I gestured at the single chair on his side of the grille. "We have a lot to go over."

This time he made no response of any kind. I waited.

Finally he said, "Don't know what you think you can do for me." His voice was deep—a large man's voice trapped in a smallish man's body.

"I'm not sure if there *is* anything I can do. That's what I'm here to find out."

My admission of uncertainty seemed to relax him; perhaps he liked the fact that I didn't pretend to have all the answers. He moved to the chair and perched on its edge.

"What did Jack Stuart tell you about me, Bobby? It is okay to call you Bobby?"

He shrugged.

"And please call me Sharon."

He regarded me from under those heavy eyelids for a moment, then said, "Stuart, all he tell me is you a private eye for that law firm of his. He say maybe there's something you can do to get me out of this mess."

"You don't seem to believe that."

Another shrug. "Don't see what nobody can do. They try me, send me up here. One of these days they gonna kill me."

"But you claim you didn't do the murder."

"Now *you* the one look like you don't believe *me*."

"I'm not sure what I think yet. A lot of guilty people claim they're innocent. But I haven't heard your side of the story. And Jack Stuart believes you."

He shifted position, leaning back in the chair. "That Stuart, he okay. Better than the PD I had for my trial, maybe."

Bobby's first attorney had been a public defender; after the conviction his mother had raised the money to retain All Souls for the appeals process. "Jack's a good criminal lawyer," I said. "If there's a procedural basis for overturning your conviction, he'll find it. But the PD you had wasn't bad, either. What it boiled down to is that there was a strong case against you."

His eyes narrowed and he leaned forward, arms on the table. "You call that a case? They never even find her body. How the hell you gas a man when you ain't even got a body?"

I knew that both the public defender and Jack had explained to him the legal basis for conviction in a "no-body" case. I also knew that he stubbornly refused to accept the explanation and argued vehemently with them every time the subject came up. What I suspected was that—lacking anything else—he had seized upon the issue as a last hope and wasn't about to turn loose of it. Determined not to let him get off on that overworked tangent, I asked, "What do you think happened to her?"

He shook his head.

"Tracy Kostakos was a friend of yours. You must have some idea about her disappearance."

"If I did, would I be here?"

"Some people think she's still alive. Her own mother, for instance. Laura Kostakos thinks her daughter disappeared of her own free will."

His gaze moved away from mine, to a point beyond my left shoulder. Immediately I felt a prickling at the base of my spine— the kind I often get when I sense someone is withholding something important from me.

I said, "Bobby? What do you think happened to Tracy?"

"Don't know," he replied, still avoiding my eyes. "But she ain't alive. If she was, she'd of heard about me and come back and put things right." He was silent for a moment, then added softly, "Tracy, she dead all right. But I didn't do it to her."

"Why did you confess, then?"

"I took that back later. That just a story."

"A story, Bobby?"

"Yeah."

"It fit the facts pretty closely."

"Facts? Ain't no facts. Ain't even a *body!*"

"*Why* did you confess?"

He clenched his fists, then tipped his head back so he was looking at the ceiling. The cords in his neck grew taut as he struggled for control.

Bobby Foster had a history of losing his temper—and a juvenile record to go with it. But while in the custody of the California Youth Authority, he'd apparently learned to cope with the impulse to violence. Life had been looking up for him—until Tracy Kostakos had disappeared one rainy night nearly two years ago.

After a bit he unclenched his fists and lowered his head. His eyes were intense but free of anger. "You ever really been scared, lady? Scared shitless?"

I had, on numerous occasions, but I sensed he was talking about a different kind of fear. I shook my head.

"Then you don't know. They hammer at me for hours, tell me what I did. They say I flunked the lie detector test I took before. Later my lawyer, he found out that wasn't true; it say I lied about some things but not about killing her. But then I believe them, and it scare me even more. I get tired, mixed up. After a while I start believing everything they tell me. The way it work, it's like you remembering some dream you had. What they tell you, you start seeing it, only you can't really 'cause it just a dream."

"And then?"

"It start getting real. You see it better. But it still be like the picture of an old TV that don't work right. You stop being scared 'cause you so tired. They hammer at you some more and you think maybe if you tell them the dream they go away. Doesn't matter, it just a dream—right? So you tell them. Then you find out it ain't no dream—it's a fucking nightmare."

I leaned back in my chair, trying to imagine what he'd told me. I could, and yet I couldn't. But it fit with certain inconsistencies I'd noticed in the trial transcript and the videotape of his confession. Police interrogation methods these days are more civilized than the old back-room tactics, but still capable of producing false admissions of guilt.

After a moment I said, "Tell me about yourself, Bobby."

His face, which had become animated while he was talking about the confession, went blank. "Why?"

"If I'm to try to help you, I need to know something about you."

"What you want to know?"

"Anything you'd care to tell me."

"Ain't nothing *to* tell."

"You grew up in San Francisco, right?"

"Potrero Hill. The projects."

"Went to school there?"

"For a while."

"To what grade?"

"Seventh."

"And then you were in and out of the CYA?"

He nodded.

Even though I already knew, I asked, "What did you do to end up there?"

Silence.

"Bobby?"

"Look, Stuart know all that stuff. Why don't you ask him?"

"I'd rather hear it from you."

He hesitated, regarding me with a mixture of suspicion and hope. "You really think you can help me?"

"I'm going to try."

"How?"

"By turning up new evidence. By finding out if Tracy Kostakos is still alive. And if she's not, I'll try to find out what really happened to her."

"Why you have to know all this stuff about me, then?"

"In my business, I never know what information is going to be important. I want to hear about your life, right up to the minute you walked into this room this morning."

That seemed to satisfy him. He nodded, took a deep breath, and said, "Okay. Where you want me to start?"

"At the point where you quit school and started getting in trouble. But first let me set up my tape recorder." I took it out of my briefcase and placed it on the table. Bobby looked dubiously at it but didn't protest. After I'd tested it, I started the tape and leaned back in my chair.

"All right," I said, "just talk. Don't hurry or leave anything out—I'll come back next week if I have to. You and I have a lot of work to do."

As Bobby began talking, I looked down at my hands. They lay in my lap, palms turned upward, fingers curled. Cupped, as if I were about to hold his life in them.

2

My visit to Bobby Foster was the result of an impromptu picnic I'd gone on with Jack Stuart, our criminal law specialist at All Souls. He'd turned up on my doorstep the previous noon—Wednesday of that last, afterthought week of the year, which serves no earthly purpose except to frustrate those of us who have had enough of the holidays and are anxious to get our lives back to normal.

I'd taken the dead time off in order to launch my campaign (I refused to call it a New Year's resolution) to once and for all have the construction finished on the back porch of my house. I'd begun enclosing it to make a second bedroom the previous summer but had run out of money halfway through. In October I'd refinanced my mortgage and received funds to complete the job, as well as to make a number of other necessary and essentially uninteresting repairs. Then I'd gotten caught up in Christmas shopping and holiday festivities. This week had been reasonably productive, but now I found myself infected with the general lassitude that was going around, and none of the contractors whom I'd had in to give estimates had gotten back to me. When Jack rang the bell, I was wandering around the backyard harboring halfhearted notions of murdering some of the blackberry vines that had taken hold there. If he hadn't shown up, I'd have been wringing my hands in boredom inside of fifteen minutes.

So I was happy to climb into his van and go off to nearby Glen Park. Jack had with him a shopping bag stuffed with French bread and cheese and salami, plus a bottle of reasonably good wine that I recognized as filched from the store laid in by All Souls for the annual New Year's Eve party. I'd brought along some catalogs I'd been meaning to study, and when we arrived at the far end of Glen

7

Canyon, I found an old blanket in the back of the van and sat down by a big tree stump to read, while Jack proceeded to climb the rocks on the canyon wall.

Jack was an avid climber, but unfortunately not a very good one. He'd taken up the hobby by way of sublimating the pain caused by his divorce the year before, but in my opinion he could have done with more psychic pain and fewer physical injuries. In early November he'd suffered three cracked ribs in a fall while climbing at the Pinnacles; he was only now getting back into shape. The dangers here in Glen Canyon, he'd informed me, were only categorized as Zone One—meaning no permanent damage was likely to result from a mishap. That was just as well, since this holiday season was the first he'd spent alone since the divorce, and he was presently sublimating with a vengeance. It made me nervous to watch him, so I kept my eyes focused on the catalog I was paging through.

The catalog was from something called the Educational Swap Meet—a loosely organized coalition of self-styled experts who jointly advertised courses they hoped to offer. For a few weeks now I'd been thinking I really ought to get back into the social swing—I'd been unattached and without much interest in pursuing a relationship for nine months—and, on the precept that Dear Abby is usually right, had decided taking a class would be a good way to Meet People with Similar Interests. Unfortunately what was offered in this particular catalog seemed odd, if not downright perplexing, and I wasn't at all sure I *wanted* to meet people with interests in those areas.

I called to Jack, "How about this one—'Spiritual Gunhandling for Gentle People'?"

Jack grunted loudly. I glanced up. He was dangling in a treacherous-looking fashion near the top of the rock formation, not all that far above. Quickly I returned my eyes to the catalog.

"What it is, is the art of Zen shooting," I said. "You're supposed to make friends with your gun and use it in meditation."

Jack gasped. I turned the page.

"Here's another—'Meeting One's Soul Mate through Visualization and Astrology.' No, wait. This is it—'Getting into Death. Face your own inevitable demise and actually *feel good* about it.'"

There was a thump. Afraid that Jack was facing his demise without benefit of the course, I looked up. He had jumped off the rocks and was brushing dirt from his jeans as he came toward me.

He said, "Why don't you just take another photography course?"

"Because I've had to face the fact I'm lousy at it."

"You'd be lousy at getting into death, too. And meditating with your gun sounds dangerous."

"True." I tossed the catalog—and my hope of meeting my soul mate through exotic means—aside.

Jack went to the van to get the sack with our lunch. I slumped against the tree stump, savoring the crisp day.

It was clear, but the sun's rays had that watery, filtered quality that tells northern Californians the rains are not far off. The canyon was heavily silent. Usually Glen Park—a recreational haven in the south central neighborhood of the same name—teems with the offspring of families who inhabit the nearby cottages and small homes, but today they must have been off enjoying such Christmas-vacation treats as movies and visits to the Exploratorium. The narrow, densely wooded canyon extending north from the playgrounds and tennis courts where we were was especially deserted.

I leaned my head back against the big stump's rough bark and stared up through the silvered, shifting leaves of the surrounding eucalyptus trees. A jay sat in a starburst of light on one of the topmost branches. Beyond him a haze of woodsmoke drifted from the fireplaces of the homes and condominiums on affluent Diamond Heights. Had it not been for the angular outlines of their overhanging balconies and the growl of a bus toiling up O'Shaughnessy Street, I could have imagined I was deep in the wilderness, rather than in one of the nation's major cities.

Jack came back, dropped down onto the blanket, and began pawing through the sack.

I said, "Well, at least you're still alive."

"Those rocks are a piece of cake. As I told you, only Danger Zone One."

"How many zones are there?"

"Three. An error in Two can put you in a wheelchair for good. Before you tackle Zone Three, you check with your life insurance agent to make sure your coverage is in force."

"Hey, what a hobby."

Jack's lean, craggy face broke into a grin. "What can I say—it's fun living on the edge."

"The only way I want to do that is on the edge of the chair while reading a good horror novel."

He began fiddling with a corkscrew. "Fear takes my mind off my troubles."

"This Christmas was a rough one?"

"In some ways. In others, not so bad. At least I wasn't constantly poking holes in somebody else's expectations."

I knew what he meant, having burst quite a few of those shiny holiday bubbles in my own day.

Jack poured the wine into plastic cups and handed one to me. "Here's to better times and new beginnings." When he touched his cup to mine, our fingers grazed.

I sipped and looked away to cover my confusion. For a while now I'd suspected that Jack was interested in me. It was an interest I didn't want to encourage.

The Stuart marriage had not been particularly happy, but it had been a long one. They'd wed while still in law school and stayed together for twenty years, in spite of radically divergent politics and career paths. But a move from Los Angeles to San Francisco and new jobs—hers with a prestigious, conservative downtown firm, his with yet another liberal law cooperative—had widened the chasm. Jack hadn't wanted the divorce, and his misery was compounded when his ex-wife married her boss a week after the final decree.

Even now, close to a year later, his pain was too fresh for him to be able to base a new relationship on anything other than "how things used to be." He would—for better or worse—compare every action of a new woman to those of his former wife. He would expect either more or less than she was actually capable of giving. I liked Jack a lot, could have felt romantically inclined toward him, but I wasn't about to let myself in for that kind of no-win situation. And I sensed that at this juncture all he could handle was a frivolous, casual relationship—the kind I no longer care to indulge in.

In spite of his self-absorption, Jack was not imperceptive. He noticed my discomfort, cut bread and cheese and salami, and changed the direction of the conversation.

"In addition to the pleasure of your company, I had a business reason for asking you along today," he said. "I'd like to discuss a case I need some help on. I've been debating whether it's worth taking up your time, and I've decided it is."

"Tell me about it."

"Do you know what a no-body case is?"

"More or less. As I understand it, it's one in which the victim's body hasn't been found, but there's enough evidence aside from the purely circumstantial to assume that a crime has taken place.

Physical evidence of the death—bloodstains, an eyewitness account, a confession—can prove the corpus delicti."

Jack looked surprised. "You read a lot of criminology?"

"A fair amount. I took a few courses in it when I was at Berkeley; given my work, it's a natural interest."

"The reason I ask is that most people think 'corpus delicti' has something to do with the actual dead body, rather than the body of the crime. Probably because it sounds so much like 'corpse.' I'm having difficulty getting the concept across to my client."

"I wasn't aware you were handling a murder case right now. Who's the defendant?"

"A twenty-year-old black kid named Bobby Foster. Already convicted and sentenced to death. Case was brought to us for appeal."

The name sounded familiar, but I couldn't place it. "Death sentence? That's pretty stringent for a no-body case—and for such a young defendant."

"The murder was committed in the course of a kidnapping. Special circumstances. There's a confession—pretty brutal stuff. The victim came from a prominent family: old money, and both parents are professors at Stanford. She herself was a young comedian whose star was rising fast."

Now I remembered where I'd heard Foster's name. "The Tracy Kostakos case."

"Right."

"Jesus."

The murder had happened nearly two years before, but I remembered it because the newspapers had given it prominence, and the chief investigator, Ben Gallagher, had been something of a friend of mine. The published accounts had intrigued me, and for a while I'd followed the case closely. Now I recalled most of the details, with Jack occasionally refreshing my memory.

Tracy Kostakos had been a very funny, highly talented woman of only twenty-two. The summer before her death she'd stolen the show at the Comedy Celebration Day at the polo fields in Golden Gate Park; for several months she'd been headlining at Jay Larkey's trendy Café Comedie south of Market, where she'd previously worked as a cocktail waitress. On a rainy Thursday night, February twelfth, she disappeared after finishing her nine o'clock show there. While the unexplained overnight absence of most women her age in a city like San Francisco would have been little cause for alarm, Tracy's parents and friends had good reason to think something was amiss: all her life she had been dependable and punctual—almost abnormally so.

From Café Comedie she was supposed to go to an improvisational session at the loft of a friend near India Basin. She'd attended the same sessions with more or less the same group of participants for close to three years and never missed one. Her absence was commented upon.

The improv sessions usually broke up about two in the morning. Tracy always returned immediately to the apartment she shared with a friend, Amy Barbour, on Upper Market Street. That morning she had promised to wake her roommate when she came in for a very special reason: the thirteenth of February was Amy's twenty-first birthday, and the friends planned to share a first legal bottle of celebratory champagne. Tracy, however, didn't come home.

Friday was Tracy's day to travel to Palo Alto for lunch with her mother, Laura Kostakos. But before that she had planned to attend an early call for actors at a casting office on Fillmore Street. The audition was for a TV commerical for Wendy's restaurants, to be shown in test markets in the Midwest. While landing the role didn't guarantee national exposure, it was a step in that direction, and Tracy Kostakos was as interested in the lucrative television market as any other rising—and largely underpaid—comedian. But she never showed at the casting office, and friends who would have been competing against her were both relieved and concerned.

In her office in the mathematics department at Stanford University, Laura Kostakos waited for Tracy's call from the train station. Tracy had assured her she would reach Palo Alto for their standing luncheon date at the usual hour of one-thirty, but when she'd heard nothing by three, Mrs. Kostakos called her husband, George, in his office in the psychology department. He had had no word from Tracy, either. Later Laura Kostakos told reporters that while she wasn't superstitious, she hadn't been able to keep from thinking about it being Friday the thirteenth.

Officially the police could do nothing about Tracy's disappearance until seventy-two hours had passed, but long before that a barely literate, poorly typed ransom note arrived at the Kostakoses's Palo Alto home. A modest ransom note, as such things go: the kidnappers wanted only $250,000.

The FBI was brought in. The Kostakoses got the ransom money together, and agents waited with them for the promised Sunday-evening call from the kidnappers. It never came. No further notes arrived. They never heard from their daughter again.

By the middle of the next week, the investigation focused on Bobby Foster, who was working as a valet parking attendant at Café Comedie. He had been seen by one of the other valets and a pair of patrons arguing with Tracy on the sidewalk in front of the club after her last performance. Bobby had an explanation: Tracy—who disliked driving so much she'd declined her parents' offer of a car of her own—had been nervous about waiting for her bus on a dark corner two blocks away and had asked him to walk over and wait with her. When he'd refused—because Jay Larkey, owner of the club, was notorious for firing valets who didn't tend to their jobs—they'd quarreled. But his story didn't ring true. Tracy reportedly had an ample allowance from her parents and could easily have afforded a cab if she were really uneasy. And besides, according to all who knew her, she was fearless when it came to walking dark city streets alone. It was unlikely she would have asked Bobby to risk his job for such a reason—not when he was such a good friend that she had a standing appointment to tutor him for his high-school-equivalency exams on Wednesday afternoons.

Bobby Foster stuck to his story, stubbornly refusing to get a lawyer, but balked at taking a polygraph test. Eventually he consented, and while he didn't pass with flying colors, the results were inconclusive enough to make the authorities lose interest in him.

By late spring the FBI had withdrawn from active participation in the case; the SFPD's investigation dragged. Then in June the wife of Jay Larkey's partner at Café Comedie—where Foster was no longer employed—came across a notebook he had left behind in the employees' lounge, and turned it over to the police. It was one he had used in his tutoring sessions with Tracy for the equivalency exams; in it were several nude sketches of a woman who resembled her, and a number of misspellings that matched those found in the badly typed ransom note.

The police moved cautiously, questioning Foster again but not holding him.

In late July a dark blue Volvo with bloodstained upholstery turned up in a ravine in the Santa Cruz Mountains, some seventy miles south of San Francisco. Its owner had reported it stolen from Café Comedie's valet parking lot the night of Tracy's disappearance. The employee who had parked it was Bobby Foster; his fingerprints appeared inside it—as did those of Tracy Kostakos. The bloodstains on the front seat matched Tracy's type and subtype.

The police questioned Foster again. At first he claimed he had not parked the Volvo. Then he said he didn't remember that particular car or its driver; he parked so many in the course of an evening. But finally he confessed to kidnapping and murdering Tracy Kostakos.

"You say the confession's grim?" I asked Jack.

He nodded. "I have a video of it. If you're going to help on this, I'd like you to look at it, as well as read the public defender's files and the trial transcript."

"What exactly is it you want me to do? What basis are you appealing on?"

"The usual technicalities. But that part of it doesn't concern you. I want you to work on the murder."

"On a two-year-old case, where there's already been a confession and a conviction? Come on, Jack!"

He ran both hands through his thick gray hair. "I know it sounds insane, Shar, but I don't think the kid's guilty."

"What about this confession?"

"He retracted it before the case went to trial."

"On the advice of his attorney."

"Before he had one. The kid was stupid, refused counsel because he thought having a lawyer would make him look guilty. And you know about false confessions."

I was silent.

Jack asked, "Did you follow the trial?"

"No. Last summer, wasn't it?"

"August. Case took a long time getting to court."

"I was away on vacation then. I never manage to catch up on the newspapers afterwards."

"Well, one of the things that kept coming out at the trial was that some people don't think Tracy Kostakos is dead—including her own mother."

"They think she faked her own kidnapping?"

"Yes. Disappeared voluntarily, using the ransom note as a ploy to throw people off her trail."

"Why would she do such a thing? Did she have reason to disappear?"

"That's one of the things I want you to find out."

"What about the bloodstained car?"

"Another ploy."

"Sounds farfetched."

"Maybe. But Laura Kostakos firmly believes her daughter is still alive—so much so that she pays Tracy's share of the rent for her apartment and keeps her room the way it was, waiting for her return."

"Maybe the woman's gone around the bend."

"Maybe. The Kostakoses separated before the trial."

"You said some *people*. Who else believes this scenario?"

"Jay Larkey, owner of the club she worked at."

Larkey, a man in his fifties, had risen to national television stardom out of the comedy clubs of San Francisco. When his popularity waned, he'd returned to the city and established a club of his own, to give other struggling comedians the same chance he'd had. "Anyone else?"

"Her boyfriend, Marc Emmons."

"That's probably just wishful thinking."

"There's something else, though. The roommate, Amy Barbour. She testified for the prosecution at the trial, but the PD had the impression she wasn't telling all she knew."

I leaned my head back against the tree stump. The eucalyptus leaves shimmered in the pale sunlight. The jay in the top branches had been joined by several others; they screeched harshly—a fitting background chorus for the tragedy we were discussing.

I asked "What does Bobby Foster think happened to Kostakos?"

"If he has any opinion he's keeping it to himself. All he wants to do is argue that they shouldn't have convicted him without a body. I'm hoping you can get beyond that subject with him."

It struck me as an incredible long shot, to pick up on a two-year-old trail that, even when fresh, had led investigators nowhere. And I feared it would be a futile effort; in order to convict in the absence of a body, the case against Foster would have been strong. In spite of the prevailing romantic belief, only a very small number of felons are convicted unjustly. I'd once heard a well-known criminal lawyer claim that 96 percent of his clients were guilty as charged; the other 4 percent, he said, were probably guilty of something.

Still, if Foster was among that 4 percent, he didn't deserve to die. . . .

I sighed. "My week off is almost over. I was getting bored, anyway."

Jack sighed, too—in relief. "Thanks. I appreciate it. After we finish eating, we'll go back to All Souls and I'll turn over the files and that video I mentioned." He paused. I glanced at him, saw his eyes had clouded. "I've got to warn you," he added, "you're not going to like what you hear."

"*I got her out the car, and I drop her there on the edge of that hollow. Then I give her a push, and she roll away down the hill.*"

"*Did you go down there with her? Try to hide the body?*"

The first voice belonged to the young black man with the weary, strained face. The other was Inspector Ben Gallagher's, but I couldn't see him or his partner; the video camera was fixed on Bobby Foster as he made his confession.

"*No, man, I didn't want no part of her no more. She just dead meat to me. Just dead white meat, something to throw away.*"

"*Go on.*"

"*That's it, man. I told you all of it.*"

"*What about the blood? There was a lot of blood in the car. Was there any on you?*"

Foster looked blank momentarily. Confused, I thought.

"*Blood. Yeah. On me, all over me.*"

I got up and switched the VCR off. Foster's face turned into that of a commentator reading the midnight news on the cable channel. It was the second time I'd viewed the tape—more than enough. I shut off the TV too and went to the kitchen for a glass of milk. Comfort food, I thought wryly.

The tape had been grim—stomach-turning in parts. Foster had admitted to kidnapping Kostakos with the intention of holding her in an apartment in the Western Addition until he could collect the ransom from her wealthy parents. He'd offered her a ride to her improv session in a car he'd earlier stolen off the Café Comedie lot, knocked her unconscious, and driven there. But once inside, she'd come to and tried to escape. In the struggle that ensued, he'd stabbed her repeatedly; then he'd raped her lifeless body. Finally he'd loaded it back in the car, driven south to the mountains, and dumped it in a ravine. The details were particularly grisly because of the flat, unemotional manner in which he related them. Still, there was something that didn't quite ring true. Many things . . .

I went back to the living room, curled up on the couch, and studied the legal pad that I'd filled with notes. There were inconsistencies in Foster's confession: he claimed the car he'd stolen was green, rather than blue; that he'd been absent from the club all night, rather than returning shortly before the two-o'clock closing, as his fellow valets had testified; that he'd abandoned the car by the side of the road, rather than in another ravine. From the trial transcript I'd learned that he'd been unable to lead investigators to the place where he'd disposed of the body. The location of the apartment where he'd killed Tracy had never been pinpointed, nor had the "dude who hangs out at the club" who had sublet it to him ever been identified. And there was the question of the quarrel he and Kostakos reportedly had on the sidewalk in front of the club: if he'd merely offered her a ride, why had they fought? Altogether I had several pages of notes on the holes in the case against Foster.

The fingerprints in the car, for instance: if it was one Foster had parked earlier, it would seem natural for his prints to be there. And the fact that he'd never followed up on the ransom demand: he had nothing to lose by doing so. True, there were damning facts in the confession, but he could have gleaned those during the hours of interrogation before the videotaping began. The others—the grim but unverifiable details of what he had done to Kostakos—could have been the product of an overactive imagination. And it bothered me that the chief investigating officer, Ben Gallagher, had seemed to prompt Foster's responses. The suspect had repeatedly employed the phrase "like you say," which led me to believe Gallagher had put quite a few ideas into his head.

Too bad I couldn't ask Ben about that. He'd been shot to death the previous month by a speed freak resisting arrest after murdering his wife and small son.

I yawned and realized my comfort drink had done its magic work. But I couldn't go to bed, not yet. I had to call Jack, who—fortunately—was a night person and would be up for hours yet.

Still, I hesitated, running my eyes over the list that Jack had provided of precedents in no-body cases: *People v. Alviso, People v. Clark, People v. Ward and Fontenot.* . . . Cases tried from 1880 to 1985, in which proof of the corpus delicti had been "legally inferred from such strong and unequivocal circumstances as produce conviction to a moral certainty."

Strong and unequivocal circumstances?

Maybe. Maybe not.

I reached for the phone and punched out All Souls' number. Jack answered; in the background I could hear the mutter of the TV, probably tuned to an old movie.

I said, "Did you get my name added to Foster's list of authorized visitors?"

"Yes, when I went up there this afternoon. I talked to him about you, so he'll know who you are and why you're there."

"Good. I'll go in the morning."

"What did you think of the material I gave you?"

"You were right—the confession's damned brutal. And I didn't like it one bit. But . . ."

"But?"

"There's something about it that makes me want to reserve judgment until after I talk with him."

3

By the time I arrived at All Souls's shabby Bernal Heights Victorian that Thursday after returning from San Quentin, I had put aside the remainder of my reservations about the Foster case and was eager to get to work on it. I seemed to be the only person around there in a working mood, however: no clients waited in the front parlor, and the doors to the offices and law library stood open, the rooms' interiors dark. Ted Smalley, our secretary, sat at his desk, but his computer keyboard was covered, and he was idly perusing one of those tabloids that are trying to outdo the *National Enquirer*.

As I came in, he murmured, "What *will* that madcap Sean Penn do next?"

"Pardon me for interrupting your studies," I said.

Ted raised the paper so I could see the headline: CRAZED KILLER CANNIBAL PLANNED TO COOK NIXON. He knows his passion for sleaze irritates me, so he takes every opportunity to flaunt it. "What can I do for you?" he asked.

"Is either Rae or Jack around?"

"Jack, no. Rae's in the attic."

It was an unlikely place to find my assistant, Rae Kelleher. "What on earth is she doing up there?"

"You'll see." He smiled mysteriously. "You coming to the New Year's Eve party?"

"Yes. I even have a new dress for it."

"So do I."

I looked more closely at him, to see if he was serious.

"Not really," he added. "This is a pretty off-the-wall outfit, but I think most people would frown upon me showing too much décolletage."

"You never know. I for one would find it amusing." I headed for the stairs, and Ted went back to his sleaze.

I dropped my coat, bag, and briefcase in my office at the front of the second floor, then followed a series of banging noises, interspersed with curses, to the attic. The noises came from the rear of the cavernous, drafty space; the cursing voice belonged to Rae Kelleher. I stopped and smiled, listening. Rae's typical expletives were along the lines of "Oh, rats!" I'd never realized she possessed such a colorful vocabulary. As I made my way back to her, I weaved through assorted cartons, trunks, suitcases, and mismatched furniture—things that staff members who lived in the small second-story rooms couldn't squeeze in, plus the castoffs of others no longer in residence.

Rae stood by the rear dormer window, holding a hammer and sucking her thumb. She is a tiny woman with curly auburn hair, who dresses with a ratty artlessness that never ceases to amaze me. Today she had outdone herself: candy-striped, paint-stained pants with the widest bell-bottoms I'd seen since 1970; a baggy purple sweater covered with those balls of fuzz I call sweater mice; a yellow polka-dot bandanna holding back her hair. There was a big streak of dirt on her forehead, and a bigger scowl on her round, freckled face. When she saw me, she took her thumb from her mouth and said, "Dammit, why did my mother teach me to sew instead of how to hit nails right?"

I looked around. There was a stack of Sheetrock leaning against one wall; insulation had been stapled between the exposed studs. "What in God's name are you doing?"

She stuck the thumb back in her mouth and said around it, "Making a room for myself. I'm sick of living in my office."

In September, Rae had separated from her perpetual-student husband and moved into All Souls. All the rooms were occupied, so she set up housekeeping in her office—my former one—which is really nothing more than a converted closet under the stairs. Being crowded was okay with her, she'd said. It was only a temporary arrangement—until a room opened up, or the couples counseling worked and she and Doug got back together.

I sat down on a rolled-up rug and said, "I take it your Christmas trip to see Doug's parents didn't go too well."

She snorted. "That's putting it mildly. His whole family blames *me* because the asshole made that fake suicide attempt last fall. His mother had the nerve to tell me if I paid more attention to him, it wouldn't have happened. It was cold in Ohio, and neither of us brought enough warm clothes. So his mother went out and bought her Dougie two new sweaters, but nothing for me. Then I found out he hadn't even told them we weren't living together anymore. When I corrected that impression, his father lectured me on a wife's duties to her husband. Never mind a husband's duties—little things like respecting his wife's rights or being truthful. Oh no, those things don't apply to their Dougie. No wonder he turned out the way he did!" She paused, suddenly shamefaced. "Sorry. I know I shouldn't rant like that. But every time I think about it, I just . . . fulminate!"

"I don't blame you." Rae had come a long way in a few months: from a woman who neglected her job to rush to her husband's side every time he snapped his fingers, to a full-scale fulminator. I motioned around us. "Does this mean you're divorcing him?"

"Yeah. The couples therapy has proved to me that we can't go on. Every week more and more things come out about both of us. Perfectly swinish things about Doug, and things I don't like much about myself, either. I can work to improve my bad character, but there's nothing I can do about his."

"So when are you filing?"

"Soon. Trouble is, I've only got twenty-nine dollars in my checking account." Momentarily she looked glum, then brightened. "But Hank loaned me a book about how to do your own divorce, and even offered to help me. I guess I can scrape together the filing fee."

I considered offering to loan it to her but decided against such partisan behavior. I'd long ago learned to stay out of friends' marital hassles; whenever I'd taken sides, they'd reconciled, and I'd ended up the villainous party.

"Hank's been awfully helpful," Rae added. "I was afraid he wouldn't want me putting in a room up here, but he said yes right away and even talked the owner into paying for the insulation and Sheetrock."

Hank Zahn, founder and nominal leader of All Souls, was great at talking people into all sorts of things. Too bad, I thought, he wasn't any good with a hammer. And speaking of marital hassles . . . "Has Hank been around this week?" I asked.

"Not much."

"Anne-Marie?" Anne-Marie Altman, our tax attorney, was my good friend and Hank's wife.

"Haven't seen her, but I only got back from Ohio on Monday."

"Well, I suppose they'll be at the party Saturday night."

"If they're speaking to each other."

"You've noticed, too."

"Can't help but. Frankly, I think what they need is separate houses. There are some people who love each other but can't live together."

"Maybe," I said, thinking of my former relationship with a certain police lieutenant. "Anyway, I need to talk to you about a case. I hate to interrupt this . . . project, but—"

"Don't worry. I need a break. I only have one more thumb, you know." She sat down next to me on the rolled-up rug.

I told her about the Foster case, pointing out what I thought were holes and inconsistencies.

When I finished, Rae was silent for a moment. "Oh boy," she finally said, "twenty years old and on death row! What sort of a kid is this Bobby Foster, anyway?"

I restrained a smile at her use of the word "kid"; Rae herself was only twenty-five. "He's okay, once you get past the tough-guy attitude—which is understandable, given where he is. Grew up in the projects—Potrero Annex. One of seven kids, father skipped out before he was born, mother's had two other husbands, both gone now, too. She's an activist—organized a watch program for her building and was instrumental in establishing the Potrero Medical Clinic."

"I've heard of it. Didn't they just get some big foundation grant?"

I nodded. "Mrs. Whitsun—Leora Whitsun—works at the clinic now, doing intake and records. She's getting a pretty good salary and wants to move her younger kids out of the projects. Her connection with the clinic has bearing on the case, too. The club owner I mentioned, Jay Larkey, was a dentist before he turned to stand-up comedy, and he still keeps his hand in. He volunteers two afternoons a week at the clinic, which is how he met Mrs. Whitsun and came to hire Foster as a parking attendant when he got out of the CYA."

"And he was in the CYA for . . .?"

"He'd been running drugs since he was nine. The last time, he was in for assaulting a dealer who had cheated him. There were other offenses relating more to his violent temper than to drugs. Right before Kostakos disappeared, though, he'd begun to turn his life around. His mother's a very gutsy woman, and underneath it all, Bobby has the same basic toughness."

Rae nodded thoughtfully. "So what do you need me to do?"

"First, set up some appointments for me. I called the victim's mother from the pay phone at San Quentin, and she agreed to see me after three." I looked at my watch. "I've got to leave in a few minutes in order to get down to Palo Alto on time. See if you can catch the roommate, Amy Barbour, at work and arrange for me to meet her at the apartment around six or seven. If that's okay, set up something with George Kostakos for tomorrow, the same with Mrs. Whitsun and the boyfriend, Marc Emmons. I'll drop in at Café Comedie and talk with the people there this evening."

"Phone numbers?"

"I'll leave the file on my desk." I stood up. "You probably should read it and the trial transcript, plus look at the video—if you can stomach it."

"If I can stomach a week with Doug's family—"

I cut her off; the tape was nothing to joke about. "I'll probably want you to verify some of the facts turned up in the police investigation, as well as run checks to see if there's been any activity in Kostakos's checking or charge accounts—that sort of thing. But that can wait until tomorrow."

"Right. What about the investigator in charge of the case? Do you want me to contact him?"

"Can't—he's dead. But there's somebody I know in the department who might pull the file for me—if I ask nicely."

Greg Marcus, my former lover, would be at the New Year's Eve party on Saturday—and my new dress was low cut and red, the color he liked best on me.

4

Laura Kostakos had told me to take the University Avenue exit off Highway 101. As I did, I felt a stab of nostalgia for my college days, when I'd dated a Stanford grad student who lived near the interchange, in the area that is actually part of the troubled community of East Palo Alto but then had been almost as desirable as Palo Alto itself. His was a long street lined with nothing but apartment buildings; they ranged from no-frills to luxury complexes replete with swimming pools and putting greens. I'd attended some of the best parties of my life on that street, but those days, a friend who lived in Palo Alto had recently told me, are gone.

Now, she said, even the most opulent of the complexes are showing signs of the hasty, poor-quality construction that dooms them to early obsolescence. Their facades are cracked; their rooflines sag; the putting greens are weedy, the swimming pools filmed with mold. Instead of Stanford students and young professionals and naval officers from Moffett Field, they are largely tenanted by working-class blacks who have moved across the freeway from East Palo Alto proper, looking for a better life.

As I drove past the bars and liquor stores and shabby businesses on the stretch of University Avenue known locally as Whiskey Gulch, I reflected on the stinginess and hypocrisy of a society that rewards its aspiring minorities with the ruling class's leavings, then tries to claim the neighborhood is declining because of the "new element" that's moved in. The decaying apartments of East Palo Alto were several cuts above the decrepit Potrero Hill projects where Bobby Foster grew up—World War II–vintage cell blocks where fear and violence lurk in every enclosed staircase and

24

entryway—but they weren't much when you considered how hard their occupants had worked to get there.

At the end of the strip of businesses, a sign announced I was entering Palo Alto itself. The neighborhood changed: stately trees arched over the pavement; handsome homes decked with Christmas wreaths stood far back on manicured lawns; the cars in the driveways were Mercedes and Cadillacs and sports models. Palo Alto is a reasonably liberal town that prides itself on culture and intellect (while determinedly avoiding the strident radicalism of such academic enclaves as Berkeley), so I was fairly sure that not all the blacks on this side of the dividing line would be wearing starched uniforms—but I also suspected there wouldn't be enough bona fide minority residents to hold a chapter meeting of the NAACP.

Chaucer Street, where Laura Kostakos lived, was one of a number in the exclusive Crescent Park district that were named after literary figures. Her house was Spanish style—a two-storied, white stucco with a red-tiled roof. The front lawn was full of big dead patches; a loose rain gutter rattled in the wind. Behind the mulberry tree that shaded the arching front window, I could see drawn drapes. The magnolia tree near the door had dropped its leaves on the brick walk, and nobody had bothered to clean them up. As I rang the bell, I noted the absence of any kind of Christmas decoration.

Mrs. Kostakos took a long time answering my ring. When the door finally opened, I saw a tall woman with graying blond hair worn loose upon her shoulders. It was a style that would have looked too youthful on many women in their late forties, but on her it seemed right, imparting a fragile air that enhanced her fine bone structure. Her blue velvet lounging pajamas—curious attire for three in the afternoon—hung loose on her, giving the impression that she had lost a great deal of weight; she'd applied no makeup to hide the dark half-moons under her eyes.

She thanked me for coming, even though I was the one who had requested the interview. Then she led me down a long, narrow gallery lined with spotlighted oil paintings and sculpture on pedestals. The air in the gallery was chill. Laura Kostakos moved stiffly, in the gait of a much older woman. As the folds of her pajamas rippled, I caught the scent of a gardenialike perfume I'd always associated with my maternal grandmother.

At the far end of the gallery was a living room whose dark exposed ceiling beams radiated out to a curving wall containing a series of five small window seats. The windows encased within the jutting sections of wall admitted little light; through them I could see a free-form swimming pool that looked as if it had been carved from lava rock. The murky midafternoon light sheened the black water.

The living room itself was gloomy. Shadows gathered in its far reaches, where glass-fronted bookcases hulked; on the table at the L of the sectional sofa, a single low-wattage lamp burned, giving off a dim halo of light. The chill I'd felt in the gallery penetrated here, too. I glanced at the stone fireplace, saw the grate was choked with dead ashes.

Laura Kostakos motioned for me to sit on the sofa. I took a place next to the table with the lamp. She positioned herself on a ladder-back chair across from me.

To establish rapport, I said, "This is a lovely room."

She glanced around, then shrugged disinterestedly. "Yes, I suppose it is. I barely see it anymore." After a brief pause, she added, "It's good of you to take an interest in my daughter's disappearance."

"I should warn you right off that my interest is in behalf of the young man convicted of killing her."

She nodded, picking at a piece of lint on her velvet-covered thigh. "I have no problem with that."

I removed a notebook and pencil from my bag. "I've come to you for two reasons. First, I'd like to get some idea of Tracy as a person, hear what she was like."'

"Is like, Ms. McCone. Tracy is still alive."

"That brings me to the other reason I asked to speak with you. You've told people that you believe she's alive, and I'd like to know why."

She nodded again and waited. Apparently she expected me to conduct a formal interview, as the police would do.

I said, "What kind of a young woman was . . . is Tracy?"

"A normal young woman. More talented than most, but quite . . . normal. If anything, her normalcy borders on the pathological. At least, that's what my husband would say—he's in psychology, you know."

"Could you explain that more fully?"

"Tracy is overly conscientious. She works very hard and is extremely self-critical. Very harsh on herself at times. With girls of her age you expect some irresponsibility: they're late for appointments; they forget to call home; they miss birthdays or Mother's

Day. But not Tracy. Even her play has a serious quality, as if she's playing for keeps. Do you understand what I mean?"

"Yes, I do. You and your husband—"

"We're separated," she said quickly.

"I see. Both of you are professors at Stanford?"

"Yes, although we've elected to take extended leaves of absence. From the university and from one another."

I debated probing into the marital situation but decided it had no bearing on the case, other than as a by-product. "I notice that Tracy was working as a cocktail waitress before she began to break into comedy. Were you disappointed that she chose not to attend college?"

"Actually she *did* attend for two years—Foothill Junior College. But when the time came for her to transfer to a four-year school, she opted to move to San Francisco and try her wings at comedy instead. Frankly, Ms. McCone, Tracy isn't academically inclined. I doubt she would have been happy or successful continuing with her education."

"So she moved to the city with your blessing?"

"Well. Neither of us was exactly delighted with her decision. It's a rough world for a young single woman with no marketable skills, and show business is even rougher. But it was what she wanted, and I knew what it was like to have parents who pressured me to succeed academically. In the end it turned out well for me, but there was a lot of pain along the way. I didn't want to do the same thing to my daughter—particularly when chances of it working out were slim—so I persuaded George to let her have her way."

That, I thought, might have been one of the causes of the breakup of the Kostakos's marriage; perhaps he blamed her for sending their daughter to her still-undetermined fate. I said, "I recall reading somewhere that you subsidized Tracy's income with an allowance. Does that mean that she couldn't have supported herself on what she made at Café Comedie?"

"Not at first. We gave her the allowance and use of our credit cards so she could afford a decent place to live and a few luxuries from time to time. She never abused the cards; she isn't that kind of girl."

"Has there been any activity in those accounts since her disappearance—activity that could be attributed to her?"

"No. During the year before she disappeared, she established her own credit. She didn't need our cards anymore." Mrs. Kostakos sounded faintly mournful. "A few weeks before she disappeared, she told me that soon she wouldn't need the allowance anymore, either. I told her it wasn't necessary to push herself to be self-sufficient. We have plenty of money; we both have good positions, and George inherited a substantial amount of money. But Tracy needed to be her own woman in every respect."

"The reason she wouldn't need the allowance anymore was that her career was taking off?"

"That's what I assumed."

Or her declaration of impending financial independence might have some connection with her disappearance. I made a note on my pad. "You and Tracy were close?"

"Yes. We had a weekly lunch date, on Fridays. We were to have lunch the day after she vanished. I'd planned a drive across the hills to the coast. We often did things like that—going for long drives, taking picnics."

"What kinds of things did you talk about?"

"The usual things a mother and daughter talk about, I suppose."

"Could you be more specific?"

"Well. My work, my students. Her career, how it was going. People we knew. What we'd done in the past week, books we'd read, movies we'd seen."

"Did she ever talk about problems? Ask your advice?"

"Tracy has always been capable of solving her own problems. And as far as I know, she had none at that time."

"She never gave any indication that she might be unhappy—with her work, her living situation, her boyfriend, perhaps?"

"No."

"Mrs. Kostakos, I've studied the news accounts of Tracy's disappearance, as well as the Foster trial transcripts. All along you've firmly stated that you believe Tracy disappeared voluntarily."

She nodded.

"Yet you say she gave no indication of unhappiness, never mentioned anything that was troubling her."

". . . That's right."

"Then why are you under the impression that she would just vanish of her own free will?"

Laura Kostakos shifted on her chair. She brought her hands together in her lap.

"Why, Mrs. Kostakos?"

Silence.

"You continue to pay the rent on her apartment. Even though

you have plenty of money, that strikes me as the sort of thing you wouldn't do unless you had a reasonable expectation that one day she'd return."

"I have never for a moment doubted that she will return."

"But *why?* And what about the ransom note, the car that was found in the mountains? How do you explain them?"

She rose from her chair so quickly that it startled me. I watched as she moved in her old-woman's walk to the center window seat and stood with her back to me, one knee resting on the cushion. The afternoon had darkened beyond the glass; the black lava rock pool made me think of a lagoon teeming with alien life forms.

"Mrs. Kostakos?"

"There's a hummingbird feeder hanging on that pine beyond the pool," she said. "Can you see it?"

I looked, spotted a smear of red. "Yes."

"I put it there last summer. I wanted the hummingbirds to come around, so I'd be less lonely. But there's one that is vicious. Every time the others come to drink, he swoops down and chases them away. It reminds me of how people have swooped down and chased away my hopes."

I couldn't think of an appropriate comment.

"Do you know what I'm going to do about that bird?" she went on. "I'm observing him, learning his habits. I've found a stone, a nice flat one that will skim through the air. As soon as I'm sure I'll get the right bird, I am going to kill him."

The words were delivered dispassionately, but there was a disturbing undercurrent of rage. I chose not to respond to it, said mildly, "If you kill him, one of the remaining birds will take up the role of the aggressor."

"I'm going to do it anyway."

Maybe it would help her, but I doubted that. Probably she'd end up trying to murder the entire hummingbird population of Palo Alto. "Mrs. Kostakos, let's get back to Tracy—"

"People think I'm crazy, you know."

I was silent again. She seemed to be approaching the subject in her own way, and I was content to let her do so.

"My husband left me because he couldn't stand living with a crazy woman anymore. He considers me dangerously obsessed with Tracy's disappearance. My students and colleagues in the math department began handling me with kid gloves, as if they were afraid one wrong word would send me screaming into the streets. Of course, anything deviating from the statistical norm is unsettling to mathematicians. You can understand why I had to take a leave of absence."

"Are you working on anything now? Articles or a book—"

"No, nothing. I can't concentrate. I hardly ever go out of the house anymore." Her words were coming more swiftly now. "The neighbors have mostly stopped speaking to me; they look at me strangely. When I do go out, people in the stores, in the street . . . it's as if I radiate an aura that frightens them. Do I frighten you, Ms. McCone?"

"No."

"Do *you* think I'm crazy?"

"I think you're lonely, and under terrible strain."

She took her knee off the bench and turned toward me. "Thank you for saying so, even if it's not true."

"I meant it. Do *you* think you're crazy?"

The question made her sink onto the window seat. "I honestly don't know."

"Perhaps you should see a therapist."

"I was, but I just can't anymore. It doesn't help. The only thing that would . . ."

"Would be finding out what happened to your daughter."

She nodded, bending her head so her hair fell against her high cheekbones. The walls of the recess cast shadows over her that made her hair more gray than blond, and totally lifeless.

"Mrs. Kostakos," I said, "please help me. You'll be helping yourself. And Tracy."

"How?"

"Tell me what makes you think that Tracy vanished voluntarily."

She didn't speak. I let the silence spin out into minutes. The gray year's-end day was drawing to a close; already the crimson of the hummingbird feeder had faded into the background of pine needles.

Finally she said, "All right. There was one thing, the week before she vanished. At lunch that Friday she asked me if I thought she was a good person. I said yes, of course—the way you do when someone catches you off guard with an important question. She seemed to sense it was a reflexive response, however, because she said maybe she once had been, but she didn't think she was anymore."

"Did you ask her what she meant by that?"

"Naturally. But she refused to be specific. She merely said that circumstance changes people, leads them to do things they never would have, as well as not to do things they know are right. When I pressed her, she said she'd done a number of things that were hurtful to others, but that her worst sin was one of omission—of not correcting a situation that was sure to harm someone she cared about. After that, she refused to talk anymore. Later when she disappeared, I assumed she'd gone away to escape whatever circumstances were making her feel she was a bad person. I've always believed she would eventually work it out and return."

I noted the approximate date of the conversation on my pad, then wrote in block letters: BAD PERSON/OMISSION/HARM. I studied them for over a minute, then said, "This may have a great deal of bearing on what happened, but it still doesn't explain why you seem to dismiss the ransom note you received, as well as the bloodstained car that was found in the mountains."

She sighed deeply. "I'd hoped I wouldn't have to. . . . Ms. McCone, this may sound horrible coming from her mother, but Tracy isn't the . . . paragon the newspapers made her out to be. She is, as I said, self-reliant and conscientious and loyal to those she loves, but she is also very ambitious and . . ."

"And?"

"She can be quite . . . ruthless when it suits her purposes. She is an achiever, and people who wish to achieve a great deal often can be self-centered and cruel. My daughter had already achieved a great deal in a very short time. It had whetted her appetite, the way the taste of blood will whet a predatory animal's."

It was an odd and disturbing comparison. "So you're saying that the note and the car are evidence manufactured by Tracy to misdirect anyone looking for her?"

"Yes."

"Would she actually let Bobby Foster die in order to keep anyone from finding her?"

Laura Kostakos raised her eyes to mine. They caught faint glimmers from the lamp beside me, seemed cut of the same lava rock as the pool. "I cannot believe that. She must be planning to return before that happens."

And in the meantime she was putting Bobby Foster—her supposed friend—through a living hell. If her mother's theory about her disappearance was correct, Tracy had chosen a strange and contradictory way of working out problems that were making her feel she was a bad person.

I said, "Can you think of anyone—a friend or a relative, perhaps—who might be hiding her?"

"I've contacted everyone I could think of. No one has heard from her, and given the circumstances, I'm fairly sure they wouldn't lie to me."

"What about a place outside the Bay Area? Someplace she has a connection to or knows well?"

She considered briefly. "We had a summer cottage on the Mendocino coast, but it was sold years ago. Otherwise, no, I can't think of any other place."

Of course, she couldn't have known of all the places Tracy might have visited after she moved away from Palo Alto. Nor could her inquiries have covered any number of people she wasn't aware her daughter knew.

I had one more question. "Why do you suppose she felt she had to disappear to work out these problems?"

"I don't know."

"But you must have speculated on it."

"Of course I have!" It was a cry of pain. "I've scarcely thought of anything else since it happened. I've gone over the conversation we had at lunch, time and time again. I've reexamined everything that she told me for weeks and months before that. But I don't have a single, solitary idea."

Her glimmering eyes moved away from mine, to a point somewhere in the encroaching darkness. The fear in them was almost a palpable presence. I came close to turning my head to see what or who stood there. But I didn't have to. I knew.

It was the amorphous shape of dread—that chimera that, once glimpsed, forever waits implacably in the shadows.

5

The icy wind gusted across Upper Market Street. It sent litter swirling along the gutters and plastered sheets of discarded newspapers against the iron bars of the fence that guarded the edge of the east sidewalk. Beyond it the hill dropped off precipitously. The lights of the flatlands below were fog hazed, the usually panoramic glitter of the Bay Bridge and East Bay barely discernible.

Traffic rushed by me on the downhill slope. The vehicles' headlights washed over me, then their taillights disappeared around a sharp curve. I hunched against the capricious gale and walked along, hands stuffed in the pockets of my pea jacket. Parking was at a premium here on the overpopulated east side of Twin Peaks; I'd had to leave my MG a long block from Tracy Kostakos's former apartment building.

The row of apartment houses that clung to the lower part of the hill started about a hundred yards from where I'd parked. When I reached their shelter, the wind was not so severe. On the west side of the pavement the buildings rose in tiers, crammed side by side on the smaller streets that snake their way toward the radio transmitter and the overlook crowning the third and fourth highest of San Francisco's forty-three hills.

The architecture on Twin Peaks is mostly rabbit-warren modern: lots of postage-stamp-sized balconies that people seldom use because of the wind; picture windows that afford spectacular views and cause the residents' heating bills to rise; standard thin walls and bland decor; too few garages and too many cars. If it wasn't for the views, the area would probably have gone the way of the "desirable" part of East Palo Alto many years ago, but the vistas keep the apartments filled and the rents high.

Of course, I thought as I walked quickly downhill, not all the

33

buildings on Twin Peaks were tacky or overpriced. My former lover Greg Marcus owned a tasteful little redwood-sided house on a cul-de-sac off Parkridge Drive. Perhaps I should stop by there after talking with Amy Barbour. I could persuade Greg to let me look at the files on the Kostakos investigation tomorrow, rather than waiting until next week. . . .

No, I decided, bad idea. It could create all sorts of complications. Better to wait and catch him at the New Year's Eve party.

Tracy's former building was brick faced, three stories, with a fire escape scaling the front wall and a plane tree growing out of a planting area in the sidewalk. A lighted entryway contained three mailboxes, and a metal security gate barred the way into the building proper. Beyond the gate was a door to the ground-floor unit; fake marble stairs rose to the other apartments. I examined the names on the mailboxes and found a plastic label—the kind you make yourself with one of those punch-out gizmos—on number two, reading BARBOUR/KOSTAKOS. As I pressed the bell, I wondered if the fact that Tracy's name remained was the doing of the roommate or the mother who continued to pay half the rent.

There was no intercom, but Amy Barbour was expecting me—Rae had assured me of that when I'd checked in before leaving Palo Alto—so I went over and put my hand on the gate. The buzzer tripped the lock quickly, and I stepped into the vestibule. The gate clanged noisily behind me; the traffic sounds were so loud that I barely heard a voice call out "hello" from the landing above.

"Ms. Barbour?"

"Come on up."

The young woman who stood in the door off the second-story landing had dark red hair, a square-jawed face, and a short beaky nose. Her hairdo looked like one of those spiky punk styles that was being allowed to grow out; it drooped in little petals that reminded me of an artichoke's leaves. She wore jeans and a red sweatshirt stenciled with a fanciful lion's head; her figure was round and a trifle bottom heavy.

I introduced myself and extended my hand. She grasped it firmly, met my eyes in a forthright manner.

"Your hand's like ice," she said. "Damned wind, I hate it. Come on in, I'll give you a drink."

I followed her inside. The door led into a living room with the obligatory picture windows facing the East Bay. The white drapes were closed against the fog. The walls were also white, but the carpet was a hideous mustard; someone had tried to hide part of it with a Mexican rug, but I could still see enough—spills and stains included—to make me wince. The furnishings were surprisingly good: a white leather sofa and matching chair, tasteful glass-and-chrome tables; plain ceramic lamps; an elaborate entertainment center. There was a single wall decoration over the couch, one of those works that is part collage, part oil painting, and totally expensive.

As I took off my jacket, Amy Barbour disappeared around a corner into a dining area. I dropped the jacket on the sofa and followed, starting when I came face-to-face with myself. The entire end wall of the dining area was a mirror.

Amy turned, smiled at my reaction. "Pretty shocking, isn't it? You can imagine how awful it makes you feel at seven in the morning. It's the landlord's idea of how to make the place look larger, so he can justify the ridiculous rent." She went through the archway into a small kitchen and sniffed at a pot on the stove.

I said, "I suppose he picked out the carpet, too?"

"I think he got it cheap because nobody else wanted it. It's being replaced in January. I can't wait to see what he comes up with this time." She fetched a pair of glasses. "Whatever it is, it still won't go with Trace's nice furniture."

"Most of the things belong to Tracy, then?"

"Yeah. She was the one with the bucks." Amy spoke with no resentment, as if it were good fortune that had befallen both of them. "I've got some mulled wine here. Would you like some?"

I sighed mentally, nodded, and watched as she ladled it from the pot. In the past three weeks or so I'd had about every variety of mulled wine known to mankind. Something bizarre happens to people at the holidays: they seize perfectly drinkable—even good—wine and put strange substances into it. Cloves, orange peel, cinnamon, and—for all I know—parsley, sage, rosemary, and thyme. They make gallons of it, more than any crowd could reasonably be expected to drink, and two days before the new year they're still serving what's left over from December fifteenth.

Amy handed me a glass and looked expectant. I took a sip, found it palatable in my present frozen state, and murmured compliments. Then we went back to the living room and sat at opposite ends of the leather sofa. Amy curled her stockinged feet under her and twisted so she could look at me. "So," she said, "who're you working for—crazy Mrs. K?"

"Laura Kostakos, you mean?"

"Yeah."

"No."

"Oh. I just kind of assumed. . . ."

"Why?"

"Well, she's so fanatical about Trace. The stuff about her still being alive. This apartment, the whole schtick." She ran a hand through her artichoke-leaf hair. "Don't get me wrong—if Trace *did* turn up, I'd probably start going to church again. But she won't. She's dead. I don't like it, but I can live with it. Unlike her mother. Who is totally . . . do you know her?"

"I've met her."

"Well, you see? She's really insane. Completely . . . you're looking kind of tolerant, like maybe you don't agree with me."

"I didn't mean to. Tell me more about her."

"Well, the main thing that's weird is about this apartment. Don't get me wrong—I benefit. I *like* having a place like this all to myself. I can have my boyfriend here, no hassle. And I get the use of this nice furniture, all the kitchen stuff." She paused, seeming to hear herself. "That doesn't mean I don't miss Trace. I *do*, dammit."

"I'm sure you do. About Mrs. Kostakos? . . ."

"Sorry. I tend to run on. Anyway, Mrs. K is creepy. She gives me full run of the place, except I can't go in Trace's room, not even to dust."

"I guess she just wants it the way it was before."

"Oh, I can understand that. If Trace ever did come back, she wouldn't want to find out I'd been pawing through her stuff. Not that I *would*, but Mrs. K doesn't really know me. So she keeps the door locked."

So far she hadn't told me anything that seemed so peculiar. I was about to comment to that effect, when she added, "What's creepy is the way she comes up here and sits for hours in that room."

"When does she do that?"

"Every Friday, at the same time of day that she used to have lunch with Trace."

But Laura Kostakos had told me she hardly ever left her house. And I knew from my files that Amy worked five days a week at a place where they silk-screened T-shirts. "How do you know that?"

"The way I caught on, on Fridays I would come home from work and the place would smell funny, like gardenias. Then, one day about a year ago, I got sick and came home early. Mrs. K was just leaving the building, and I realized the smell was that perfume she wears. Pretty strong stuff. The next Friday, I left the answering machine off and kept calling the apartment from work. Around one-thirty she answered." Amy paused dramatically. "And do you know what she said?"

I shook my head.

"She said, 'Tracy, is that you?' You see what I mean—creepy."

Somehow I doubted Amy had enough imagination to make up such a story. I said, "Are you sure she comes every Friday?"

"Yep. You go in that room, you can smell the gardenias."

"I thought you weren't supposed to go in there, that she keeps it locked."

Amy looked mildly abashed. "The locks on these doors, there's a little tool you can use to open them from the outside."

"And you've used it."

"Only because I wonder what she does in there—at first I thought maybe she'd set up a shrine or something."

"And had she?"

"No, nothing like that. All she'd done was move a rocker that used to be out here—I wondered at the time why she'd taken it away—in there by the window. I guess she just sits there, waiting."

I compressed my lips and frowned, concerned for Laura Kostakos.

Amy said, "Yeah, that's how I feel. It's creepy, coming home on Fridays and knowing she's been in there . . . just waiting. I mean, I never know what to expect. What if she *does* something?"

"Like what?"

She flung a hand out wildly, almost knocking her wineglass over. "How do I know what a crazy person will do? She might kill herself. I'd come home, find her. Yuck. Or what if she turns violent? I'd walk in, and it'd be all over."

In spite of her dramatics, I sensed Amy was genuinely afraid. "I don't think she's violent or self-destructive," I said, "but maybe it would be good to talk to someone about it. Have you thought of contacting Tracy's father? After all, he's a psychology professor."

"Old George? Forget it."

"Why?"

"He's just . . . all psychologists are weird."

Maybe it was just as well she hadn't talked to him, I thought. If he didn't already know about his wife's weekly vigils in Tracy's room, it would be best if he heard it from someone more tactful and less prone to histrionics than Amy. "Tell you what," I said, "I'll ask him about it. If he thinks there's potential danger, you should probably move out of here."

Amy sipped wine, her gaze skipping around the room, as if

taking note of all the possessions she would lose use of by such an action. Then she sighed. "Maybe it would be for the best. Maybe it's time I move in with my boyfriend. If he'll let me."

"Would you mind if I look at Tracy's room?"

"Why should I? The only one who might mind is Mrs. K, and she'll never know. By the way, if you're not working for her, who is it? I started to ask, and then I forgot."

"Bobby Foster's lawyer."

Her eyes widened and she became very still. After a moment she said, "Bobby. God, it's so *awful!*"

"You know him?"

"Not well, but to even have an acquaintance on death row . . . I've had bad dreams about that."

She was beginning to wear on me. I stood and moved toward the hallway to the bedrooms. "So has Bobby."

Amy opened her mouth, shut it, and gave me a reproachful look. Then she followed me, wineglass in hand.

Two of the doors off the hallway were open: to a bathroom midway down and a small bedroom to the left at the end. The door to the right room was closed. I said, "Where's the tool for unlocking this?"

"Here in the linen closet." Amy rummaged around and handed me a slender metal probe.

I fitted it into the slot in the doorknob, pushed, and the lock snapped open. As it did, I realized there was something wrong with Amy's story about Laura Kostakos. "How does Mrs. Kostakos get into this room if it's kept locked?" I asked.

Amy hesitated, frowning. "I never thought about that. The door locks if you set the button before you close it, but there's no key other than . . ." She looked at the probe in my hand.

"She must use this, then. Is it always kept in the same place?"

"Yes, sort of. But . . . oh shit!"

"What?"

"Sometimes when I've gone in there, I've put it back on a different shelf. If she realizes I've been using it to check out Trace's room, she'll throw my ass out of here!"

"She's probably known all along and doesn't care. She may even be aware you know of her visits." I turned back to the door, opened it, and felt for a light switch. Behind me, Amy was silent.

When I flicked the switch, an overhead fixture came on. The room, its dim light revealed, was fairly good sized—about twelve feet square—but so crammed with furniture and possessions that it seemed a cell. A king-sized waterbed covered with a white goosedown comforter stood against the wall perpendicular to the window. Part of the window itself was blocked by a huge antique armoire; the rocking chair Amy had mentioned stood in front of the unobstructed portion. The dresser was laden with cosmetics and jewelry in clear acrylic stack boxes; the floor space between it and the bed was taken up by a stand with a portable TV and VCR, in spite of there being similar equipment in the living room.

I stepped all the way inside. Through the closed window I could hear the swish of tires on the pavement of Upper Market; headlight beams slid over the bedroom's walls and ceilings. That, I thought, was the price tenants paid for the view: bedrooms on the street side, inconducive to sleep.

The bed was piled with pillows. There was no room for nightstands, so the things one usually keeps there were on the floor: a clock radio, water carafe and glass, Kleenex box, TV remote control. In addition to these commonplace items, I noted several paperback biographies of celebrities, yellowing copies of *Variety*, and an ashtray filled with what looked to be marijuana roaches. I went to the closet—a large one in which my wardrobe would have taken up maybe a third—and found it crammed with clothing. The shelf above the pole was stacked with sweater boxes, the floor covered with a jumble of shoes. The armoire was in a similar state—the clothing jammed so tightly that it would have required ironing before it could be worn. On top of the armoire sat a big stuffed unicorn; it stared haughtily down at me.

Amy lounged in the doorway, sipping wine. "Trace was into *things*," she said.

"I can see that."

"She loved to shop, was always charging stuff. Clothes, cosmetics, furniture, stuff for the apartment."

Laura Kostakos said Tracy had never abused their credit cards. What did "abuse" mean to people of their financial standing? And what about last year, when Tracy had established her own credit? She couldn't have been earning enough to pay cash for everything, and most companies place low limits on new cards.

Amy seemed to take my silence for disapproval of her friend's spending habits. She said, "Look, Trace might have been into things, but she was a good person. She was generous, always buying people presents. And she only bought quality. The stuff for the kitchen, for instance—there's a Sharp microwave, a Cuisinart, a whole set of Calphalon cookware. The stainless is Dansk—"

"Amy, would you mind if I look over the room alone? I could concentrate better."

She shut her mouth abruptly, turned, and strode back toward the living room.

Touchy, I thought, looking after her. Touchy, and quite mercurial. I wasn't sure about the public defender's claim that Amy hadn't told everything she knew at Bobby Foster's trial, but there was more to her than initially met the eye.

I searched the room carefully, taking my time. Few things that I found interested me, except for a thick notebook in which Tracy had written sketches of characters she portrayed in her comedy routines. I set it aside to take with me; it would help me get to know her better, and I could copy it and return the original before Laura Kostakos realized it was gone.

What did interest me was how few things of a personal nature I found. There were no letters, postcards, souvenirs, diaries, not even an appointments calendar. Of course, I thought, they might have been removed by the police or Laura Kostakos. Or perhaps Tracy had not been one to save things or keep a journal. Finally, noting it was after eight o'clock, I took the notebook containing the character sketches and returned to the living room.

Amy slumped on the couch, working on another glass of wine. When I came in, she looked up sulkily.

I said, "I'd planned to ask if you'd noticed whether any of Tracy's things are missing, but after seeing her room, I can't imagine how you could have."

"Yeah." Her good humor returned—marginally. "Given what she owned, there was no way to keep track."

"I gather the two of you were good friends."

"The best."

"How did you meet?"

"Through a roommate referral service—one that matches people up according to their preferences. Where they want to live, how much they can pay, whether they smoke or not. You know."

I knew. Such services could be iffy, but apparently this one had done well by Amy and Tracy.

I ran through my routine questions—some of which I already knew the answers to, ones that merely served as checks on Amy's truthfulness. She answered them all without hesitation: they had lived together for two years before Tracy's disappearance; they'd squabbled about the usual things, such as boyfriends staying overnight too often; they'd confided in each other, given parties and dinners together, played racquetball at a health club a couple of times a week. As far as Amy knew, Tracy had had no serious personal problems; her career had come before anything else.

"She was all set for a big breakthrough," Amy said. "Her appearances at Café Comedie were terrific exposure, and Jay— that's Jay Larkey, the owner—had renewed her contract for another six months. She'd landed a couple of TV commercials, and a Hollywood agent had agreed to take her on. She could have been another Carol Burnett, only then this . . . thing happened to her."

"You say 'this thing,' but I got the impression before that you're convinced she's dead."

"I say 'thing' because I can't stand to use the other word. But like I told you, I know she's dead, and I can live with it. Bobby killed her. He confessed, didn't he?"

"There are a lot of discrepancies in that confession."

"But there was *evidence*."

"Tracy's mother thinks she disappeared deliberately and faked the evidence. Tracy said some things that make her believe—"

"What things?"

"That she felt she had turned into a bad person. That circumstances were forcing her to do things she never would have before."

Amy drew her feet up on the sofa and locked her arms around her knees. "God," she whispered.

I looked inquiringly at her, but she shook her head, refusing to elaborate.

"You testified for the prosecution at the trial," I said. "Bobby's public defender thought you were holding something back."

She tightened her grip on her knees. "What could I hold back? All I did was testify that Trace was supposed to wake me when she came home that night, but didn't." Her voice had changed, gone high and shrill. "All I said was that she was dependable, like clockwork. I don't *know* anything else. And it wasn't my testimony that put Bobby where he is—it was his own confession."

"You sound as if you feel bad about testifying against him, though."

She wouldn't look at me.

"*Do* you?"

"Look, I don't like having had any part in sending somebody to the gas chamber, if that's what you mean. But I told the truth, and I *wasn't* holding anything back. There isn't anything I *could* have held back."

I didn't reply. After about thirty seconds of silence, Amy squirmed uncomfortably, her eyes still focused on the opposite side of the room.

I said, "What about the things Tracy told her mother? Do you have any idea what she might have meant?"

"Look, everybody knows Mrs. K is crazy. She probably made the whole thing up." But Amy's voice was even more shrill now; hearing what her roommate had told her mother had frightened her.

"I don't think so, Amy. And that doesn't really answer my question. Do you have any idea—"

"No!" She unwound her arms from her knees and stood. "It's way after eight, and I've given you a lot of my time. My boyfriend's . . . I have a date. You'll have to go now."

I regarded her levelly for a moment, and she again looked away from me. Finally I stood, putting on my jacket. When I picked up Tracy's sketchbook, I expected her to protest my taking it, but she didn't seem to notice.

6

Café Comedie was located on South Park, in the area known as SoMa, or South of Market. At a little after nine, I drove along Bryant Street, past the Hall of Justice. The offices of the bail bondsmen were brightly lighted and doing a brisk business. I smiled as I passed my favorite: Cable Car Bail Bonds, housed in a spiffy little trailer that I just knew had to also be the sales office of the used-car lot next door. I've never been able to decide which of the establishments I'd patronize were I to require their services; Cable Car has a nice San Francisco ring (and is probably a favorite with tourists), but what greater feeling of security could be engendered than by taking one's business to Dad's Bail Bonds, just down the way?

Beyond the neon strip near the hall, the streets became darker, somewhat deserted. The warehouses and light industrial concerns were shut down for the night; here and there lights blazed at one of the legion of trendy restaurants and clubs that have sprung up in SoMa, and I spotted an art gallery that appeared to be holding some sort of showing. South of Market is an eclectic neighborhood where auto repair shops and factory outlet stores vie for space with clubs and leather bars. Landmarks such as the Old Mint, the Flower Mart, China Basin, and the Moscone Convention Center attest both to the area's rich heritage and bright future, but winos still stumble down the sidewalks, and pawnshops and transient hotels abound. I find SoMa fascinating because of its inconsistencies and contrasts, and now I wondered why I'd taken so little time to explore it.

I turned off Bryant onto Second Street and began looking for a place to leave the MG. Although parking is relatively plentiful in that part of the city, especially after the employees of the various businesses have gone home, I was certain that South Park itself would be jammed with vehicles belonging to residents and patrons of Café Comedie. Around the corner on Brannan Street I found a space just the MG's size and wedged it in there. Then I locked up and walked back to the entrance to the parkway—more of an alley than a street.

South Park is a perfect example of where SoMa has been and where it's going. Originally a fashionable retreat for the Gold Rush gentry, it began to deteriorate as early as the 1870s, when its stately Georgian homes were converted to rooming houses for Japanese immigrants. During the Depression its grassy ellipsoid was set aside by the city's parks commission for "soapbox speeches." I didn't know how successful that venture was, but I did know that when I last visited it, in the early 1980s, it had been taken over by derelicts and drug dealers. But now, if the presence of Café Comedie and a couple of small eateries was any indication, the curious little parkway might eventually be restored to respectability.

I walked between two warehouselike buildings to where the roadway split and curved around either side of the small park. A row of sycamore trees hugged its perimeter; through their bare branches I saw odd, hulking shapes that appeared to be playground equipment. Café Comedie was easy to spot among the small houses and squat functional buildings facing the park.

It was on the far end of the north side, sandwiched between a packing company and a brightly painted Victorian. Its floodlighted brick facade was whitewashed, the mortar between painted blue; a red-white-and-blue striped canopy emblazoned with the club's name extended out from the front door. In a small fenced-off area on the sidewalk stood two wrought-iron tables with similarly striped umbrellas. A pair of white-coated valet parking attendants waited at the curb.

As I approached, an Audi swung around me and stopped at the canopy. One of the young men rushed forward to open the car door. I followed the well-dressed couple inside, suddenly conscious of my casual jacket and jeans. A quick glance at the other patrons reassured me, however; their attire ranged from fancy cocktail dresses and tuxedos to basic thrift-shop and L. L. Bean.

The club was one large room—I guessed it had formerly been a warehouse—with a bar along the left wall and a raised platform at the front. Small round tables with white cloths were crammed close together; those at the rear were tiered for better visibility. A couple of waitresses were seating people—quietly because a show was in progress. I shook my head at the one who looked questioningly at me, then took a seat at the bar.

When the bartender came up, I gave him my card and asked to speak with Mr. Larkey. He studied the card for a few seconds but didn't comment; he was in the upper reaches of middle age and somewhat jaded looking, so I assumed nothing surprised him. When he said he'd check, I ordered a glass of sauvignon blanc and swiveled to watch the show.

The comedian was probably in his late twenties, a big man encased in soft baby fat, with a clown's mobile face. His first routine involved cruising the main street of Modesto on a Friday night; next he segued into a bit about a sex-starved teenager. He wasn't all that funny, but the audience seemed to find him hilarious. Something to do with his delivery, I supposed, the contortions into which he could twist his rubberlike mouth. After a while I grew weary of watching him wander around the stage mumbling inane things, then pausing to loudly announce, "I'm *hoorny!*" I turned back to the bar.

The bartender was approaching with my drink, my card still in his hand. He said, "Mr. Larkey would like to know what this is all about."

"Tracy Kostakos."

I actually succeeded in surprising him; he blinked and went away again. I sipped wine, trying to shut out the voice of the comic, who was now imitating the sex-starved kid's father.

After a while the bartender returned again. "Mr. Larkey will see you. He's in his office. Through the door that says Yes."

I stood, leaving payment for the wine on the bar. "'Yes'?" I asked.

"'Yes,' meaning, 'Yes, this is the way to the restrooms.'"

"Cute," I said in a tone that conveyed exactly what I thought of that.

"Yeah, well, it goes with the territory." He looked glumly at the howling, snorting clientele.

As I went through the door that said Yes, the comic asked in the father's baritone, "Just how do you explain this, son?" In a slurring falsetto he replied, "I'm *hoorny!*" For some reason, that brought down the house.

Halfway down the hall beyond the restrooms, the door marked OFFICE stood partly open. I knocked, and a voice told me to come in. Jay Larkey sat on an exercise bicycle in the middle of the cluttered space; he wore a bright blue sweat suit and was pedaling furiously.

When he saw me, he backpedaled and stopped. The dentist-turned-comedian-turned–club owner looked much the same as the last time I'd seen him on TV: curly brown hair that stuck out in wild tufts and cascaded down onto the nape of his neck; narrow foxlike face; mouth full of sharp little teeth that always seemed to bite off the ends of his tart, needling punch lines.

I'd once read an interview with Larkey, in which he'd said that in order to be funny, comedy had to hurt, à la Don Rickles. I wasn't sure I agreed with that—I dislike humor at an innocent person's expense—but Larkey often made me laugh in spite of myself. And a friend who had been the target of one of his attacks on audience members at Harrah's Lake Tahoe had told me that afterward Larkey had come up and thanked him for suffering such abuse. Maybe, I thought now, it was the dentist in him that made his humor vaguely sadistic.

Tonight, however, Larkey didn't look as if he were about to crack jokes. He glared at me, then snapped, "All right—what's this shit about Tracy Kostakos?"

I came all the way into the room and shut the door. "I'm working for Bobby Foster's attorney, on the appeals process. I understand you don't think Tracy is dead."

Larkey frowned, then began pedaling again. "Well, you heard wrong. At one time I did, but she's been gone too long. If she was alive, she'd have surfaced by now. But I'll tell you one thing: that kid didn't kill her—he wouldn't kill anyone. So sit down, if you can find a place."

I looked around. There were a couple of chairs, but they were buried under a welter of cardboard file boxes, weight-lifting equipment, discarded clothing, newspapers, and trade journals of both the entertainment industry and the dental profession. Larkey noticed my confusion, waved an arm, and said, "Take my desk chair."

I moved behind the desk and sat. It was mounded with papers, many of which appeared to have to do with a real-estate transaction.

Larkey continued to pedal. "I'm doing a public-TV fund-raiser on New Year's Eve," he said through gritted teeth. "Part of the proceeds'll benefit the Potrero Medical Clinic—one of my charities. Otherwise I wouldn't do it. I hate to go on looking like an overweight, washed-up comedian. I thought maybe I could ride off some of the Christmas flab on this thing."

"You don't look overweight to me. And you're certainly not what I'd call washed up."

"Then you must have a vision problem, as well as seriously warped perspective. I'm both, and I know it." He paused, puffing slightly and wiping sweat from his forehead. "Thing is, I think I should care, but deep down I really don't. I've got enough money, the club is turning a profit, and for the first time in my life I'm enjoying myself."

"You didn't enjoy yourself when you had your TV show?"

"Shit, no. You know what pressure you're under in that life? The punishing schedule? The lack of privacy? Your time's not your own, everybody wants a piece of you. When I was practicing dentistry up in Red Bluff, I would have killed for that life. But once I was actually in it . . ." He shook his head.

"How long were you a dentist?"

"Five years. My short-lived career was a disaster. I was funny, and who wants funny in their dentist? Cavities and plaque are serious stuff. So there I was, tossing out one-liners when my patients couldn't laugh because I had my hands shoved in their mouths, cackling my head off while I was performing root canals. My practice fell off so much that I decided I might as well move down here and take a crack at the funny business."

"Well, you certainly succeeded."

"Yeah, but you pay a price for that success. I tried to warn Tracy about that, but she wouldn't listen. Any more than I would have at her age."

"You were close to her?"

"In a fatherly sort of way, like I am with all the kids who work here. I care about my people—pay them well, offer a full medical and dental package through the Potrero Clinic. Anyway, I tried to advise Tracy, be her mentor. Not that she needed one."

"Why not?"

"She had her career well in hand. For a funny lady, Tracy didn't have much of a sense of humor when it came to getting ahead in the world. Way back when she was still in junior college, she read every damn book there is on stand-up. Watched every comedy show on TV, went regularly to the clubs, the competitions. Took notes, too."

I'd seen the shelf of books on comedy in her bedroom; they were well thumbed.

Larkey went on, "She was constantly refining her act. You know how she worked?"

"I gather she created characters, like Carol Burnett."

"Yeah—contemporary women, the situations they find themselves in, their problems. Social commentary that made you laugh but also made you think. Offstage she'd discuss them very seriously, as if they were real people: Would Annie really do such-and-such? Was it in character for Lizzie to go out with so-and-so? When she tried out a new routine, she'd have somebody videotape it, and she'd study the tape for hours, concentrating on word choice, small nuances. She approached comedy in a scientific way."

"I take it that's not how it's usually done."

"Comedy's like any other art form: it comes from deep within, it's more intuitive than scientific. Most of us just wing it, let our material evolve. The ones who have to analyze usually don't have much of a flair to begin with. But Tracy combined the scientific with the intuitive—with brilliant results."

"If she was that intent on success, do you think she would have just dropped out of sight? Everything I know about her indicates she was on the verge of a breakthrough."

He took his feet off the pedals, let them spin to a stop. Then he got off the bike and sat on a corner of the desk, one leg drawn up on it, half facing me. "I don't know what to think," he said. "I wish to hell I did."

"Any ideas?"

"None."

I leaned back in his chair, propping my feet on an open desk drawer. "I've been trying to think of the typical reasons a twenty-two-year-old woman disappears," I said. "She's on drugs, or pregnant, or suicidal. She sees her life as at a dead end, or she's angry at her friends or family and wants to hurt them. None of those motives fits with what I know of Tracy."

"No."

"I thought of another reason: maybe her disappearance and kidnapping was staged as a publicity stunt, to further her career. But that doesn't wash, because in order for it to have been effective, she'd have to have surfaced long before this."

"Right. Now she's old, old news."

"Unless something went wrong with the stunt."

"Like what?"

I shrugged.

"So what's left?" he asked.

"Tracy's mother has the impression something was weighing on her mind before she disappeared," I said. "Tracy indicated that she thought she'd turned into a bad person."

Larkey's eyes flickered with interest.

I asked, "Do you know what that might have been all about?"

He got up and moved back toward the exercise bike, but instead of riding it again, he balanced on the seat, feet on the handlebars. "Maybe the business was destroying her youthful idealism."

"It sounded like more than that. She mentioned a 'sin of omission'—a situation she hadn't dealt with that could hurt someone she cared about."

He was silent, compressing his lips in thought. "Ms.—what's your name?"

"McCone, but you can call me Sharon."

"Sharon, a club like this is a little world all its own . . . sort of a scaled down version of the real world, only it operates at a much higher level of intensity. Most of my people are young, and a fair number of them are highly creative. They thrive on excitement, drama, intrigue—and if some doesn't come along naturally, they'll conjure it up. So you get undercurrents, rumors, secrets. Everybody's up to something, but they're not letting on what it is because usually it's pretty mundane, and if people find out, the fun'll be over."

Larkey paused before continuing: "I'm used to that; Hollywood's the same way, although the stakes are higher. So I try to ignore what goes on here. I've got other interests, the Potrero Medical Clinic, for instance. I keep out of what goes on here, and by and large nobody tries to drag me in on it. But just before Tracy disappeared, I had the sense something was wrong here. I couldn't put my finger on it, but the atmosphere was more frenetic than usual."

"Can you be more specific?"

"It was just a higher level of intensity—and it didn't feel good."

"Did you sense it in all your employees or just certain ones?"

He considered. "Well, when something like that starts going around, it spreads like brushfire. But if I had to name the ones who were most caught up in it, I'd say Tracy and our bartender Marc Emmons."

"Tracy's boyfriend? Not the guy at the bar tonight?"

"God, no. Marc still works here, but that's not him."

"Which one is he?"

"Marc's the not-terribly-funny fat boy onstage." Larkey flashed his famous foxy grin. "Why do you think I'm back here pedaling my ass off? I can't stand to watch him work. But it's the kind of thing that goes over with the crowd we attract these days."

"He wasn't one of your performers when Tracy disappeared?"

"No, although he was a hopeful. I kept telling him he ought to stick to tending bar."

"Why on earth did you give him a chance, then?"

"That was my partner Rob Soriano's bright idea. He thought it would be good publicity to let him fill in for Tracy. Anguished boyfriend helps the show go on while he waits for news of his beloved." Larkey made a disgusted face.

"Well then, why do you keep him?"

"What can I tell you? They *like* the sucker."

I was about to comment on the level of his clientele's taste when the door opened and a man's voice said, "Jay, do you have a minute to go over those loan papers?" Seeing me, the new arrival stopped on the threshold.

He was a tall, well-built man wearing a tuxedo and steel-rimmed glasses. He held himself with soldierly precision, shoulders squared, arms and spine rigid. His hair was clipped short, in a flattop style that I'd noticed had been making a comeback in certain conservative circles of late, and was so uniformly dark brown that it had to have been dyed. I judged his age to be in the early fifties.

"Speak of the devil," Larkey murmured. More loudly, he said, "Sharon, this is Rob Soriano. Rob, Sharon McCone. She's a private investigator working on the Bobby Foster case."

For a moment Soriano's square-jawed face was blank. "Foster . . . oh, right. The kid who murdered Tracy Kostakos."

"Well, it seems there's a difference of opinion on that—" Larkey broke off as the phone buzzed. He snatched it up and barked, "Yes?" After listening for a few seconds, he said irritably, "I'll be right out." As he moved toward the door, he said to Soriano and me, "Sorry. Trouble with some drunk at the bar wanting credit. I'll be back."

Rob Soriano eyed me curiously. "Investigator, eh?" he finally said.

"Yes, for All Souls Legal Cooperative." I remained where I was, my feet still propped on the desk drawer.

"Never heard of them."

"A lot of people haven't. Mr. Soriano, did you know Tracy Kostakos?"

"Not well. I caught her act a few times. She had a nice little talent."

"What about Bobby Foster?"

"He was just one of the kids who parked cars."

"Are you an active partner in Café Comedie?"

"No, I prefer to keep a low profile. My wife enjoys the glamour, such as it might be."

"Is it a profitable enterprise?"

"So-so."

"It's certainly crowded tonight."

"We manage to pack them in. Comedy's hot in San Francisco, and people like clubs. Gives them a chance to dress up, get out, be seen doing the 'in' thing. But the real profit isn't in the small independent clubs; it's in the franchises like the Improv."

I recalled that an Improv club had opened downtown recently. "They're a chain?"

"Some people call them the 'Baskin-Robbins of comedy.' Squeaky-clean stuff, no offensive material; they're tied in to a couple of TV shows. Good clubs, but they really have more appeal to tourists or suburbanites than locals. But to get back to your question, Café Comedie is more or less Jay's hobby. Some people retire and play golf; Jay became a champion of young aspiring comics."

"When you came in, you mentioned loan papers, and I see there are real estate contracts here on Jay's desk. Is he thinking of expanding or changing locations?"

A smile flickered across his thin lips, then vanished as quickly as it had appeared. "You're quite interested in Jay's affairs. But it's no secret: he and I have a second partnership, in real estate development. We've been buying up SoMa properties and holding them to see which way things go here."

The SoMa real estate market, I had heard, was a fluctuating one whose eventual direction could mold the development of San Francisco business for decades to come. The area was currently caught in a tug-of-war between those who advocated increasing the number of industrial and service businesses, and an older community of residents and artists—including the clubs—who favored maintaining the status quo. Multibillion-dollar developments such as the Mission Bay complex and Yerba Buena Gardens had served to stimulate property trading, and once-low rents had risen tenfold in only a dozen years.

"What do you mean—holding?" I asked.

"Just as it sounds. We're maintaining the existing structures and renting them out. We'll develop the properties after the city adopts definitive growth controls. I've a theory that runs contrary to what most developers would tell you: too much money has been pumped into commercial property in the last few years. There's bound to be a downswing. I've always survived the down cycles by buying undervalued parcels and holding onto them until the upswing. That's the policy Jay and I are—"

The office door opened. I looked that way, expecting to see Larkey. A woman stood there instead. She was tall, close to six feet, and clad in a long red leather coat, boots, and a floppy red hat. Black curls framed a face whose handsomeness was marred by a slash of blood-red lipstick. She wore numerous rings, a great deal of Giorgio perfume, and a suddenly sour expression. After she recovered from her initial surprise at seeing a stranger in Larkey's chair, her eyes flicked over me appraisingly, then dismissed me as no competition.

The look told me more about her than she'd probably care for me to know: she was one of that type who don't like other women, would have no close women friends. To her the rest of us represented the enemy, who might steal her man or her place in the spotlight. I instantly distrust a woman like her, just as I do a man who dislikes others of his gender.

Rob Soriano seemed amused by the look. He said, "Kathy, this is Sharon McCone. She's a private investigator working on the Kostakos murder. Sharon—my wife, Kathy."

Kathy Soriano frowned at me. "I thought the Kostakos case was a dead issue, pun intended." Before I could reply, she added, "Look, Rob, we need to check out the new girl in the ten-o'clock slot. Where's Jay?"

"Right behind you," Larkey's voice said. He pushed around her and said apologetically to me, "Sorry I had to cut our conversation short. Can we continue it another time?"

I stood up and came around the desk. "Sure. If it's okay with you, I want to talk with Marc Emmons and your parking attendants. I'll check back with you later."

Larkey gave me a card printed with both his numbers at the club and at home. The four of us left the office and went down the hall, Kathy prattling about how she and Rob didn't think the new comedian in the ten-o'clock slot was going to work out. Wasn't it a pity, she said, that the Kostakos case really *was* a dead issue? The little girl had shown a lot of talent.

"I'll never forget the routine about the feminist. It wasn't even what she said but how she said it: 'If God had meant for us to have hairy armpits, would She have given us Nair?'"

Rob Soriano grunted in annoyance and strode ahead of us. Larkey said, "I hate it when you mimic her like that. It's as if she's right here with us—but she's not."

"Oh, Jay, lighten up!"

Larkey didn't reply, merely hunched his shoulders inside his sweat suit. Whether the woman was embarrassing him or had seriously upset him, I couldn't tell. When we entered the club itself, he winked at me and followed the Sorianos to a reserved table at the rear.

I went to stand by the bar, watching the new comedian begin her routine until the busy barkeep could get to me. She was actually pretty funny, delivering a rapid-fire commentary on some of the more outrageous headlines in the tabloid newspapers; I made a mental note to tell Ted Smalley he should catch her act—quickly, in case Kathy and Rob Soriano's opinion of it prevailed.

The bartender spoke over my shoulder. I declined a drink and asked where I could find Marc Emmons.

"He left as soon as he finished his routine." The man paused. "Funny about that—he asked me if Jay was free, and I said he was talking to a private eye about Tracy. I thought he'd be excited, want to sit in on the conversation, but all of a sudden he split."

Now, that was odd, I thought. "Did you know Tracy?"

"Some. But the younger crowd, they keep to themselves."

"What about Bobby Foster?"

"Not too well, but from what I saw of him, he was a nice kid."

"Who was he friends with here at the club, besides Tracy?"

The bartender thought a moment. "I guess that would be Lisa McIntyre, one of the waitresses."

"Is she here tonight?"

"No, Lisa quit a long time ago. I don't know where she is now."

I could check on Lisa McIntyre's address with Larkey in the morning. I thanked the bartender and went outside.

It had started to drizzle, but the wind no longer blew and the air felt warmer. The pair of parking attendants I'd seen earlier stood under the canopy. I went up to them and said I'd like to ask them some questions.

At it turned out, neither had known Bobby Foster or Tracy Kostakos; they'd hired on at about the same time, only six months before. They were able to explain how the parking setup worked, however.

"There's a lot over on Brannan," the older one, a dark-haired man with a beard, said. "City law says restaurants and clubs can't use street parking, so Larkey rents space. Thing is, it's shared, and on the busy nights it gets pretty hairy in this neighborhood. So you bend the law some. First you try the lot. If it's full, you find a place on the street, tag the keys with the location. Jog back here, do it all over again." He held up his foot, which was shod in a good brand of running shoe.

"What about the keys? Do you keep them on you?"

His coworker, a redhead, went over to a metal box hanging unobtrusively from the top rail of the fence that enclosed the area containing the wrought-iron tables. "Too much chance of losing them or being on break when the owner wants to leave." He opened the hinged front of the box; inside were rows of keys hanging on hooks. The labels above them designated various streets.

"Does this box lock?" I asked.

"No."

"So anybody could reach in there and take a set of keys."

"Sure. But there's usually somebody here—we've got a couple of guys off sick tonight—and you'd have to know about the box to begin with."

"Would other employees of the club know?"

He looked at his coworker, who shrugged. "Probably, if they bothered to watch us work."

A Porsche pulled up at the front of the canopy. The bearded man said to the redhead, "Your turn."

I watched him hand out a woman in a fur coat, then take the keys from the man. "Is business always this slow?" I asked the remaining attendant.

"No. Christmas holidays, a lot of people busy with parties or out of town. But it's never like North Beach. That's a bitch. You get crazy drivers, drunks, dangerous characters. There's a lot of hostility coming from the customers and other valets. Private parties in places like Pacific Heights are a little better, but folks up there think the street belongs to them and call the cops if you park next to their driveways. Plus the guests look at you like you're some kind of a servant and stiff you on the tip. This is a good gig here; I'm gonna try to stick around."

"The other guy mentioned a couple of attendants who are off. Did either of them know Kostakos or Foster?"

"Nah, they only been here a couple of months. None of us're real steady workers."

"Does anybody at the club ever talk about the murder?"

"Sometimes. In whispers."

"What do they say?"

"That Foster was railroaded. But face it, nobody wants to think somebody he knows can do a thing like that."

The redhead returned, jogging. Another car approached; the man I'd been talking with went to the curb. I thanked them both for their time and started down the sidewalk.

The drizzle had become a full-blown rain by now. Most of South Park's buildings were dark; here and there light showed behind closed blinds or around yellowed shades. Along with the rain, the wind kicked up again; it rattled the bare branches of the sycamore trees ringing the park; their leaves lay sodden on the ground.

I glanced at my watch and shivered. Ten-thirty on a rainy Thursday night in winter. A little less than two years before, Tracy Kostakos had gone to her unknown fate at just about this time on just such a night. Had she walked this way, feeling the drops on her head and wishing for a hat, as I was? Or had she ignored them, moving purposefully—and if so, to what end? And had Bobby Foster walked beside her, or was he telling the truth—that they'd argued and parted?

Not for the first time I was afraid I'd prove unequal to feeling my way through the dark maze that lay between the present and that long-ago night. But the desire to shed light on its events had taken firm root within me. It wasn't even desire, but raw necessity—for the sake of the man whose life I held in my hands.

7

George Kostakos said, "Do you realize what it will do to people, your resurrecting this tragedy?"

"I'm afraid I can't get beyond the fact that it may save a young man's life."

He lowered his handsome, rough-hewn face into his palms, ran long fingers through thick black hair that was frosted with gray. "Christ, I know it's unconscionable to put my own feelings first, while that kid's sitting up there waiting to die. But we've all been through such agony, dammit. I don't want the people I care about to suffer that again. And I certainly don't want to relive it myself."

I remained silent, giving him time to get his emotions under control. It was eleven o'clock Friday morning. We were seated in the living room of his borrowed house in the Marina district, directly across the street from the Palace of Fine Arts. Through the front window I could see the icy-gray lagoon bordered by wind-warped cypress trees; beyond it the tan colonnade and domed rotunda—relics of the 1915 exposition celebrating the opening of the Panama Canal—were shrouded in mist. Kostakos had explained that a friend who was temporarily living in Europe had offered him the use of the house when he'd separated from his wife the previous summer. Even if he hadn't told me that, I would have guessed it wasn't his, because nothing about it went with the man seated across from me.

The house actually had a schizoid quality. The exterior was Mediterranean, as many of the buildings in that quiet, affluent area of the city are: white stucco, with black ornamental grillwork and decorative yew trees; possessed of the obligatory postage-stamp front lawn; two storied, with a garage below the living room window and a door enclosed in a Moorish arch. From the outside

56

it seemed an ordinary-enough house for the Marina, although its location would make it more expensive than most.

Inside was another story. The owner had taken it upon himself to create a designer's showcase dream that would be a nightmare to anyone desirous of living comfortably. The walls of the first-floor entry were starkly white; it contained nothing whatsoever except a polished black rock on a pedestal. The uncarpeted stairs rose to a living room off a gallery—also white, with bare, bleached wood floors. Two pairs of spartan chrome-and-leather chairs faced each other at right angles to the fireplace; they struck me as the modern-day equivalent of those prissy antiques that are guaranteed to be unsittable and will probably fall apart if you try. A second grouping of chairs and tables at the far end of the room looked similarly inhospitable, and the only sign of human habitation was a book- and paper-heaped desk in front of the window. I assumed that was Kostakos's import.

The chairs had proved as unsittable as they looked, at least for any length of time. I shifted on mine now, waiting for Kostakos to speak.

Finally he raised his head and looked me in the eye. His were gold-flecked hazel, the kind that can surprise you by sometimes appearing either green or blue. He said, "I'm not going to try to obstruct your investigation, but I don't care to help you, either."

I hesitated, framing my reply carefully. "I'm not asking you to help, not in any material way. The reason I wanted to talk with you is that I'm trying to form some kind of impression of your daughter. I've heard various things about her—from her mother, her room-mate, her employer—and it will round out the picture to hear what you have to say."

He regarded me intently for a moment, then got up and moved restively around the barren room. He was tall and lean, and his body—clad in a blue chambray workshirt and jeans—seemed to hum with a pent-up energy. This man, I sensed, would do nothing halfway. Whatever he turned his hand to would receive his total concentration and effort—be it teaching, writing, research, or things personal.

Face it, McCone, my often annoying inner voice said as I watched him pace, your prim-and-proper "things personal" is a euphemism for sex.

Not totally, I countered. But if so, what of it? I'm not allowed to think about sex? I certainly *ought* to be, after all these months without it.

But the thought was unsettling nonetheless, and when Kostakos sat back down, I had difficulty meeting his eyes.

He said, "You've talked with Laura?"

"Yesterday afternoon."

"How is she?"

"Lonely."

His eyes became shadowed, their color edging toward the green; the fine lines around them grew tight, as if he were in pain. After a pause he said, "I'm sorry about that. I've told her she ought to get out, go back to the university, start seeing her therapist again—anything but sit there in that house or that wretched apartment."

"You know about her weekly visits there?"

"I know." His lips pursed; the knowledge had left a bitter taste.

"Amy Barbour knows, too," I said. "She's afraid Laura might be self-destructive or dangerous to her."

"Amy Barbour is a twit. Laura's incapable of harming herself or anyone else. She's much too selfish for that."

The harsh judgment shocked me. It showed on my face, because Kostakos immediately added, "Selfishness isn't really a negative trait, you know."

"If you say so—you're the psychologist."

"There's a difference between selfishness and self-centeredness," he said. "Self-centered people are narcissists, engrossed in only what concerns them. Selfish people, on the other hand, tend to put their own welfare first, but they realize they're not the center of the universe. They're often able to do extremely well by others, because they take care of themselves and can be quite effective in their endeavors. When I say Laura is selfish, I mean she looks out for herself. It's her way of getting through."

"She doesn't seem to be doing too good a job of it recently, though."

"No." He hesitated, eyes clouded again. "But there's nothing I can do about that."

"You mentioned her way of getting through. What's yours?" It was a very personal question, but Kostakos seemed candid enough to answer it, and I wanted to keep him talking.

He motioned at the desk in the front window. "My work. It takes me outside myself."

"Laura said you've both taken leaves of absence from Stanford. Are you teaching somewhere else?"

"Something like that. I'm involved with a group called Living Victims. Have you heard of it?"

"No."

"It's a support group for friends and relatives of murder victims. Sort of like Parents of Murdered Children, except it's not limited to blood relatives. They helped me a lot when I first moved to the city, and now I'm trying to return some of that by assisting them with grant writing. And I'm also working on a book that I'd started . . . before."

"What's the book about?"

"It outlines a psychological model—" He broke off. "You don't really want to hear about it."

"Actually, I do. I was a soc major at Berkeley, and I took a good bit of psych, too."

Kostakos looked pleased. I assumed he spent a good deal of time alone, and although his involvement with Living Victims would bring him into contact with a fair number of people, most of them would have little interest in his psychological theories.

"The model is a system of personality classification, based on whether a person is primarily action oriented, emotional, or intellectual," he said. "Within the various categories there are three levels—the healthy, the normative, and the pathological. That's nothing new; it's a synthesis of various models that have been around for a long time. What I'm trying to do is explain it in layman's terms as well as develop guidelines that people can use to move in the direction of the healthy level."

"A self-help book, right?"

He smiled ruefully. "I know—one more to add to the legion in the stores. But I've got a lot of confidence in this project; what people don't realize is that within any one personality category there are individuals who don't seem to have anything in common because they're operating at different levels. But all of those— except for the most severely disturbed—are capable of moving toward the highest level without making any fundamental changes in who or what they are."

"Can you give me an example of one of these groups?"

"Sure. Think of historical figures, leaders—the good guys. Who comes to mind?"

"Well, since we've had a shortage of those lately, John Kennedy, Martin Luther King."

"Okay. Do you know who those people would share a group with? The Reverend Jim Jones and Charles Manson."

"Good Lord."

"Pathological to healthy. Now this model—" Again he broke off. "Look, would you like some coffee?"

"Sure, that would be nice." As he stood up, I added, "Let me help you make it—I'm curious about the rest of this house."

"Strange, isn't it? I still haven't gotten used to it, and I doubt I ever will."

Kostakos led me around the stairwell to the other side of the gallery. A dining room opened off it. The walls in there were desert orange, the table a slab of something that resembled petrified wood. Tall cacti stood in the corners like entrapped outlaws, their arms reaching for the sky—or in this case, skylight.

"The southwestern room?" I asked.

"Yes—a decided contrast to the North Polar living room."

Kostakos pushed through a swinging door into the kitchen. It was large and high ceilinged, with more skylights, more bleached wood and white walls. The starkness was alleviated by shelves of colorful cookbooks, a great many hanging baskets, and large bunches of dried red peppers. Beneath the bentwood table lay an enormous black-and-white cowhide rug.

"The peppers and baskets carry on the southwestern motif," I said, "and that rug's definitely Texas."

Kostakos laughed. "This house suffers from an extreme identity crisis. There's a game room downstairs that's Hollywood kitsch. The master bedroom's all antlers and moosehide—north-woods theme. The guest bedroom's southern—flower prints and white lace and little lavender-scented pillows. If you woke up in there, you'd half expect Butterfly McQueen to come sashaying in with your breakfast tray."

"What in God's name is the owner like?"

"He's a mild-mannered medical researcher at UCSF. But I suspect he has a rich fantasy life." Kostakos went to the U-shaped workspace at the end of the room. "What kind of coffee would you like? We have Brazilian, Zimbabwe, Colombian-Armenian, and Plantation Blend dark roast."

I was embarrassed to tell him that to me coffee is just coffee, despite my efforts to educate myself to the contrary.

Kostakos grinned at my confused silence. "I don't care, either. Coffee's good if it's strong and drinkable. I've been using the dark roast because there seem to be cases of it in the pantry." He busied himself with a grinder and beans.

I sat at the table, stooping first to pat the rough cowhide. "About your personality classifications—which one are you?"

Without hesitation he replied, "My group's the one described as the intellectuals."

"Fitting, considering you're a professor."

"You'd be surprised how often a person's group doesn't mesh with his or her profession. But I must say I like my group. We're perceptive, analytical, produce very original ideas. Some of us have been on the genius level. Freud, for example." He set the coffee-maker going and faced me. "Of course, there are those who claim Hitler may have been one of us."

"That's not too encouraging. I wonder which group I am?"

He got out coffee mugs and set them on the table. Even the mugs in this house were at odds: one was a caricature of Richard Nixon, ski-jump nose and all; the other was Jimmy Carter, big white teeth agleam.

Kostakos regarded me thoughtfully. "I'd have to know you a lot better to say for sure, but if I were to hazard a guess from what I've observed of you and from knowing your profession, I'd say your group is the same as mine."

"Oh, come on! I'm no intellectual."

"That's just a convenient label. You're straightforward, give evidence of being analytical. You think before you speak, phrase what you say precisely. In your business, you're certain to be logical and perceptive. I also sense you might have what's known in psychological jargon as 'the third ear'—the ability to hear meanings beyond what a person's actually saying. You've got intuitive and emotional qualities. You just don't let them get in the way."

He made me sound like quite a sterling character. I basked in the flattery as he fetched the coffeepot.

"Of course," he added as he poured, "there's another side to our group, as exemplified by Hitler's presence. We tend to become rigid in our ideas. We develop theories and won't turn loose of them. We can become extremists." He replaced the coffeepot on the warmer and sat across from me.

"I knew it sounded too good to be true." I sampled the coffee and found it excellent, even to my unsophisticated taste. "How'd you know that I don't use milk or sugar?"

"It's a characteristic of people in our group." At my incredulous look, he added, "Actually, I don't use them, and I just forgot to offer any."

"Those negative things you mentioned, a lot of them are valid for me," I said. "That rigidity? . . ."

He nodded.

"Once, right after I'd gotten my degree and couldn't find a job, I took a personality test to see if I was suited for—don't laugh—a career in life insurance sales. Do you know what the results said? They said I could be 'pushy, severe, and dominant.'"

He raised Nixon to me. "That's our group."

"What else can you tell me about us?"

"Well, do you ever get reclusive? Standoffish? Kind of prickly?"

"I've felt that way for close to a year now—as if I've built a wall around me so nobody can come too close."

"Bad sign. Unhealthy end of the scale. Look out for creeping paranoia. You may become obsessed with peculiar ideas, feel prey to any number of indefinable threats. When that happens, insanity with schizophrenic tendencies lies just around the bend."

I choked on my coffee. "You sound just like a fortune teller I used to know."

He smiled and patted my hand. "Cheer up. When you go nuts, I'll recommend a good psychiatrist."

I drank some more coffee, feeling relaxed and companionable and oddly unwilling to bring the conversation back to the reason I'd come. But finally I said, "What group was Tracy?"

He was silent, looking down into his cup.

"From what people have told me, she must have inherited your sense of humor."

"Actually she was more like her mother. Laura has very little sense of humor, and Tracy didn't have a funny bone in her body."

I thought of what Jay Larkey had told me—that for a funny lady, Tracy had taken herself very seriously. "How do you explain her becoming a comedian, then?"

"That was an outgrowth of her analytical ability. She knew what made other people laugh, and how to create it. She just didn't laugh much herself. Sometimes people standing on the outside see what's going on inside more clearly than those of us who are there." He was silent for a while, then looked at me. "You did it, didn't you?"

"Did what?"

"Got me talking about her, even though I said I wouldn't."

"It wasn't all that calculated."

"I didn't think it was. But now that you've got me started, I might as well go on. Let's go back to the living room, though; it's too cheerful here to talk about somebody I loved who's dead." He listened to his words, then shook his head. "On the other hand, Tracy's memory is so warm that it might do a great deal for that icy room up front."

We went back to our unsittable chairs by the fireplace, and George talked of his daughter. He talked not in terms of his psychological model, or even with the detachment of one in his field, but as a still-grieving father.

Tracy's birth had been premature; for a couple of days he and Laura had feared they might lose her. But her will had proved larger than her tiny body, and she quickly grew strong.

As soon as she could talk, she'd clamored for a baby sister. Laura could have no more children, but it wasn't something a small child could understand.

She'd had five kittens. Each had met with disaster—speeding cars, leukemia, the neighbor's dog. After the fifth died, she'd announced to her parents that she never wanted another pet. And she never acquired one.

George had worried for a while because she always had more imaginary friends than real ones. But she'd outgrown them, and when he'd first seen her perform comedy, he'd realized what fertile material those old pals had become.

She'd gotten pregnant during her senior year in high school; he and Laura had gone along with her decision to have an abortion. It had left no apparent emotional scars.

They'd both known she was unhappy at Foothill Junior College, and had noted her growing preoccupation with comedy with a certain unease. When she'd announced her desire to move to San Francisco, he'd been opposed at first. But Laura had convinced him of the damage an overprotective family can do, and in the end he'd given in.

No, he said, he didn't resent Laura for pressuring him to allow the move that eventually led to Tracy's death.

No, he and Tracy hadn't talked much in the last three or four years of her life. He'd just assumed it was part of the natural separation process.

Had she abused their credit cards? He'd never had that impression, but Laura was the one who handled the bills, and she did have a tendency to be overindulgent where Tracy was concerned.

No, he guessed he hadn't really known his daughter. Not at the time of her death.

Yes, he honestly believed she was dead. He had no illusions, unlike Laura.

"Why?" I asked.

"I went to the trial. I watched the evidence being presented day after day. There's no doubt she's dead."

His hands were locked together between his bluejeaned knees; the knuckles showed white through his tan. His eyes were more greenish now; when I tried to hold his gaze, it slipped away from mine.

Finally he sighed. "Maybe it's more that I have to believe it."

"Why?"

"Because if she's not dead, she has done a monstrous thing. If she's not dead, she is someone I don't want to acknowledge as my own."

After a moment he added, "Please don't find Tracy alive, Sharon. And if you do, don't bring her back to me."

8

After I left George Kostakos, I stopped at a phone booth and called Café Comedie. Larkey wasn't in, but the woman who answered gave me the last address and phone number on file for Lisa McIntyre, the waitress who had been Bobby Foster's friend. I called the number but found it now belonged to someone else, who had never heard of McIntyre. Next I tried to call Marc Emmons but got only a machine. Rae had had similar results the day before when she'd tried to arrange an appointment for me, so I decided the best place to catch Emmons would be at the club that evening.

Directory Assistance had no current listing for McIntyre, but her old address wasn't far away, on Pacific Avenue just off Polk Street. I decided to drive over there and see if anyone knew where she'd moved; possibly one of the neighbors was still in touch with her.

The building on Pacific was a fairly large one, part commercial, with a furniture reupholstering workshop, bakery, and drugstore downstairs and apartments on the second floor. As I'd expected, none of the mailboxes in the vestibule bore McIntyre's name. I rang the manager but received no response; next I buzzed the seven remaining apartments. Two people were home; neither had heard of McIntyre. None of the people working in the downstairs businesses remembered her, either; they didn't pay too much attention to the tenants, one man told me.

I decided to turn the search for McIntyre over to Rae. Since separating from her husband, my assistant had displayed boundless enthusiasm for all sorts of routine chores. Besides, McIntyre wasn't really central to my investigation; I only wanted to talk with her to see if she could shed some light on the unusually high level of tension that Larkey had sensed in his younger employees shortly before Tracy vanished.

I went back to the MG and considered what to do next. Leora Whitsun, Foster's mother, was visiting relatives in Los Angeles and wouldn't be back until New Year's Day, when she was scheduled for duty at the Potrero Medical Clinic. There were other friends of Tracy's I could interview—members of her improv group, for instance—but they struck me as even more peripheral than McIntyre. About all they'd be able to tell me was what kind of person Tracy had been, and I felt I already had enough of a handle on that. Besides, the Friday before New Year's Eve was a bad time to find people at home.

I thought some more about Marc Emmons: his answering machine always being on, his abrupt departure from the club the night before. It could be he was monitoring calls, ducking me. Since his address on Potrero Hill wasn't too much of a detour on my way home, I might as well swing by there and check for signs of his presence.

Emmons lived on Mariposa, not far from Missouri Street, in the heart of the upscale, newly trendy part of the hill. The transformation of this predominantly blue-collar, ethnically diverse area began in the seventies, when the middle class discovered its sunny weather and as yet reasonable property values. Now the neighborhood is largely mixed: renovated houses and new apartment buildings and condominium complexes are interspersed among older, shabbier dwellings; hardware stores and corner groceries and bars that have been there for generations stand side by side with patisseries and wine shops and restaurants that cater to the new element.

Emmons's building was one of the new ones: bastardized Victorian, with skylights and decks and greenhouse windows, painted sky blue. A developer's sign advertised one, two, and three-bedroom units, hot tub, sauna, and exercise room, plus a complete security system. I was surprised that a man who made his living as a stand-up comic could afford such a place, but then I didn't know how much Larkey was paying him. He also might—like Tracy—have well-to-do, indulgent parents.

I rang the bell for 7A but received no response. Then I went to the security gate and peered through it at the lower-level parking area, trying to see if there was a car in that unit's space. As near as I could tell, there wasn't.

I was beginning to feel this wasn't my day. Probably the best thing to do was go home and start over at Café Comedie that evening. I began driving south on Missouri, planning to take Army

Street across town to my quiet little neighborhood near the Glen Park district. But before I got there, I turned east, toward the Potrero Annex housing project, where Bobby Foster had grown up.

After a few blocks Missouri curved and took a sharp downward slope, and I found myself looking at a whole other Potrero Hill. Only minutes from the luxury apartment houses with their saunas and hot tubs was a housing complex so alien from them—from most of the rest of the city—that it might have been in an alternate universe.

The two-tiered dun-colored buildings sprawled over an entire hillside. The view of the bay and the bridge connecting the city with Oakland would have been spectacular from their windows—except they were heavily meshed and barred. I stopped at a corner where a couple of burnt-out, vandalized cars stood. Farther down, against other battered and rusted vehicles, leaned small knots of black men, drinking and most likely doing drugs. A ghetto blaster stood on the hood of one of the cars, and rap music filled the air. Some kids were scrounging around among the rubble in the gutter; as I watched, one of them held up a used hypodermic syringe.

I stayed at the top of the rise viewing the war zone below—an embattled piece of turf that armed drug dealers and addicts were doing their best to wrest from the honest citizens. A few months back, San Francisco's public housing projects had been declared "out of control" in a federal government report; a HUD official had admitted in print to being "terrified" on a tour of the large Sunnydale complex. For a time a great many solutions to the problem had been proposed; what they mainly amounted to was shifting the responsibility from the Housing Authority to the police to the Department of Social Services, and back again. As far as I knew, few plans had been implemented, and after a while the media had lost interest in the subject. If anything had improved in the projects, you couldn't tell it by looking at Potrero Annex.

As I sat there contemplating the despair and hopelessness trapped within those barrackslike buildings, a silver stretch Mercedes topped the rise behind me. The driver and his passenger—both young black men with eyes masked by mirrored sunglasses—looked hardened beyond their years. They weren't pro ballplayers come to dispense New Year's cheer to the old neighborhood; they were here to dispense death. This other, alien San Francisco was no place for me, unarmed and alone—even in the middle of the afternoon.

* * *

When I arrived home, my brown-shingled cottage on the tail end of Church Street seemed even more inviting than usual. One of the contractors I'd had in to give an estimate earlier in the week was just coming down the front steps. He wanted to check a couple of things, he said, and then he'd be able to quote me a price. The price was agreeable, and since none of the others had so much as bothered to call back, I told him to draw up a contract, and he said he could start next Wednesday. After he left, I puttered around until six, then called Café Comedie.

Marc Emmons had called in sick, Larkey told me. I dialed his home number and again spoke with the machine. Not my day, I thought, and not my night, either.

The videotape of Foster's confession had been stuffed in my mailbox when I'd returned, but Rae had included no note. I called All Souls and talked with Ted, who said she was in the attic, mudding and taping the Sheetrock she'd put up.

"She says she wants the room finished by tomorrow night," he added, "so she can start the year in a real room."

I could understand that, so I told him not to bother her. Then I wandered around listlessly, thinking about Bobby Foster's plight.

Capital punishment was an issue on which I felt oddly ambivalent. I agreed with the usual arguments against it: it hasn't been proven a deterrent; it is used discriminatively against the poor and minority group members; more than a few innocent parties have been unjustly condemned and executed; and contrary to what its proponents would have you believe, most methods of execution are neither painless nor humane.

On the other hand, the sight of a bloodied, broken victim of violence called up a primal rage in me—an atavistic bloodlust that made me want to exact the proverbial eye for an eye. I'd encountered enough unrepentant killers to know that there were those who couldn't be redeemed, certainly not in an overloaded penal system such as we have in California. I had to admit that there were instances when I'd subscribed to the just-blow-them-away viewpoint.

As of today there had not been an execution in California since 1967. In the interim, some three hundred people, including my client, had been sentenced to die in the gas chamber. Within the next couple of years the legal carnage mandated by the reinstatement of the death penalty would begin, and at that time I suspected that those of us who were undecided would quickly have our fill of retribution. In my rational moments, I abhor killing of any kind, so I knew which side of the issue I would then champion.

To take my mind off that subject I went to the kitchen and put on some leftover spaghetti to heat slowly. Then I gave in to the impulse I'd been trying to resist, and looked at the video of Foster's confession again. That depressed me thoroughly, so I gathered together my notes and what files Rae didn't have and went over them, paying particular attention to various "sightings" of Tracy that the authorities had investigated before the bloodstained car had turned up.

As usual in missing-persons and kidnapping cases, reports from individuals both sane and mad had poured in to the authorities. Most had been easily dismissed as mistakes or outright fabrications, but there had been two leads promising enough for the various law enforcement agencies to commit themselves to a significant number of man-hours.

A Walnut Creek woman had spotted someone strongly resembling Tracy driving a car across the San Francisco–Oakland Bay Bridge at around twelve-thirty in the morning after she was last seen at Café Comedie. The informant had taken note of her because they'd gone to school together at Foothill College prior to the woman's marriage and move to the Contra Costa County suburb. She could say nothing definite about the make or model of the car, however, nor had she noticed if there was anyone with Tracy. East Bay authorities assisted in the search, but no tangible evidence of Tracy's presence there ever surfaced.

Another lead backed up the sighting on the bridge. A clerk in a twenty-four-hour convenience store just off Interstate 80 outside of Berkeley identified Tracy as having stopped and bought a quantity of groceries at around one that morning. At first she'd thought she didn't have enough cash to pay for them, and had asked if the store would accept a traveler's check left over from a recent vacation in Hawaii (where Tracy had gone with her parents for the Christmas holidays that year). While she searched for the checks, the clerk asked her where she had stayed in Hawaii, and she named the resort on the big island where the Kostakoses had spent a week. Then she discovered she had enough cash after all, paid, and left. Together with the first lead, this one had seemed promising, but eventually the East Bay inquiry was back-burnered.

I flipped through my legal pad to the notes I'd taken on the two sightings. They both seemed significant to me, but I also had questions, such as whose car Tracy had been driving. She hadn't owned one, didn't like to drive. I supposed I could speak with the Walnut Creek woman and the clerk—assuming either could be located—and see if they could supply additional details, but that was an unlikely possibility, given the passage of time.

Frustrated, I grabbed another legal pad and began making a list of things for Rae to do on Monday—or more likely Tuesday, since January second was the legal holiday.

1. Ask our contact at the realty co to pull credit rept on T. Check for activ in chg accts aftr date of disapp. If we have a contact at her bank (see my Rolodex) check for activ in accts there.
2. Call my friend at DMV & see about vehicles registrd to T. Check driving recrd for viols after disapp.
3. Call Mrs. K & get names of T's drs, dntsts. Ask if any reqs for med recs.
4.

I stopped, chewing on the pencil top. Why on earth was I doing this? Rae knew the elements of skip tracing, had probably gotten started. All I had to do on Monday was tell her to look for Lisa McIntyre as well.

Besides, I knew skip tracing wouldn't turn up anything on a woman as bright as Tracy. If she were alive and unwilling to be found, she wouldn't be using her own name. She wouldn't be stupid enough to use her charge or checking accounts. She would long ago have acquired a new identity. I would let Rae go through the motions, because it's always wise to do so, but I was certain she would be wasting her time.

Finally I tore the list off the pad, balled it up, and tossed it on the floor. For a moment I considered reading through the notebook of character sketches I'd taken from Tracy's room, but decided to save that for the next day. In case I was still unable to contact Marc Emmons, it would give me something to do before I had to get dolled up for New Year's Eve.

I put the files and the video aside, then dished up some spaghetti and settled down with it and a tape of *Airplane!*—my all-time favorite lunatic comedy movie and cheerer-upper. After a while, my fat old spotted cat, Watney, came to sit on my lap, and together we whiled away a few more hours of the waning year.

9

The shabby brown Victorian on the hill above Mission Street was ablaze with light and awash with New Year's Eve revelers when I arrived at nine on Saturday night. The living room chandelier and wall sconces had been turned on, and for once all the bulbs worked; a fire crackled on the hearth. I noted with amusement that someone had tried to disguise the fact that most of the needles had fallen off the Christmas tree in the window bay by draping it in extra tinsel. A bar had been set up on the big coffee table; the punch bowl would surely contain the bourbon punch for which I had long ago provided the recipe. I knew if Hank had tinkered with it, it would be doubly lethal—and that the coffee in the urn in the kitchen would be doubly strong.

The crowd was an odd mixture of All Souls clients, personal friends of staff members, pillars of the local liberal establishment, and even an occasional Republican. Across the room by the fireplace I spotted Charlie Cornish, an antiques—well, really junk—dealer who had figured prominently in the first major case I'd investigated for the co-op. He raised his punch cup to me, and I waved. On the other side of the room was my old friend Claudia James, who used to own my answering service until it went bankrupt due to the increasing popularity of answering machines. Tonight she looked prosperous in a dyed suede outfit; it seemed to me that I'd heard she was now doing something with computers.

I hurried upstairs to my office, dumped my coat and bag, then went to the hall mirror and examined my appearance. The dress had been my Christmas present to myself: red silk, long sleeved and low necked, with a slightly flared, indecently short skirt. I'd piled my hair high on my head, liberated my grandmother's garnet earrings from the strongbox where I usually hide them, and put on

71

a pair of high-heeled black suede pumps. All in all, it was a far cry from my usual sweater and jeans. Spiffy enough to make me feel hopeful. Maybe there would be an interesting man downstairs— one who wasn't into Zen gun handling or death. My "soul mate"? Well, at least somebody who could be taken out in public.

Before I joined the party, I went to the kitchen to see if I could help out with the food. Jack was there, arranging a platter of cheese and cold cuts. His eyes brightened when he saw me; they moved from my face to the dress's neckline to my legs. I gave him what I hoped was a sisterly smile.

Ted was there, too, getting out more wineglasses and examining them for those unsightly spots. "*Love* your dress," he said.

"Thank you. Where's yours?"

"Didn't come back from alterations in time."

I patted the sleeve of his burgundy velvet smoking jacket. "This is more you, anyway."

I looked for the bread knife so I could start cutting slices of sourdough, and saw Rae leaning against the stove, talking to a chubby man whom I thought held some position in the mayor's office. She had upgraded her fashion image tonight with a silk blouse and black skirt splashed with red things that were probably supposed to be cherries. I smiled affectionately as I noted that there already was a wine spot on the blouse, and her shoes—a pair of those spike-heeled, open-toed sandals that always look tarty—were at least seven years out of date. When she saw me, she motioned for me to come over, and the man excused himself.

"You look great!" she said.

"You too." She did—for Rae. "Did you get the room finished?"

"Sort of. It's not painted, and I've still got to do something about carpet and a door, but I can start sleeping there tonight."

"Good for you."

Behind me Jack yelled for someone to get a move on with the bread. Rae went over to the cutting board of the Hoosier cabinet, and I followed.

"Listen," she said, "your friend from the DMV stopped by for a few minutes a while ago. She had another party and said to tell you she's sorry she missed you. But she brought the data I requested on Kostakos, and I put it on your desk."

"You got her records pulled already?"

"I started the skip trace yesterday. Things were slow, so your friend was able to speed it up."

"Anything there?"

"I didn't have the time to look."

"Well, thanks for getting to it so quickly." I'd been absolutely right about not needing to make a list for Rae; she was turning into a first-rate assistant. "I've got another person for you to trace, but I'll go into it on Monday. If you're planning to work—it's a legal holiday."

"I'd as soon work as anything else. By then I'll have done all I can on the room, until I get some money."

"Good. Have you seen Hank and Anne-Marie tonight?"

A funny look came onto her face. "Hank's in his office."

"Where's Anne-Marie?"

"Home."

"Uh-oh. I better go talk with him."

As I left the kitchen, however, a loud whoop resounded at the far end of the hall. A tall, lanky man in Levis, a leather vest, and cowboy boots charged at me, grabbed me by the waist, and swung me high off the ground. Jack, who had been following me with the plate of cold cuts, looked startled, then chagrined.

It was Willie Whelan, a longtime client. Willie had once been a fence, operating out of local flea markets, but he'd since gone legit, as he put it. Now he owned a chain of cut-rate jewelry stores, the kind that extend credit to anybody and charge usurious interest rates for the favor. He even did his own commercials, and for a couple of years now, I'd been accustomed to seeing him leering at me on late-night TV, asking, "Need credit? Come to Willie's Jewelry Mart. . . ."

He set me down, planted a big kiss on my forehead, and backed off to look me over. Jack scowled and tried to edge around us, with no success.

"McCone, you look great!" Willie exclaimed. "Jesus, what's it been—two years? Three? Got no call for your services now that I've gone legit."

"You look great, too. But I've seen a lot of *you* lately."

"Yeah? How do you like those commercials? Clever, huh? The way that happened, one day my ad man comes to me and says, 'Willie, there's not a thing I can do for you that you can't do for yourself. You're a walking advertisement for the Jewelry Mart'— this was when I only had the one store—'and what I want to do is put you on TV.' Well, I thought about it. This fellow owns the Diamond Center has had a lot of success with it. So I said, 'What the hell, let's try it.' And we did, and it worked, and now I've got seven stores all over the Bay Area."

"Excuse me," Jack said plaintively.

"And you know why it works?" Willie went on. "Sincerity. I love my customers, every one of them. That comes through in the ads. They come in, they got no credit, lousy credit, and I help them. Those commercials? I write them myself. None of this speech-writer crap like the politicians. I just say what I feel, and the customers keep pouring in." He winked at me. "And so does the money."

"Excuse me," Jack said again.

"Say, where can I get a drink around here?" Willie asked.

"Front room." I pointed.

"Think I'll go grab one. We got to sit down and talk later. I want to know all about what's going on with you."

As Willie ambled back down the hall, Jack sighed in relief. I stepped aside so he could deliver the platter, then went to Hank's office and knocked on the half-shut door.

Hank sat tipped back in the chair in front of his rolltop desk; the room was illuminated only by his green glass lamp; his coat hung over the head of his emaciated-looking cigar-store Indian. Recently he had begun spiffing up the office, buying the desk and the Indian. It should have been a good sign, indicating he was becoming less slovenly and taking more pride in his surroundings, but I viewed it with alarm. The improvements were a result of his spending more time there than at the flat he and Anne-Marie owned in Noe Valley. He was also spending more time at the Remedy Lounge on Mission Street, playing pinball and drinking too much.

Now I saw the scotch bottle on the desk and the glazed look that not even his thick horn-rimmed glasses could hide, and realized he was quite drunk. I came into the room, shut the door, and sat in the client's chair.

"Happy New Year," Hank said. He gestured at the bottle. "Want a drink?"

"You know I don't drink scotch."

He shrugged and poured himself some.

"What're you doing in here?" I asked. "Why don't you join the party?"

"Don't care to. How're you? I hardly ever see you anymore."

It was on the tip of my tongue to reply that he hardly ever saw me because I didn't spend my every waking hour at the Remedy, but I restrained myself. "I know. We'll have to rectify that."

"What're you working on these days?"

"The Foster case, for Jack."

"Jack. Jack's a good man. He's hung up on you, you know."

"Jack's at the stage where he'd be hung up on any woman who was nice to him."

"You could do worse. Have done worse." He paused to drink. "Greg's here. Have you seen him?"

"Not yet."

"He broke up with What's-her-name."

"So he told me."

"You been seeing him?"

"Occasionally. But there's nothing between—"

"Greg's hung up on you. Always has been."

"According to you, the whole world's hung up on me."

He waggled his finger at me. The motion almost tipped the chair over. He righted it with exaggerated dignity. "You'd do well to heed my advice."

"Why are you always trying to fix my love life?"

"Somebody's got to. You need a man of sh . . . substance. Solid, like Greg or Jack. Look at you."

"What's wrong with me?"

"That's a man-hunting dress if I ever saw one."

"So?"

"So if I don't take you in hand and advishe . . . advise you, you'll go and fall for some yoyo like that disc jockey you just got rid of. God knows what it'll be next. Another surfer, probly."

I'd come in here to discuss his troubled marriage, and he'd managed to turn it into a dissection of my romantic history. "The surfer was way back in high school. Hank, where's Anne-Marie?"

"Home. Fuck her."

That shocked me so profoundly that I couldn't think of a reply.

"She wants to stay home, entertain the assholes upstairs, let her. This is where I belong. Celebrate New Year's with my friends, like always. So fuck her."

"I realize you two are having problems—"

"Problems?" He laughed bitterly.

"Do you want to talk about it?"

"No."

"Will you at least come out and join the party?"

"No."

"Hank—"

"*You* go out and join the party. Trample on Jack's feelings. Snub Greg. Find a surfer and take him home and screw him, for all I care. Just leave me alone."

I had long before learned not to try to reason with a belligerent drunk. I went.

The party was in full swing now. Voices babbled and laughed, glasses clinked, and ice rattled. I went to the living room, got some punch, and looked around for Greg. He was over by the Christmas tree, talking to a tall redhead whose expression said she was captivated by his gray-blond good looks. I felt a flash of irritation, which quickly faded when he saw me, smiled, excused himself, and made his way through the crush.

He put his hand on my shoulder and kissed my cheek. "Hi. You look great."

"Thanks. But so many people have said that in such tones of wonder that I'm beginning to suspect I look terrible the rest of the time. How're you?"

"Not too bad. Overworked as usual. I really had to do some finagling to get off tonight." Someone jostled him from behind and his punch sloshed dangerously. "Why don't we go out in the hall where it's not so crowded?"

We weaved through the crowd, found the hallway jammed, too. Greg motioned at the stairs, and we went halfway up and sat.

"So what's new with you?" he asked when we were settled.

"Not a great deal. I finally got the house refinanced and they're going to start work on the new bedroom next week."

"It's about time. What's your next project?"

"I may actually be done." I paused, wondering how to broach the subject of the Foster case.

"You seeing anybody?" he asked.

"No. You?"

"No."

The silence that followed was not a comfortable one. Greg watched me speculatively. I looked away, saw Willie Whelan performing one of his commercials for Rae's benefit. She was laughing uproariously. Maybe they— No, that was too unlikely a combination.

"Greg," I said.

He raised his dark eyebrows, looking hopeful.

"Greg, there's something I need your help with."

The eyebrows pulled together in a frown. "Uh-huh. Here it comes."

"Hear me out. You remember the Bobby Foster case?"

". . . Kid who kidnapped and killed the Kostakos girl, right? Gallagher headed up the investigation."

"Right. Jack Stuart's handling the appeal."

"And he believes those cockeyed rumors about Kostakos not being dead."

"I think there might be something to them. That investigation was full of holes."

"Look, Gallagher wasn't one of the department's brightest, but—"

"I'd really like to take a look at the case file."

"Why do you always have to ask me for things like this?"

"It's been a long time since I asked for a favor."

The speculative look was back on his face. "What'll you do in return?"

"Well, not that!" The words popped out before I could consider them.

Greg threw his head back and laughed so loudly that several people looked at us.

My face got very hot. "Hush," I said, tugging on his sleeve. "I didn't mean—"

"You meant exactly what you said, but don't worry—it wasn't what I had in mind. Although I have to warn you, I'm not counting us out just yet."

It was the first time he'd so much as hinted that he would like to get back together, and it silenced me.

He added, "What you can do is buy me dinner one night next week. Why don't you come down to the hall tomorrow morning? I'm on duty, and things will be quiet."

"Thanks. I really appreciate it."

"No problem. If there really are holes in the investigation, I want to know." He stood up, reached for my glass. "I'll get us another drink."

Halfway to the punch bowl, however, he was buttonholed by one of the city's watchdog activists, and I could see he would be a long time fielding her criticisms of the department's policies. Finally I got my own drink and wandered about, talking with friends and renewing old acquaintances. And waiting for the time when we could all sing that such things should be forgot, and then go home.

The party had begun to depress me. Every time I turned around Jack was there, looking wistful and staring at my cleavage. Hank never emerged from his office, and I was afraid he had passed out in there, but didn't want to appear to be checking up on him. Greg's speculative gaze kept following me around the room, and I sensed he would make some move before the evening was out. My soul mate had failed to materialize, and I didn't so much as spot a surfer. Finally, at half past eleven, I slipped upstairs for my coat, shoved the envelope from the DMV into my bag, and went home to usher in the New Year alone.

I had a bottle of champagne on ice—perhaps I'd subconsciously expected I'd leave the party early—and I opened it, then turned the TV to the replay of the Times Square celebration. Even that was depressing. The big red apple that had been installed there some years before in an ill-advised burst of civic pride had finally been supplanted by the more traditional golden ball that I remembered from my childhood, but it now looked tacky to me. The drunken revelers seemed asinine, and I kept looking for pickpockets in the crowd. It was a relief when the ball dropped and I made my solitary toast to new beginnings.

And then the phone rang.

I looked at it, afraid it might be Jack or Greg or somebody else wanting me to come back to the party. Or a maudlin, drunken Hank. Or my mother, whom I love but didn't particularly want to speak with just then. Or worst of all, a wrong number. But it also might be something important, so on the fourth ring I answered.

"Happy New Year," George Kostakos's voice said.

I felt a surge of warmth. "Happy New Year to you, too."

"I wasn't sure I should call, but I wanted to share the moment with someone—and who could be better than a fellow personality-group member?"

"I'm glad you did call. I can't think of anyone I'd rather share it with."

We talked for a while, about other New Year's Eves—good ones, bad ones, pleasant surprises, disappointments, disasters. Long after we'd hung up, the warm glow persisted.

When I poured the last of the champagne, I again toasted to new beginnings.

10

On the way to the Hall of Justice the next morning, I thought about Tracy's character sketchbook, which I'd read the previous day before the New Year's festivities began. It contained some 50 two- or three-page descriptions of women in the young-to-middle-aged range. They were less physical descriptions than psychological profiles—reflecting the kind of insight her father possessed—and the way she turned a phrase led me to believe that had she not gone into comedy, she might have become a writer. I was particularly interested in the first entry because, having seen Tracy's room, I suspected she might have been describing herself.

In part, it read: *No need for a physical description. She is superiorly average, almost nondescript. What stands out is her greed—for material things, for life itself. Why such neediness? Easy to blame it on her family. The mother was cold. She never hugged her. She wanted to be a mentor. But there's no place for mentors in families. The girl needed a mother. The beloved father, for all his academic knowledge, was little better. Vague, fondly absent. Sometimes she thought him only half-alive.*

As I read the other profiles, I realized that Tracy had based a good number of her characters on actual individuals. Although she had given most fictional names, the brief physical details in two of them allowed me to recognize people I'd recently met: Kathy Soriano, Larkey's partner's wife; and Amy Barbour.

The interesting portion of Kathy's profile read: *Not for her the garden club, the volunteer work, the kiss-kiss luncheon-and-fashion-show circuit. She prefers to hover on the fringes of power, a sort of exalted gofer for those who control. But she has no power herself. That belongs to the husband, the man of steel-rimmed glasses and steelier eyes. Deceptively mild-mannered, he watches his wife jump at whatever fingers are snapped and remains amused and detached. She knows this, so she indulges in petty revenge, nasty little affairs designed to wound a man who is unwoundable. A circular bind here, because he will never let her have power over him—which is what she wants the most.*

Beside the entry in another color of ink, Tracy had noted: *Can't use. Too grim, and she's likely to recognize herself.*

Amy's sketch was gentler, more affectionate, but most of it still damning: *She's a poor thing, clinging to each current craze, desperately hoping to define herself by externals. The tough facade easily gives way to anger, the anger to fear, then to tears. A bundle of rage, despising whoever is convenient for what her parents have done to her, but actually despising herself because she believes their neglect was deserved. She thinks if she finds someone to love, she will belong. An impossibility, because she is incapable of loving even herself.*

Tracy had merely drawn an X through the entry.

In the latter pages of the notebook the profiles became more brief and even more grim than Kathy Soriano's, as if Tracy had lost her ability to see humor in those around her. The last five or so did not even bear fictitious names, and the final one was only a paragraph.

It has become her habit to milk every emotion, even her own, for personal gain. Everything is useful. She sleeps with this one and that one solely for the exotic experience. She sleeps with another for his influence, all the while professing love. But if she does love him, shouldn't she take steps to protect him? It's a form of paralysis, her inability to act.

Reflecting on the sketchbook now, I thought of Laura Kostakos's claim that her daughter had been upset and disillusioned with herself shortly before her disappearance. If her impression was correct—and I had no reason to doubt it—it would account for the apathy and disinterest shown in these last pages.

When I arrived at the hall, I found a parking space directly in front on Bryant Street and hurried inside. The Hall of Justice is normally a noisy, bustling place, but on this Sunday and holiday, with the courts closed and the various offices minimally staffed, it seemed strangely quiet. I found Greg in his cubicle upstairs, looking cheerful. Perhaps, I thought, he'd gotten together with the tall, admiring redhead after I'd left the party. Whatever the reason, his mind was on business this morning, and after a perfunctory inquiry about where I'd disappeared to the night before, he sat me down at an out-of-the-way desk with the bulging files on the Foster/Kostakos investigation.

I plowed through the material for more than three hours, even though much of it was familiar because I'd read it in the files Foster's public defender had turned over to Jack. I took notes on a few details that had previously escaped me: what Tracy had been wearing when last seen (a red llama's-wool cape, jeans, and matching red rubber rain boots); the registration of the blue Volvo that had been stolen from the club's lot and later abandoned in the Santa Cruz Mountains (Atlas Development Corporation); the statements of witnesses who said her performance had been off that last night, and that she had made a phone call shortly before leaving the club.

I'd saved a stack of Ben Gallagher's scribbled notes for last, and I went through them quickly, dismissing most as unimportant. There was one sheet that interested me, however: jottings on a phone inquiry to the DMV. Tracy had apparently received a citation for reckless driving (left turn across oncoming traffic) at a location in Napa County two days before her disappearance.

What had she been doing up there? I wondered. And in whose car, since she didn't have one of her own? I studied the notes more carefully, trying to decipher the crabbed writing, then remembered the envelope from my friend at the DMV, that I'd stuffed in my bag when leaving All Souls the night before. I pulled it out, found it contained a computer printout of Tracy's driving record. But on it, the date of the final entry was different.

Gallagher's scribblings showed the citation as having been issued at two-ten in the morning on February eleventh. The printout said the thirteenth. If the printout was correct, Tracy had been in Napa County a good four hours *after* she was last seen outside Café Comedie quarreling with Bobby Foster. And around fifteen minutes after Foster returned to the club, according to the testimony of his fellow parking attendants.

I held up Gallagher's notes and studied the date. That wavery "1" could easily have been intended to be a "3." The significance of the date might not have registered when Ben wrote it down; he might have been interrupted and not gotten back to the notes for some time. And by then, he would merely have read the number as "11," two days too early to have any bearing on the disappearance.

The location of the violation was given as Cuttings Wharf Road at Highway 121 in Napa County. I had no notion where that was, but it had to be at least an hour away from the city. The car Tracy had been driving was a Volvo, license plate number—

I looked back at the information I'd copied down about the stolen car belonging to Atlas Development Corporation. The license plate number was the same.

There was no written confirmation of Gallagher's inquiry from the DMV, but that didn't surprise me. It might never have been sent, or it might merely have been another piece of paper that got lost in the shuffle.

One piece of paper that would have invalidated Bobby Foster's confession. A piece of paper whose absence had condemned him to death.

I stared at Gallagher's notes for a moment. Although I told myself not to get too excited yet, feelings of elation spread through me. It was the first break—and a major one—in a case I'd initially thought unsolvable. I checked the date and time of the citation once more, then got up and went to the door of Greg's cubicle. "Would you come here a minute?" I said.

Since it was New Year's and the next day was also a legal holiday, there wasn't much Greg could do to check out the discrepancy. He would request verification of the date, time, and vehicle license plate number from the DMV when their office opened on Tuesday, as well as contact the highway patrol, to see if the issuing officer remembered anything about the incident. But, as he cautioned me, that was unlikely; officers give so many tickets that they're not apt to remember one from that long ago—unless there had been something exceedingly unusual about the circumstances. My spirits refused to be deflated by that, though.

When I left the hall and climbed into my MG, I took the packet of maps from the side pocket and found one for Napa County. Cuttings Wharf Road ran south from Highway 121, just beyond where it split off from Highway 29, the main arterial into the city of Napa and the wine-producing valley to its north. The smaller road seemed to be an accessway to the Napa River. To get there, I would take the Bay Bridge. . . .

There was an entrance ramp to the I-80 freeway and the bridge less than a block from the hall. I drove down to Fifth Street and joined the light flow of eastbound traffic.

On the other side of the bay, the freeway took me past Berkeley, where I had lived for four years but now seldom visited. Beyond Richmond, the land became gentle, rolling hills; as I approached the Carquinez Strait, the hills were dotted with pastel-colored oil storage tanks, and I could see smoke-belching refineries spread out on the shores of San Pablo Bay. Another bridge took me across the strait, and at Vallejo—a bland town whose only distinctions are the Mare Island Naval Shipyard and Marine World/Africa U.S.A.—I cut over to Highway 29. The traffic was even sparser there; the businesses that fronted the road were closed for the holiday. After about ten miles, Highway 121 curved off to the northeast, toward Lake Berryessa. I stayed on the main route, crossing a high-arching bridge over the river, then took the other branch of 121 toward Sonoma.

Cuttings Wharf Road appeared in less than a mile; a sign indicated it was the way to the Napa River resorts. There was a turn lane, the one from which Tracy would have made the dangerous left across traffic that had attracted the attention of the highway patrol. The officer would have followed her onto Cuttings Wharf Road and stopped her immediately, I thought, perhaps here in front of these small houses or next to that high-tension tower.

A good deal of the land was planted in grapes here, black knotty vines devoid of leaves. Windbreaks of eucalyptus edged the road. I drove slowly, looking at names on mailboxes, searching for some clue as to what Tracy might have been doing here in the dead early hours of a February morning. When the road branched, I hesitated, then took the arm that went toward the public fishing access.

There were more vineyards and a Christmas tree farm down there, as well as a number of cottages that looked to be closed up for the winter. A large boat- and RV-storage yard spread out on the right, its signs advertising groceries, bait, and beer. Beyond it was a mostly deserted parking area.

I drove to the edge of the water, stopped, and got out of the car. The river was perhaps a hundred yards wide at that point, edged on both sides with rocks and tule grass. A couple of lonely-looking fishermen wearing heavy parkas hunched over their poles on the wharf; neither bothered to glance my way. I stood there for a few minutes, listening to the ripple of the current. Black rain clouds massed over the distant hills; closer in I saw the towering super-structure of a drawbridge, its steel gray a darker complement to the gray of the sky. Finally I turned back to the car. There was nothing here for me, no one to question. Even the bait-and-tackle shop at the water's edge—called, so help me, The Happy Hooker—was closed for the holiday.

I drove back the way I'd come and took the other fork—a winding road that led through more vineyard and past small farms. The land was flatter here, the cloud-shrouded hills many miles away. I met with no other cars, and the only signs of human habitation were vehicles parked in driveways and occasional wisps of smoke from the farmhouses' chimneys.

The road took a sharp turn in the direction of the drawbridge I'd glimpsed earlier. Now it was built up on only the left side: a solid row of houses set close to the pavement on narrow lots that backed up to the river. To my right was a flat plain that signs announced as belonging to a salt company; a railroad spur cut across it and the road to the drawbridge. I bumped over the right-of-way, nearly in the shadow of the great clockwork structure.

More houses hugged the river's edge, some of them large, others mere cottages. Now I spotted a few people in the small yards, encountered a couple of joggers loping along the pavement. I slowed, continued to study mailboxes, looking for . . . what? I wasn't sure.

After about a mile, the houses were more widely spaced. The road narrowed, became potholed. Then there were several vacant lots, covered in scrub vegetation and iceplant, which rose to a levee beside the river. Beyond them I saw three more cottages set far apart from one another, and a turnaround where the road ended. I slowed in front of the first of these, a house that was screened from sight by a tall wooden fence overgrown by vines. A weathered sign attached to the sagging gate said BARBOUR.

My breath caught and I jammed on the MG's brakes, almost killing the engine. That was not your typical spelling of the name, I thought. Not likely to be mere coincidence.

I left the MG next to the fence and went up to the gate. It was secured by a hasp and padlock, but its hinges had given way on one side, providing enough of an opening for me to wriggle through. Inside, a rutted driveway led through a thicket of pyracantha bushes. I followed it, batting their berry-laden branches aside.

The cottage was weathered shingle, with a sagging front porch and an equally sagging roofline. All its windows were shuttered. To the left was a dilapidated garage, its double doors also secured by a padlock. An ancient apple tree spread its branches over the porch's roof; as I walked toward the cottage, I breathed the sour odor of many seasons' windfall fruit.

The wooden steps groaned as I mounted them. In the shadows of the porch lurked a motley collection of wicker furniture and a rusted old-fashioned glider swing. I was certain no one had sat on any of them in years. I tried the door, found it locked, then checked the shutters and found them secure. Next I went down the steps and over to the garage.

The padlock held its doors firmly, but there was a side window that hadn't been shuttered. I went up to it, rubbed off some of the accumulated grime, and looked inside. Nothing but a potting shelf with a rusted metal watering can on it, and a jumbled assortment of garden tools.

I circled the house, hoping to find a similarly unshuttered window, but met with no success. Behind the building was a stand of pepper trees that blocked the view of the river. I made my way through them and climbed the levee. Beyond it, the land dropped off to a dilapidated dock; a derelict fishing boat was beached on its side perhaps twenty yards from the shoreline. The boat lay under the drooping limbs of a willow; a flat-armed cactus had grown up over its gunwales. Once the gunwales had been trimmed with blue, the rest of the boat white, but now it was all speckled with rust and faded. The sides of its tall cockpit had caved in.

The river was wider here than at the public fishing access; its gray waters rippled and gleamed dully. To my left I could see the docks of the houses I'd passed earlier, and the power- and sailboats tied up at many of them, even at this time of year. To my right the river stretched toward San Pablo Bay; the bridge I'd crossed earlier spanned it, soaring and graceful. Several powerboats moved in the channel.

The wind blew cold and steadily here. I shivered, stuffed my hands in my pockets, and moved toward the shelter of the willow tree. There I leaned against the splintered bow of the boat, turned my collar up, and thought, *Why?*

I felt reasonably certain that this deserted cottage had been Tracy's destination on that winter night. The Barbours who owned this place had to be connected with her roommate Amy; it would be too much of a coincidence otherwise. Also too much of a coincidence that she'd received a traffic citation at the beginning of a road that dead-ended here. A citation in a stolen car, the report on which hadn't yet been entered into the computerized network when the highway patrol stopped her. A car that had been stolen off the lot at Café Comedie, where she worked and had access to keys.

But why *steal* a car? Why not just borrow one? Or rent one? And what had someone with Tracy's dislike of driving—a dislike so strong she refused to own a car—been doing journeying over dark country roads in the middle of a rainy night? Why come here at all? And where had she gone next?

The wind blew stronger. The storm clouds had moved down from the hills and over the bay. I glanced at my watch. Only two-fifty. It seemed later because of the impending storm. There was nothing else to see here; I'd do well to go back to my car—

But there *was* something more to see. Over to one side, in my peripheral vision. A motion, something wafting about in the wind.

It was a long strand of yarn. No, a piece of cloth that looked to have been torn from something. Wool. Once red, perhaps, now faded to pink.

I scrambled up onto the boat and reached for the strand. It was wool all right, held firm between the jagged edges of one of the cracked boards of the pilot house. I fingered it, looking down into the sharply canting cockpit. My flesh rippled unpleasantly. I felt in my bag for my flashlight, shone it through the opening.

Nothing but warped planking. And a hatch cover that shouldn't have been there . . .

I lowered myself into the cramped space and shoved at the hatch cover. It moved only a few inches. I set the flashlight down and tugged. It came up with unexpected ease, throwing me off balance. I let it crash backward and regained my equilibrium. Then I grabbed the flashlight and shined it through a large hole in the floorboards.

What I saw first were the exposed ribs of the boat. The air in there was dank and musty. I moved the flash down, to where the ribs formed a V at the keel.

She was there. What was left of her.

Nothing but bones now, and those appeared to have been disarranged by small animals. The llama's-wool cape and jeans were largely eaten away, but most of the red rubber rain boots remained, faded and pitted like swiss cheese. I drew back, grasped the hatch cover for support, shut my eyes against the sight.

Even in the blackness behind my lids I could still see her pitiful skeleton.

Poor funny lady—all that talent and ability to bring forth laughter reduced to bone fragments and a few scraps of cloth. Somehow degrading that the red rubber boots could outlast the human being.

I opened my eyes, felt them sting with tears. Then I snapped off the flash and backed out of the cockpit. When I jumped down from the boat, I took in the fresh, ozone-charged air in great gulps. My knees were trembling, but I didn't want to lean against the ruin that had served as Tracy's coffin.

The feelings of elation that had buoyed me as I drove up here were gone now, replaced by a deep gloom. I'd found what I wanted—indisputable proof that Bobby Foster's confession was false—but while it would open up a whole new line of inquiry, it might still lead right back to my client. The police could claim that he'd concocted the confession expecting not to be believed, as a smoke screen to keep them from finding out what he'd really done with her. Given the condition of her remains, there would be no way of pinpointing the exact time and date of death; even though Bobby had been at the club at about the time Tracy had received the traffic citation, it could be argued that he'd come up here at some other time and killed her, then ditched the car down south in an effort to confuse investigators.

But whatever had happened, she had certainly been dead the whole two years. Had probably been dead since the early hours of that February morning. All this time, while the people who loved her had waited and hoped and suffered. . . .

And then I thought of George.

What was it he'd said to me?

Please don't find Tracy alive, Sharon. And if you do, don't bring her back to me.

Well, I hadn't. But I doubted that would ease his pain. What he had thought unbearable two days before would now seem infinitely preferable to the reality of his daughter lying for close to two years in this makeshift grave. And what he had thought bearable would now seem intolerable.

Much as I dreaded it, I felt that I had to be the one to break the news to him.

11

The windows of George's borrowed house were dark when I arrived there at a little after eight that evening, but a light shone in the Moorish arch that framed the front door. A piece of paper was taped to the door itself, fluttering in the chill wind. I hurried up the walk to read it.

I was tired and edgy after spending over two hours dealing with the Napa County sheriff's department. They'd been understaffed due to the holiday, and therefore slow in responding to the call I'd made from a cottage several doors down from the Barbour place. The medical examiner's people were even slower, their work hampered by the rain. The investigator in charge—a man named Stan Gurski, who looked like a former linebacker and spoke as softly as a minister—questioned me in detail about my case. Afterward he said he would contact Tracy's parents to break the news and request the name of her dentist so records could be obtained for making an identification. I explained that her mother was in poor emotional health and ought not to be notified by a stranger. And, I added, I would like to break the news to her father; I knew him and felt I owed him that much.

Gurski was agreeable, so I called George and told him how I had found her. He was badly shaken but in control. When I asked about dental records, he said he didn't know who Tracy had gone to in recent years; the family dentist had died shortly after she'd moved to San Francisco. Then I remembered Jay Larkey mentioning that he offered his employees a full medical and dental package at the Potrero Clinic. George said yes, he recalled that, too, and asked that I tell the sheriff's department to contact the clinic.

Then he was silent a long time before adding, "When you're done up there in Napa, would you come here, please?"

88

I didn't have to ask why. I simply agreed.

After I hung up, I told Gurski about the clinic and offered to expedite the release of Tracy's records by calling Jay Larkey. Reaching the club owner proved to be a problem, however. Café Comedie was closed, and there was no answer at Larkey's home number. Finally I thought of the Sorianos; perhaps they knew where he was. Gurski obtained their unlisted number in the affluent Marin County suburb of Tiburon and again allowed me to make the call. I spoke with Kathy, explaining briefly about finding Tracy's body. She displayed no emotion whatsoever, just said she and Rob had no idea of Jay's whereabouts but, if he got in touch, would tell him to contact the Napa authorities.

"He's going to be upset about this," she added accusingly, as if I'd deliberately contrived to wreck his holiday. When I hung up, I banged the receiver down harder than was necessary.

Gurski gave me a sympathetic look and said, "Thanks for your help. If we can get hold of her records today, we can make an ID tomorrow. Tuesday, latest."

"That's fast, considering tomorrow's a holiday."

He smiled thinly. "This is an important case. Capital case that was mishandled badly from the start. We'll move on it." From the way he spoke, I gathered he harbored visions of showing up the SFPD; a case like this could be a career maker for Gurski.

I said, "I hope there's not going to be a lot of publicity until you know for sure."

"Do you see any reporters around here?"

"Well, no, but there might be a leak—"

"I don't tolerate leaks in this office."

I believed him. After telling him I'd check in with him the next day, I sped back to the city, keeping a wary eye out for the highway patrol.

Now, as I approached George's door, I saw that the piece of paper taped to it was a note, addressed to me. It said, "Look for me by the lagoon."

I went back down the path and crossed the street. Unlike up in Napa, the weather here was clear. The rotunda and colonnade of the Palace of Fine Arts were floodlit, pinkish against the black of the trees and sky. Occasional arc lights shed a soft-white glow on the cement path and set the lagoon's water glimmering; the gently sloping lawn was deep in shadow. Not a soul was in sight save the dejected silhouette of a man slumped on a bench near the water's edge. I quickened my pace and went to stand in front of him.

George looked up at me, his eyes as sheened and unfathomable as the lagoon, his rough-hewn features sharpened by pain. For a moment I couldn't speak. Then I said, "I'm sorry," and extended my hands toward him.

He grasped them and drew me down onto the bench beside him. His fingers were icy, but he didn't seem to feel the chill.

I asked, "Are you all right?"

"Yes. I just couldn't stay in that ridiculous house. Even the dark is preferable. Did the sheriff's department arrange to get hold of Tracy's records?"

"Not yet, but they'll have them soon."

He merely nodded.

"Have you told Laura?" I asked.

"No, no one. Not until . . . No one."

We sat holding hands for a while. I had no words of comfort to offer him; there were none that could comfort. He asked me for no more details, and I didn't volunteer them. It was too soon for that, or to discuss the implications of when and where she had died. The wind rose, rippling the water of the lagoon, and I shivered, thinking of the rippling water of the Napa River. George pulled me into the circle of his arm, his fingers tangling in the hair that tumbled about my shoulders.

He said, "I must have sounded like a high-minded son of a bitch the other day, loftily telling you I didn't want my daughter back because of the 'monstrous thing' she might have done."

"To some people you might have sounded that way. To me you didn't because, frankly, I didn't believe you."

His arm tightened around me. "Oddly enough, I believed myself—at the time. But when you called and told me you'd found her—where and how you'd found her—I knew how badly I'd deluded myself. Anything—no matter how monstrous—would have been preferable to this."

"I know."

Now he shivered. I moved closer to him, my cheek grazing the front of his down jacket. He put his other arm around me and held me tight; his body pulsed with restrained tension. When I looked up at his face, I saw a white stone mask, immobile except for two tears, one sliding slowly down either cheek. I reached up, wiped one away. He touched my hand with his lips.

For a moment I wanted to pull back, to run from this man who had already make a crack in the wall I'd so carefully erected around my emotions. But I remained still as he put his fingers under my chin, tilted my face up toward him, and kissed me. He drew away, looking quizzically at me, then kissed me again. And I felt the foundations of my self-protective isolation begin to crumble.

After a time he moved back, smiled at me, smoothed my hair, straightened my collar. He said, "I've wanted you since you made me open up about Tracy. You touched me in a primal way that no one's come close to in a very long time. And because you made me remember her as she really was, rather than the idealized version I'd manufactured out of my grief, in a sense you gave my daughter back to me. Gave me hope."

"And then took her away again. Took away the hope."

"No, at a gut level I've always known she was dead. And the hope was for myself, for a life beyond all of this."

I tried to read what was in his eyes, to confirm that he really believed what he'd said, but they were like shiny pebbles in the reflected light. I couldn't help but wonder if in some way he didn't blame—

"No," he said, "I don't feel any resentment against you for bringing me the news. I don't, and I never will."

Promises, I thought. If only we could always keep our promises.

"We'll go to the house now," he said.

"Yes."

"The psychologist in me warns that this is a predictable and banal reaction to a death. The man in me doesn't give a damn."

The investigator in me warned the same thing. But the woman in me didn't give a damn, either.

The master bedroom was all antlers and mooschide, just as George had described it. Somehow the tasteless decor didn't matter. As I'd so coyly speculated on the occasion of our meeting, he was a man who gave himself wholeheartedly, and in our lovemaking we managed to leave death and tragedy behind. But dreams are another thing entirely. . . .

The first time I awoke, George was thrashing about in the throes of a nightmare. I shook him awake and held him for a while; then he slept more peacefully. Later my own sleep was disturbed by visions of rain and wind and darkness. The rain's sound was persistent, and I woke to realize it was pelting the roof. I reached for George, but he wasn't there. When I sat up, I saw him standing naked by the window, staring out through the water-streaked glass. I went to stand beside him, and he drew me into the circle of his arms, fitting my body to his.

A pair of security floodlights were mounted on the wall of the house beyond the back fence. They silvered the rain. The black bushes and trees were whipped about by the wind. I could imagine what George was envisioning: the lonely stretch of riverbank and rotting hulk of a boat where she'd lain through the damp and cold of many such rains; through fragrant spring days that promised life to everything and everyone but her; through the relentless heat of two long summers; through the dying, swiftly cooling days of two autumns.

As if he realized I understood his thoughts, he said, "Nearly two years. Such a long time for her to lie there."

"I know."

"I thought I'd done all my grieving. Now it starts again."

"I'm sorry I ever went up there."

"Don't be." He released me, then cupped my face in his hands. "I had to know. And now I have you to help me through it."

"I'll do whatever I can."

"Then do this for me—find out what happened."

"I'll try."

That seemed to satisfy him. I led him back to bed, and we made love again. Then he slept deeply, while I lay awake and thought about the death of his daughter.

I dozed off at some point and woke before dawn to find him gone again. I slipped out of bed, the moosehide of the throw rug rough against my bare feet. There was a robe hanging from a bad-taste clothes rack fashioned from a set of antlers; I put it on and went out onto the gallery.

Sound came from the living room—the TV tuned low. A woman's voice, then laughter. George hunched in one of the uncomfortable chairs, watching the screen intently. I went over there, stood behind him with my hands on his shoulders, and watched, too.

I'd seen photographs of Tracy in the newspapers, but they didn't begin to do justice to the living, moving young woman on the video tape. Blond-haired like her mother, strong-featured like her father, tall and spare, she moved expressively while delivering her lines in a deadpan fashion, never once spoiling them by laughing at her own humor. As she slipped effortlessly from character to character— from a single mother named Gloria to a bewildered feminist named Fran—she became immersed in each new persona, portraying her so convincingly that I could forget momentarily that this was Tracy

Kostakos, the daughter George mourned, the subject of my investigation. I found myself laughing at the feminist's dilemma, which ended in the punchline: "If God had meant for us to have hairy armpits, would She have given us Nair?" It was the line Kathy Soriano had quoted on Thursday night, and the triviality of the problem made it ring true.

George was laughing, too. "Jesus, she could be funny," he said. "I don't even like stand-up comedy much, but I could watch her for hours."

"Do you have a lot of tapes of her?"

"Dozens, of practically every character she ever performed. They were in her apartment, and I brought them home, thinking I'd watch them. But I never had the heart to, and when I left Laura, she didn't want them. She said she didn't need the tapes to remember Tracy because she would be back soon. So I brought them up here with me. I've never watched any of them until now."

I glanced back at the TV. Fran the feminist had metamorphosed into a lesbian waitress named Ginny. "I wonder," I said.

"Wonder what?"

"Those tapes—there could be something in them."

"You mean something that would explain what happened to her?"

"Maybe . . . no, it's probably a stupid idea. Besides, I can't see myself watching dozens of them—not when there are more promising leads I could pursue."

"You might want to look at the ones that were made close to the time she died. Everything I have is dated."

"Maybe I'll do that." I glanced at the clock on the VCR. It was almost six, still dark outside. "Right now," I added, "why don't we brew some of that fancy coffee? There are a couple of people I want to catch off guard, before their morning shots of caffeine have time to take effect."

12

When I arrived at Amy Barbour's building at a little after seven, a man in a sweat suit was leaving. I caught the iron gate before it swung shut, and he started to say something. Then he shrugged and turned downhill on the sidewalk. I climbed the stairs and pounded on Amy's door.

For about thirty seconds nothing happened. Then Amy's voice shouted for me to hang on, she was coming. The lock turned, a chain rattled, and Amy's face peered through the crack; she was pasty complexioned and bleary eyed, and her dark red hair stood up in little tufts. I wondered if she always looked this bad in the morning or if her appearance was a consequence of too much New Year's celebrating.

"What the hell are you doing here at this hour?" she said.

From her manner I gathered she hadn't heard about me finding Tracy's body yet. I'd told Detective Gurski about the probable connection between the cottage and the victim's roommate and had given him Amy's address and phone number, but there were a variety of reasons he might not have spoken to her yet.

I said, "There's been a new development, and I need to talk with you."

Her mouth twitched irritably, but she stepped back, removed the chain, and let me inside. The apartment was dark and frigid. Amy shivered inside her long white terrycloth robe, then turned away from me and fiddled with the thermostat of the electric heater. "It's just as well you came by, I guess," she said. "I've got something to show you."

It surprised me that she didn't ask about the new development, but maybe she hadn't fully comprehended what I'd said. "What is it?"

She moved away, flicking on lights and heading for the kitchen. When she caught sight of herself in the mirrored wall of the dining area, she grimaced. "There, on the table. Shit, I feel terrible. I've got to make some coffee."

I looked at the table. It was covered with all manner of things: dirty dishes, an ashtray, sections of newspaper, books, playing cards, a basket of moldy-looking fruit. "Where on the table?"

"Oh, for Christ's sake!" She strode over, picked up one of the books, and thrust it at me.

It was a red and black paperback titled *You Can Create a New Identity*, by an individual described as a "world-famous private eye." I'd never heard of him. The book looked well thumbed, and a great number of its pages were dog-eared. I turned to one, captioned "How to Establish a Mail Drop," and saw various phrases had been underlined in blue ink. In the margin was the notation "Los Angeles?" The handwriting looked to be Tracy's.

I said, "Where did you find this?"

Amy dumped coffee into a paper filter before she spoke. "In Tracy's room."

"When?"

"Yesterday."

"What were you doing in there?"

"Just looking around."

"I thought you were afraid Mrs. Kostakos might catch you and throw you out of here."

She shrugged. "I'm not anymore. I talked my boyfriend into letting me move in with him. I'm sick of Mrs. K and her weirdness."

"Has she done something since we last talked?"

"You bet your ass she has. She showed up on Friday like usual, so I thought I was rid of her for the week. Then she turned up on New Year's Eve. My boyfriend and I came back from having dinner, all set for a nice quiet evening, if you know what I mean. Then we smell the old gardenias. Surprise! She's in there. Stayed there all night, too. We didn't want to drive across town to his place—we'd been drinking, and the sobriety checks, you know. So we stayed here and we couldn't . . . well, do anything because of the walls being so thin. Anyway, I got mad and said fuck it. As of tomorrow I'm out of here. I haven't paid my share of the rent for this month, and I don't intend to. If Mrs. K wants, she can. Then she can sit there all day every day for all I care."

I frowned, disturbed both by Laura Kostakos's actions on New

Year's Eve and by the book in my hand. This slim but colorful volume was not something I would have overlooked in my search of Tracy's room; I was certain it hadn't been there on Thursday night. "Exactly where did you find this?" I asked.

"The bookcase, along with her stuff on comedy."

Then it definitely hadn't been there on Thursday; I'd examined those books thoroughly. Someone had planted it—but who? Laura Kostakos? Or was Amy lying? And if so, why? The only reason I could think of was that she was trying to make it look as if Tracy had planned her own disappearance well in advance. If that was the case, the identity of the person who had killed Tracy was obvious.

My silence made Amy uncomfortable. She got coffee cups from one of the cabinets, took out milk and sugar, then glared at the teakettle on the stove, tapping her fingers on the counter. "Look," she finally said, "just take the book and go, will you? I've got to get ready for work. Everybody else has a holiday, but do I? Hell, no."

She wanted me to leave immediately, but she'd taken out two cups. "Is your boyfriend here, Amy?"

"What? No." She looked down at the cups. "All right—yes. Just go, okay?"

She seemed excessively evasive for an emancipated young woman who had just declared her intention of moving in with the man. I pulled out a chair at the table and sat down.

"What're you doing? I told you to—"

"Don't you want to know about the new development in the case?"

"The new . . . oh, I thought that was just an excuse to get in here and hassle me some more."

"It was no excuse. Tracy's body has turned up. At a cottage on the Napa River, owned by people named Barbour."

What little color she'd had drained from her face. Her mouth went slack, and she sagged against the counter.

"She's been dead the whole time, Amy. Hidden in that old fishing boat on the riverbank. She's nothing but bones."

"No no no no!"

"All this time she's been there—and you knew, and you never told."

"I didn't! I—" Toward the front of the apartment, a door opened. Amy swung horror-struck eyes in the direction and shouted, "No!"

"Ame, what the hell?" A man came through the living room in a rush: a big, chubby, bathrobe-clad fellow with a clown's face. The wide mouth turned down in dismay when he saw me.

I stood up. "Marc Emmons," I said. "I've been trying to reach you for days."

"Who . . . ?" He looked at Amy. "This is her?"

She nodded.

Emmons quickly went to stand beside her, one arm thrown protectively around her shoulders. Both their robes and their early-morning unattractiveness were a perfect match.

"What have you been doing to her?" Emmons demanded.

"Relaying some news you should hear, too. Tracy Kostakos's body has been found. She's probably been dead since the night she disappeared. But perhaps you knew that, Marc. Amy did."

"I didn't! I swear I didn't!" Amy said.

Emmons barely reacted to the news—a tightening of his mouth, but nothing more. He put his other arm around Amy, as if to shield her from my accusation. "What makes you think that?" he asked.

"She was found near a cottage on the Napa River. I believe the property belongs to Amy's family."

Emmons looked down at her. "The old summer place?"

She nodded, teeth chattering.

"So that's what happened," he said softly.

"You don't seem particularly upset by the news."

"I'm not a person who likes to show emotion in front of strangers. Besides, Tracy's been gone a long time, and I've made a new life for myself."

"Obviously."

"Look, let's sit down and have some coffee." He released his hold on Amy. "Honey, get us some, huh?"

As if it understood his words, the kettle shrieked. Amy started and turned toward the stove. Emmons motioned at the chair I'd been occupying. "Please?"

I sat, and he took a chair on the other side of the table, in front of the window. Dawn had broken over the East Bay hills; a thin line of opalescent light showed between their tops and the clouds that lowered over them. Emmons's face was in shadow, but I could see that his clown's mouth pulled down at its corners; though he stared at the table in grim concentration, I sensed he wasn't really seeing it. Was he thinking of Tracy? Or had he other things on his mind—things he wanted to hide?

When Amy brought the coffee, her hand trembled so badly that the cups rattled in their saucers. She scurried around the table and moved the chair beside Emmons's several inches closer, so that when she sat, their shoulders touched.

I said, "How did Tracy come to be at your family's cottage?"

She glanced at Emmons before she spoke. "She took the keys. She used to go there a lot, whenever she wanted a quiet place where she could be alone for a few days and think things over. Nobody else ever went there. My father—the old bastard—is living in Mexico with his fourth wife. My mother's back in New York with her third husband. And my sister's too busy with her big-deal career in Silicon Valley to bother. *I* haven't even been there in years."

"What were the things Tracy wanted to think over?"

"How should I know? Trace never told me anything."

"You said the two of you confided in one another. That you were best of friends."

"I made things sound better than they were. *I* confided, she listened. She was that way with everybody—and then she used them. You think I haven't read what she wrote about me in her character sketchbook? I'm not so stupid that I didn't recognize myself." Her lips twisted bitterly.

"You say she went to the cottage often?"

"Yeah. Whenever she wanted to."

"How did she get there?"

"Get . . . ?" Amy looked puzzled.

"She didn't have a car. She didn't like to drive."

"Trace didn't like to drive in the city or deal with the parking hassles, but she didn't mind it so much on the freeway or in the country. She'd rent a car, or borrow one." Amy glanced at Emmons again. "Sometimes she'd take someone with her."

"All right—when did she take the keys that time, and from where?"

"I don't know when. I keep a set on my key ring, and there was always a duplicate set on the pegboard in the kitchen." She motioned to it, next to the stove.

"Can you approximate when?"

"Not too long before she disappeared, or I'd have noticed they were gone. She might even have come back here that night and taken them. I'd gone to bed early—she was supposed to wake me for champagne for my birthday when she got home—and I'm a pretty sound sleeper."

"When *did* you notice they weren't there?"

Her gaze slid away from mine. "Oh, not until after all the stuff about the kidnapping."

"When you finally noticed, did you try to call her there?"

"There isn't any phone."

"Didn't it occur to you to tell the police to check the cottage?"

"Why? There'd been a ransom note, for Christ's sake! The kidnapper wouldn't have taken her to the cottage."

"But after that, when no more notes came and the kidnapper never recontacted her parents, why didn't you tell someone about the missing keys then?"

"I . . . oh, shit." She looked at Emmons for help, but he was staring at the table again, a distracted expression on his face. "All right! I went up there, about a week later. I borrowed a car from this girl I work with. Trace wasn't there. But there was this blue Volvo in the garage, and there was dried stuff all over the upholstery in the front seat that looked like blood."

That startled me; for some reason I'd assumed the car had been in the ravine in the mountains since shortly after Tracy had been killed. It also angered me that Amy had been sitting on an important piece of information all this time.

I said, "Why in God's name didn't you call the sheriff?"

"I was afraid. I mean, Trace wasn't there, but there was the car and all that blood. And it was my family's cottage. And Marc—"

Emmons looked at her and frowned.

I said, "Marc told you not to."

She was silent.

"Why, Marc?"

His expression was still distracted, as if he was listening to the conversation and thinking about something else at the same time, but now it betrayed more than a touch of fear. He said, "I felt the same way Amy did. They'd think she'd done something to Tracy. And if not that . . . well, Tracy and I had some serious problems, and a lot of people knew about them. I was also afraid they might suspect me."

"What sort of problems?"

"Well, basically we'd broken up. She still came around when she needed something, but we weren't a couple anymore. She was seeing others."

"Who?"

" . . . That wasn't something she'd discuss with me."

"All right, you were both afraid of being accused of something, so you decided to forget about the car with the bloodstains. But why didn't you come forward later when it turned up in the mountains and Bobby Foster make a confession you knew had to be false?"

Now both of them were silent.

I added, "You'd have let Bobby go to the gas chamber to protect yourselves, wouldn't you?"

Emmons moved a hand as if to deny the possibility. "By the time we found out the details of the confession, it was too late. If we'd said anything, they'd try to pin it on us."

"Were the two of you involved before Tracy disappeared?"

Amy looked genuinely shocked at the suggestion. Emmons said, "No. We just sort of came together afterwards. Even though we'd broken up, I missed Tracy. Amy missed her. It just happened."

"You both missed Tracy, but you said nothing about what Amy had found at the cottage. What if she'd still been alive at that point? You might have saved her."

"But she wasn't," Amy said. "I could feel it, when I saw the blood in that car."

"Great. Yet for nearly two years you've watched Marc going around acting lovelorn and pretending he believed she was still alive. For all that time, you let her body lie there—"

Amy turned her face against Emmons's upper arm and started to cry. Through her sobs she said, "We didn't know she was there. And we *did* miss her. Ask anybody. We *did!*"

Emmons smoothed the tufts of her ragged hair. "Haven't you upset her enough?" he said. "Neither of us needs a lecture. We know what we did was wrong."

"Maybe you do, but both of you have certainly capitalized on her death. Amy has this entire apartment for half the rent, plus use of all Tracy's things. And you built your career on her disappearance."

He stood up so fast that Amy was thrown off balance. She clawed at the edge of the table, looking up at him in teary panic.

"I've had enough of this," he said. "Just get out of here and leave us alone."

"I'll do that, but I think you should be prepared to hear from the authorities. If you think I've been rough on you, wait until they start talking to you about a charge of obstructing justice." I stood, picking up the book on creating a new identity. "Did you plant this in Tracy's room," I said to Emmons, "or is Amy lying about where she found it?"

His face became mottled with rage. I retreated into the living room. He took a step toward me, but Amy's sobs became louder, her breath rasping and fast, as if she were having an anxiety attack. Emmons glared at me, then turned and put his arms around her.

I left the apartment, struggling to contain my own anger. It was a relief to be out of there and not have to hear any more self-serving explanations of what was simply cold-blooded behavior.

13

Early that afternoon Jack Stuart and I sat together on a bench in the visiting area at San Quentin. We'd been waiting to see Bobby Foster for over two hours. The delay annoyed me, but Jack took it stoically; attorneys were used to long waits until one of the segregated visiting rooms became available, he told me. At first we'd discussed the case but after a while had run out of things to say and lapsed into silence. Jack seemed remote today; I wondered if it had to do with my avoidance of him at the New Year's Eve party.

At about one forty-five, a slender black woman wearing jeans and a thick turquoise sweater entered the area. Her head, crowned by a short afro, turned from side to side as if she was looking for someone; plain gold hoop earrings danced with the motion. Jack roused himself and waved to her. "That's Leora Whitsun, Bobby's mother," he said. "I spoke with her earlier, and she mentioned she would be coming up here."

I watched Leora Whitsun make her way toward us, realizing with some shock that she was no older than I—several years shy of forty. The woman had had seven children and three husbands; I knew from the files I'd read that she'd put herself through two years of college in night sessions while organizing community watch programs and working days at the clinic. I'd expected a much older, wearier-looking person, rather than this attractive, vigorous woman in the prime of her life. And I certainly would not have expected her to be smiling.

Jack made the introductions, and Leora Whitsun sat down beside me, taking my hands in hers. "I can't thank you enough for what you've done for my boy," she said.

I shrugged, embarrassed by what I considered undue gratitude.

"I was just doing my job. I'm only happy that things may work out after all.'"

"*Will* work out, I know it." She flashed us an even more brilliant smile. "I'm into the power of positive thinking today. Yesterday, when I found out about that girl's body turning up, I was just in heaven. Been there ever since."

"Yesterday?" I said. "Jack didn't even know until this morning."

"Leora found out at the clinic," Jack said. "She was working intake yesterday, and Larkey's partner's wife came in, looking for Larkey, so she could break the news about Tracy personally."

Maybe Kathy Soriano had a heart after all, I thought. "Was he there?"

"No," Leora said. "None of our dentists work on holidays, although we always have one of the regulars on call. Anyway, somebody must of got hold of Jay, because he took the records up to Napa himself first thing this morning, so he could help with the identification."

I knew that forensic dentists appreciated the assistance of the subject's own dentist whenever possible; the records, especially X rays, were open to wide interpretation, so it helped to have a person who was familiar with them on hand. I said, "How did Larkey seem to be taking the news?"

"Poor man was upset, even though he was glad that my boy'll go free."

Jack said, "Leora, I have to caution you: we've got a long pull ahead of us yet. What this evidence does is pave the way for a new trial. But Bobby could be convicted again."

She frowned. "But the body being up there in Napa proves his confession was no good. And from what you"—she looked at Jack—"told me on the phone this morning about that girl getting a traffic ticket, there wouldn't have been time for Bobby to go up there and be back at the club before closing."

I said, "There's no proof of exactly when she died. Given the state of the remains, there's no way the medical examiner can pin it down. And even if it were possible, a jury might not believe the testimony of the parking attendants who claim Bobby came back to the club at closing."

Jack added, "We have no way of knowing how the prosecution might structure a new case against him."

Leora shook her head, earrings swinging violently. "But he didn't kill her."

"We know that," I said, "and what we're going to do is work to find out who did."

For a moment she continued to look downcast but then rallied. "I just know you can do it, because you've already done one miracle."

Jack touched her shoulder reassuringly and got up to confer with the visiting desk officer. When he came back he said, "We're on. Do you want to come with us, Leora?"

"I better see my boy alone," she said. "Gives him more visiting time. I don't mind the wait."

Jack and I said good-bye to her and went to the segregated room assigned to us. After the door had closed and locked, he set his briefcase on the table and began taking files and a legal pad from it. He said, "How do you want to handle this?"

"You explain to him about me finding Tracy's body, and I'll take it from there."

"Just what is it you're looking to get out of him?"

"Bobby's hiding something. It has to do with his quarrel with Tracy when she was leaving the club that night. I've an inkling of what that was all about, and I want to get him to confirm it."

Jack looked curious but merely nodded.

After about ten minutes Bobby was let into the room on the opposite side of the grille. He seemed wary as he greeted Jack and me, and he held himself stiffly as he sat down. I supposed that each of Jack's sessions with him required a certain amount of time for rebuilding their rapport. Jack explained quickly about the break in the case, cautioning him first about becoming overly optimistic. Bobby listened intently, wetting his lips and then compressing them, as if to keep his emotions contained.

He was silent for a bit after Jack finished. Then he looked at me. "You say you'd try, and you did. Thanks. For that, and for believing me." Quickly he glanced at Jack. "You, too."

Jack nodded.

I said, "As Jack explained, we're by no means in the clear yet. I've got a lot of work to do. We need to establish the facts—all of them.

"The facts, Bobby," I repeated. "Such as what you quarreled with Tracy about the night she disappeared. It was something that you felt would make you look even worse, wasn't it? Something you're so ashamed of that you've kept it to yourself all this time."

". . . Don't know what you mean by that."

"You do—and you'd better tell me about it."

"Tracy, she dead. It don't matter now."

"It matters a lot."

He was silent.

I reached into my briefcase and took out the notebook containing Tracy's character sketches, opened it to the last page. "Does this sound like someone you used to know, Bobby?"

He looked at me, then at the notebook, puzzled.

I read, "'It has become her habit to milk every emotion, even her own, for personal gain. Everything is useful. She sleeps with this one and that one solely for the exotic experience.'"

He moved his hand, as if to push the words away.

"Tracy used people," I said. "She let her friends confide in her, then built characters for her routines based on those confidences. When she ran out of material, she created it. Like she planned to create it by sleeping with you."

Jack grunted in surprise. Bobby lowered his head into his hands, his fingers pressing spasmodically against his skull.

"If it's any comfort," I added, "she regretted what she'd done. She told her mother she thought she wasn't a good person anymore, said she'd done things to hurt others."

He mumbled something.

"What?"

"Wasn't the way she told it to me. That why we had the fight. I knew what we did was wrong. We were *friends*. I loved her, but not that way."

"When did you sleep with her?"

"Two, maybe three weeks before."

"How many times?"

"Just the once."

"And that Thursday night . . . ?"

"I wanted to talk about it, tell her no way it gonna happen again. I want to know why— She started it, see. But she wasn't having any talk. I say we got to have it out, and she say . . ."

"She said . . . ?"

"That it wasn't no big deal. She done it 'cause she was gonna use a white girl who slept with black men in her act. She wanted to know firsthand what it was like. You know how she make me feel? Like some slave put out to stud. I say that to her, and she say some ugly things. That the last I saw of her."

He raised his face; his eyes were bleak and moist. "Now we can't never put it right. She dead, and I can't tell her I'm sorry."

Beside me Jack cleared his throat and shifted on his chair. I didn't feel any too comfortable myself, but I pressed on. "Okay—you fought, and then what?"

Bobby wiped his eyes on his sleeve before he answered. "She run off, something about going to Marc's."

That gave me pause; Emmons had said nothing about an appointment with Tracy that night. "He wasn't working the bar?"

"Guess not. He only a part-timer."

"Marc told me they'd broken up."

"Yeah, but every time she want something, she go to him. And Marc, he love her, so he give it to her, no matter what."

But love has its limits, I thought, and when they're reached, it can turn nasty. "All right," I said, "then what did you do?"

"Just walked. Stopped for a couple of drinks."

"Where?"

"Some bar, I don't remember where."

"Think."

He thought. And shook his head. "The way it was, I'd done some crack, to get up for talking to Tracy. With the booze and all . . ."

"Well, if you do remember anything, let me know right away. So you walked around, stopped for a couple of drinks, then went back to the club around closing?"

"Yeah. I wanted to see if the other guys covered for me with Larkey."

"Had they?"

"Yeah."

"Then what did you do?"

"Look, I told you all this the other day."

"Tell me again."

He sighed. "I went to see this girl I know, but she not home. After that I go back to my ma's place. She working all night at the clinic. My brothers, they off someplace. The old granny from next door, she sitting with the little ones. She the only one saw me, and that don't help 'cause she die the next month, before all this shit start to come down."

Now I sighed. He'd told it as he had before; it bore the unmistakable stamp of truth. But it wouldn't be of much use in establishing his story.

Bobby looked from me to Jack and back again. "Still don't look good, huh?"

I began gathering my bag and briefcase. "Things are better than they were last week. We'll just take it one step at a time." I wanted to get back to the city now, to call Stan Gurski in Napa to see if he had an identification on the remains. And I needed to check with Rae about what she'd turned up on Lisa McIntyre. And then there was George. . . .

Jack said, "You going?"

"Yes. I'll check in with you later." We'd come in separate cars, so there was no reason for me to wait for him.

Bobby said, "I thank you again."

"You're welcome. Try not to feel discouraged. We'll work this out yet."

"I wish . . ." He hesitated.

"Wish what?"

"I don't know. All this time I been hoping you'd find her alive. So I could of got things straight between us."

I had no answer for that. I knew from bitter experience that every death diminishes us, but those that leave differences unresolved and things unsaid are the most painful of all.

14

"According to Larkey, McIntyre worked at the club the night that Kostakos disappeared. She was scheduled to have Friday and Saturday off that week, and they're not open Sundays, so her next shift was Monday night. She never showed, never picked up her last check. In my book that's a big coincidence. . . . Sharon, are you listening to me?"

I was, but with only half my attention. The rest of it was turned inward, focused on Marc Emmons. I'd called Detective Gurski that morning and relayed the information about Barbour's visit to the cottage and Emmons's counseling her not to go to the authorities. Gurski had said he'd request the SFPD to pick them up and hold them for questioning. But when I'd called him again after returning from San Quentin and told him Tracy might have been on her way to Emmons's apartment the night she disappeared, he said neither had been located yet. That probably meant I'd panicked them into running, and I was now regretting my poor handling of the situation.

In response to Rae's plaintive query I said, "A big coincidence. You're right. Did anyone at the club make an attempt to locate McIntyre?"

"Larkey got worried and sent his partner's wife around to her apartment later that week, but she'd vanished."

I'd been turned toward the bay window of my office, watching dusk fall over the monotonous expanse of the Outer Mission district, but now I swiveled to face Rae. She was pacing on the old oriental carpet, following its geometric pattern in precise steps. She often did that when we talked about a case; I assumed it was her way of slowing down and ordering thoughts that were frequently rapid-fire and chaotic..

"What do you mean, 'vanished'?" I asked. "Had she moved out?"

"Apparently. Most of her stuff was gone. The manager told Kathy Soriano that she didn't give advance notice and nobody saw her go."

"Interesting. The police should have been told about that. I want you to look into it more thoroughly. Talk to the manager, and to Kathy. Were you able to get any leads on where McIntyre went?"

"No. There's not much to go on. She'd recently moved here from out of state—she was originally from Oklahoma, Larkey thought— and hadn't bothered to get a California driver's license. I got the impression he wasn't too surprised by her just up and going. He said a lot of would-be comedians drift from place to place."

"McIntyre wanted to be a comedian?"

"That's what he implied."

"Well, keep on it."

"Sure. Anything else?"

"Not at the moment." I glanced at the silent phone, then at my watch. A few minutes before five. Gurski hadn't yet received confirmation that the remains I'd found were Tracy's when I'd talked with him earlier; he'd said he'd call me as soon as he heard. When I'd phoned George, I'd gotten his answering machine. Wait for the beep; So-and-so will get back to you. That, and doorbells ringing in empty residences: sometimes it seemed they were all my days consisted of.

Rae had stopped on the central block of the rug's pattern and was looking hesitantly at me. "What?" I said, more snappishly than I'd intended.

"Well, *excuse* me!"

"Oh, come on, don't be so touchy."

"Then you don't be so much of a grouch."

"Sorry. What is it?"

"Hank."

Now she had my full attention. "What's wrong?"

"He slept on the couch here last night."

"Uh-oh. Have you seen Anne-Marie?"

"She hasn't been in."

It didn't sound good.

Rae shifted from foot to foot, then said, "I was thinking maybe you should talk to him."

I recalled Hank's abrupt dismissal of me on New Year's Eve and shook my head.

"Somebody's got to help him, Sharon. He looks terrible. And I saw him head downhill to the Remedy right after noon. He's still not back."

"Oh, for God's sake . . . all right. I'm not accomplishing anything by sitting here. Are you going to be around for a while?"

"Yes."

"Good. If Detective Gurski or George Kostakos calls, take a message and call me down there, okay?"

Rae gave me a thumbs-up sign and left the office.

The Remedy Lounge has long been my litmus test for discovering kindred souls among the co-op's staff. One of Mission Street's many working-class bars, it is totally devoid of character—unless you count cracked plastic booths and gouged formica tables, fly-specked mirrors and suspiciously clouded glassware, decrepit pinball machines and an often broken jukebox as hallmarks of individuality. But friendships at All Souls have blossomed or withered depending upon the person's attitude toward it.

Hank loved the Remedy; had, in fact, the dubious distinction of having discovered it. Anne-Marie liked to disparage it, but until she and Hank started having problems, she was almost always found on the next barstool. Jack and I spent a disproportionate amount of time there. Rae had felt I'd bestowed an honor upon her the first time I invited her down the hill for a drink. Even Ted—who despaired of the clientele's staunchly heterosexual orientation—stopped in several times a week and, in fine neighborhood tradition, was tolerated by the patrons. Let others from All Souls sip their blush wines in fern-infested bars, we often declared. *We* knew where the good times were to be found!

Only the times at the Remedy weren't so good anymore. Hadn't been for quite a while.

Tonight the evidence of that was slumped over the bar at the far end, a glass of scotch in front of him. The happy hour was just getting started, and most of the customers were giving Hank a wide berth. Even Brian, the bartender, was keeping his distance. I waved at him and pointed to Hank, a signal that he should bring my white wine down there.

When I slipped onto the stool next to him, Hank didn't glance my way. But when Brian set down my wine and took a dollar and a quarter from the pile of bills and coins on the bar, he looked up in surprise.

"You owe me," I said.

"I do?" Behind his thick lenses, his eyes were vague and unfocused; he was badly in need of a shave.

"Yes. You were downright nasty to me on New Year's Eve."

"I was?"

"Uh-huh. You ordered me out of your office, told me to go find a surfer and take him home and screw him."

"I did?"

I nodded and sipped wine.

"Jesus." Hank ran a hand over his thick curly hair.

"Of Anne-Marie, you said, 'Fuck her.'"

"Ah, I'm beginning to remember." He took a gulp of scotch.

"Do you want to talk about it now?"

He was silent, turning his glass round and round between his palms. The bar beneath it was wet with spills from many earlier drinks.

"I've held off asking you anything for months," I added, "because I hoped things would improve, or that one of you would talk to me. But I can't hold off any longer."

"So why don't you ask her? I'm sure she'll be happy to give you all the explanation you need."

"I plan to, but right now I want to hear your side of it."

"Why?"

"Because you're my friend, dammit! We go all the way back to the old days in Berkeley. What the hell's wrong with you, that you can turn your back on that kind of friendship?" My voice had risen; the people two stools over looked at me, then hastily glanced away.

Hank said, "Shar, I just can't talk about it."

"You talked to Jack. He gave me a brief outline way back last fall."

"That's different. Jack's been through it."

"You think I haven't? Just because Don and I weren't married—"

"Ah, Shar, I know that. But you handle things. You're . . . in control."

His words brought a sense of déjà vu. I remembered my older brother John, just after his divorce, telling me I couldn't understand what he was going through because I was a person who "played it safe." At the time I'd wondered if I really presented such a cold, constrained facade to others; now I wondered again.

"Yes," I said, "I'm in control. That's why it took me months to break it off with Don—months that I spent drinking too much and fussing over little things so I wouldn't have to face the real issue.

That's why I've holed up and avoided another relationship ever since." Until last night.

Hank peered at me through his smudged lenses. "I didn't know any of that."

"That's only because I'm better at hiding my emotions than you. Talk to me, Hank."

He drank the rest of his scotch—courage, I supposed—then said, "What it all boils down to is that I can't live with Anne-Marie. She wants order, I create chaos. I hate sharing household chores and entertaining graciously and going out for Sunday brunch. I want to let the flat go to hell and have old friends over for a pot of my chili and sleep till noon all weekend. We're just different, and I should have realized that and never married her."

"Do you still love her?"

"Yes."

"Does she still love you?"

"If she still does after New Year's Eve, she ought to be institutionalized."

"What happened—besides your going to the All Souls party without her?"

He motioned for Brian to bring him another drink. Brian looked doubtful but poured it when I nodded at him.

"Okay," Hank said when the drink was in front of him. "What happened was Anne-Marie invited the Andersons—the people we rent the upstairs flat to—for dinner. I wanted to be at All Souls, where we've always spent New Year's Eve, so I left. But then I couldn't face people, so I drank in my office."

"Do you remember me coming in and talking with you?"

"Oh, yes. I remember it quite clearly now. I'm not so bad off that I'm blacking out. And I remember the rest of the evening. In hideous detail."

"Go on."

"I gave up and went home a little after midnight. Took a cab—I'm not enough of an asshole to drive in that condition. The Andersons were still there. Anne-Marie had this made-of-porcelain look she gets when she's pissed off but trying to remain civil. I'd hoped they'd be gone so we could talk. Just seeing them there . . . Are you sure you want to know what a swine I am?"

"We all behave swinishly upon occasion."

"Some of us more than others. Well, I started yelling at her for letting 'those people' in our flat. Said I was sick of them, sick of hearing about their car phones and computers and their vacation condo with the view of some golf course fairway, and their stupid, boring jobs on Montgomery Street."

"Oh, Lord!"

"It gets worse. Then *she* started yelling at me. Said that the only reason she ever had them down to dinner was so she wouldn't have to spend the evening arguing with me. Said that she'd only asked them for New Year's Eve so we wouldn't go to the All Souls party and get drunk and scream at each other in front of our *real* friends. Said that she found car phones and computers and condos and Montgomery Street boring, too, and besides, Bob—he's the husband—is an ass grabber. By that time the Andersons were on their way out the door."

Hank's expression was woebegone in the extreme. I, on the other hand, felt a welling up of relief. For months now Anne-Marie had avoided me, not returning my phone calls. From what I'd heard of her behavior, I'd been afraid that my friend had turned into someone I wouldn't even want to know. But her New Year's Eve outburst in front of the dreadful Andersons proved that the candid, unpretentious Anne-Marie of yesterday still existed.

I said, "Well, you won't have to worry about having them to dinner again."

"It gets worse."

"How could it?"

"Then we *really* got into it. I'm sure the Andersons were upstairs with a glass pressed to the floor. Hell, they wouldn't even have needed one. I told her I couldn't stand living her life-style. She told me I'm a slob with the social graces of a pit bull. Then she said my chili was awful." Hank drew himself up indignantly. One elbow slipped off the bar, and I had to steady him.

I'd been having difficulty controlling the laughter that was building inside me. Now it rose and spilled over. The more I laughed, the more indignant Hank looked, and his expression only gave fuel to my hilarity. Finally—gasping and wiping my eyes—I said, "Hank, I don't know about all the rest, but she's right on one point—your chili is *horrible!*"

". . . You always ate it."

"That's because the company was always so good."

He thought about that for a moment. "Anne-Marie always ate it, too. Guess my company isn't good anymore."

"For the time being, probably not."

He knocked back half the fresh drink and said, "Do you want to hear the rest of it?"

"There's more?"

"It still gets worse. She stomped off and locked me out of the bedroom. Then I threw up and passed out on the bathroom floor, sort of wrapped around the toilet. And in the morning there was an envelope from the Andersons shoved under the door. They gave thirty days' notice. That's when I decided I'd better stay at All Souls."

I leaned my forehead on my hand and groaned. Finally I said, "A nice flat like that'll be easy to rent."

"It's not keeping the flat occupied that worries me," he said. "It's the prospect of sleeping on the All Souls's couch for the rest of my life."

I knew what he meant; the couch was a maroon relic of the 1930s with badly sprung springs.

Before I could offer any optimistic comments, however, Brian signaled that I had a phone call. "We'll talk more later," I said to Hank and went to the end of the bar to take it.

George's voice came over the line—high and shaky, infused with an element that I wouldn't have expected. As he said, "Sharon? Your assistant told me to call you here," I heard joy—no, elation.

"What's happened?"

"I just spoke with Detective Gurski. About the identification from Tracy's dental records."

"I've been trying to get in touch—"

"Sharon," he said, "it wasn't her! *The body you found wasn't Tracy's!*"

15

For a moment I couldn't speak. The implications of this new development were staggering, that much I knew. But I couldn't quite grasp them yet, couldn't put them into words.

"Sharon?" George said.

"Yes, I'm here."

"Do you realize what this means? Tracy may be alive after all!"

Not necessarily, I thought. And if she was, we'd be back to the monstrous thing he feared.

George interpreted my silence correctly. "Yes, I know," he said. "But at least there's hope. After believing her dead—really believing, the way I did last night—I know I can handle anything."

"I hope so." I thought of the pitiful collection of bones I'd found, and the tattered remnants of Tracy's clothing. The obvious had already occurred to me, and it was extremely unpleasant.

"Well," I added, "this certainly changes things. I hardly know how to proceed."

"I wish you'd come over here, or let me come there. I'm so hyper that I feel as though I'll come apart if I don't see you."

The need and desire in his voice cut through my confusion. I glanced up and saw Jack come through the door, probably looking for Hank. He and I would have to talk right away.

"Let me come there," I said. "But first I have to talk this over with Bobby Foster's attorney. That may take a while. I'll be there as soon as I can."

"I'll be waiting."

I hung up the receiver and waved at Jack. He changed course and came to the end of the bar. "What's wrong?" he asked.

"It's that obvious?"

"You should see your face."

"Well, what's wrong is this: the body up at the river *wasn't* Tracy Kostakos." Quickly I explained about George's call.

Jack's craggy features went blank as he shifted mental gears and assimilated the news. Then he rubbed his chin and said, "Of course they have no idea who the bones *do* belong to."

"No, and the ID on that is going to be a tough one—if not impossible."

"Meanwhile, we're back to square one."

"Not quite. We have proof that Kostakos was alive at two-ten in the morning—well after Foster confessed to killing her. And we have Barbour's story about the car being at the cottage a week later."

"Sure, and it's enough to move for a new trial, but then we've got the proof of Foster's whereabouts to worry about. The parking attendants who alibied him were easily the weakest defense witnesses at his first trial. Neither presents himself in a way that exactly inspires belief. Ah, shit!" Jack slapped a hand on the bar so hard that it made the man sitting around its corner jerk.

"Look," I said, "why don't we go up the hill and kick this around in private?"

"Fine by me." He glanced the length of the bar, to where Hank still hunched over his drink. "Is he okay?"

"Going to be, I think."

"Then let's go."

I waved good-bye to Hank and followed Jack outside.

Winter darkness had settled over Mission Street. Cars, their headlights ablaze, jammed the pavement; buses and jitneys pulled up to the curb and disgorged commuters. Some hurried into the warm shelter of bars and restaurants, others went toward the nearby Safeway to pick up things for dinner. Still others trudged uphill with us, to the hodgepodge of dwellings that line Bernal Heights' steep streets. I watched them, feeling the beginnings of the depression that often settles over me at that hour of the evening.

At times it seems as if I'm always out of step with the world—set apart by both my temperament and my habits. On nights when people are rushing home to their families or lovers, I'm often at loose ends or about to go to work on an interview or a stakeout. While others round out their days with cocktails and dinner, TV and helping the kids with their homework, I'm likely to be chasing an elusive witness all over the city, or sitting cramped and cold in my MG in front of somebody's apartment building.

It isn't that I mind my erratic schedule; it's the only way of life that will ever really suit me. And I live for those cut-crystal moments when a difficult case finally begins to come together. But in the early evening, with the lights of other people's residences glowing warm around me, I'm more often than not reminded of what a lonely life I've made for myself, and sometimes I wonder what it would have been like had I made other, more traditional choices.

On this night, however, I was able to banish the depression quickly. I had George to think of, the touch of his hands and lips and body to anticipate. Because of the new, fragile thing between us, I had no reason to feel lonely. No reason not to expect it would grow stronger and prosper, unless this new development . . .

I pushed the thought aside and followed Jack into the big brown Victorian.

Rae and one of the attorneys sat on the couch in the living room watching the TV news; the half-denuded Christmas tree hulked in the bay window behind them. A lone industrious soul perched on a stool in the law library, the trestle table covered with books and crumpled sheets of yellow paper. Oddly enough, the kitchen was deserted. Jack and I got glasses of wine and sat down at the round oak table in front of the window. I kicked off my shoes, propped my feet on one of the extra chairs, and waited to hear his thoughts on the matter at hand.

He began to discuss the impact of this latest development on Foster's legal situation, weighing each factor carefully, speaking slowly and precisely. After his initial frustrated outburst at the Remedy, he had settled into a calm, professional mood, displaying the sharp insight and cool logic I'd come to expect of him. Hard to believe that this was the same man who two nights before had mooned around the New Year's Eve party like a lovesick teenager.

Unfortunately, what Jack concluded was that the discovery of the body had even less impact on the status of his case, now that we knew it wasn't Tracy's. While he still had enough evidence to move for a new trial, to bring the case before a jury in its present unresolved state would only invite another conviction. "As I've said before," he added, "what we need is to find out what happened that night. And now we seem to be further than ever from that."

"Well, let's look at what we've got, item by item," I said. "Tracy: a pretty cold user, if we accept what she told Foster about sleeping with him for the exotic experience."

"Do we?"

"I do. The sketchbook backs it up. She may have had qualms

about her behavior, but they didn't prevent her from throwing it in his face." I made mental apologies to George for my harsh assessment of his daughter. But then, as he admitted, he hadn't really known the woman his little girl had grown into. "Next," I said, "we have a stolen car. That's something that bothers me: why *steal* a car? I'm going to have Rae find out more about the car's owner."

Jack nodded in agreement.

"All right," I went on, "now we have Foster's claim that Kostakos was on her way to Emmons's apartment that night. Truth or excuse, so she could get away from him? No way to know until the police locate Emmons."

"What's the status on that?"

"He and Barbour are missing. My fault, I'm afraid. I panicked them. But they'll turn up. Anyway, the next thing we know is that Kostakos was driving the car in the vicinity of the Barbour cottage at two-ten the next morning. Driving badly, so perhaps she was nervous or frightened. We can safely assume that the cottage was her destination. We don't know if anyone was with her, and it's unlikely the officer who issued the citation will remember. We do know that the car was at the cottage a week later but that Kostakos was not."

"How did she leave there? From what you've told me, it's a long way from the main road."

"It is. There aren't too many options." I began ticking them off on my fingers. "She hitchhiked or got a ride with someone from a neighboring cottage. But in that case, when all the publicity started, someone probably would have recognized her picture in the papers or on the news and come forward."

"Unless they didn't read the papers or watch the news. Or just didn't want to get involved."

"That's possible, too. Another possibility is that someone she knew came to get her. She could have prearranged that or called from a neighbor's. And here's another possibility: that the person whose bones I found arrived at the cottage in a car which Kostakos later left in."

I paused, sipped wine, all too aware of what neither of us had yet put into words. Finally I said, "The clothing remnants I found with those bones were what Kostakos was wearing when she left Café Comedie. What they suggest to me is that the body was dressed in them after death, in an attempt to make it look like hers. The killer must have realized that the chances of it being discovered in the near future were slim, but if it ever was, the clothing would indicate that Kostakos was the one who died."

"Naive, considering identification techniques."

"Well, Kostakos probably didn't have too much knowledge of forensic science."

"You think she was the killer? Or an accessory?"

I nodded, feeling a different kind of depression than I had earlier. For a while there I'd been caught up in the process of reasoning; now I couldn't help but personalize the facts. If my theory was correct, the aftermath of my investigation would inflict pain and suffering on the man I was beginning to care for a great deal.

"And the victim?" Jack asked.

"Well, someone who hasn't been missed or had no one who cared enough to mount a full-scale search. Someone who might be expected to just pull up stakes and go."

"Any specific ideas?"

"One. A waitress named Lisa McIntyre who worked at the club. She disappeared at roughly the same time Kostakos did. Larkey was concerned enough when she didn't come to work that he sent his partner's wife to check on her. McIntyre had moved out without notice. Larkey didn't pursue it, because in his mind she was something of a drifter."

"Coincidence?"

"Could be, but I don't like the things. Let me call Larkey."

I got up and followed the phone cord across the floor to where the instrument sat on the drainboard of the sink, and grabbed it up irritably. The long cords on the All Souls's phones had annoyed me for years—both because of their tendency to tangle and the staff members' tendency to abandon the instruments wherever they were when they hung up. Since the introduction of cordless phones, I'd been lobbying for us to buy some for our restless talkers, but so far no one had listened to me. I supposed I would indefinitely continue to follow cords, like trails of crumbs in the woods, to some highly peculiar places.

Larkey answered the phone at Café Comedie, sounding down. "I heard about you going up to Napa to assist in the identification," I said.

"The least I could do. And it was a relief to know the body wasn't Tracy's. But Jesus, what a depressing experience. Somehow in my spotty career I'd missed out on having to do that. I hope I never have to again."

"I don't blame you. Jay, I know my assistant questioned you

about Lisa McIntyre earlier today, but I'd like to ask a few more things."

"Sure, go ahead."

"Did anyone come around asking about her after she left town—family or friends, for instance?"

"Not that I know of. She hadn't been here long enough to make close friends, and as for family, she mentioned something about having been on her own since she was fifteen. She was from Oklahoma, but I gathered she'd drifted around the country for the past ten years—Boston, New York, L.A. The usual places would-be comedians gravitate to."

"Was she any good as a comedian?"

"Not really. Comedy is like any other branch of show business: you've got to have discipline, and Lisa lacked it. I wasn't really surprised when she up and left town. Her kind are always looking for those fabled greener pastures."

"And you say she had no close friends. What about lovers?"

"Lisa was a lesbian, but I never saw her with another woman."

I thought of the videotape George had been watching in the early hours of the morning, and the lesbian waitress named Ginny whom Tracy had portrayed. Had Lisa been the inspiration for that character?

"What does Lisa look like?" I asked.

"Tall, thin, light brown hair worn longish and curly. Fairly attractive."

"One more question, and I'll let you go. Did you ever work on her teeth?"

Larkey hesitated. I assumed the question had surprised him. "As a matter of fact, I did."

"And you still have her records?"

"Yes." There was an inquiring note in his voice now.

"Then Napa County will probably be in touch with you about getting hold of them."

"You think it was *Lisa* up there?"

"It's worth checking out."

"Hmm." He hesitated. "Now that you mention it—this isn't a hard-and-fast recollection; no dentist can be expected to remember the teeth of all his patients—but I think Lisa's and Tracy's may not have been all that dissimilar. Few cavities, no capping or irregularities. That would explain why, when I first started making the comparison, it seemed to be Tracy. There were slight differences, but not all that many."

THE SHAPE OF DREAD / 121

"I'll call Napa and tell them to get in touch with you." I thanked him and hung up quickly, before he could ask any time-consuming questions.

Jack had been listening to my end of the conversation closely; he made no comment as I called NCSD and asked for Stan Gurski. I wasn't sure if the reasoning that I laid out for Gurski made a great deal of sense, but it didn't take him long to say he'd request McIntyre's records from Larkey and let me know what the medical examiner concluded.

It was now well after seven. George would be wondering what had happened to me. I called him and said I had to go home to feed the cat, but that I was on my way. He asked me what I liked on my pizza, and when I hesitantly admitted to a fondness for anchovies and Italian sausage, he laughed.

"Do you realize how hard it is for me to find someone who also likes that combination?" he asked. "We must be made for each other."

"I'll hold on to that thought."

When I replaced the receiver in its cradle, Jack was looking quizzically at me. "Was that George Kostakos you were talking to?"

". . . Yes."

"Sounds as if the two of you really hit it off."

"Yes, we did. He's an interesting man, and easy to get to know."

Jack's expression grew guarded; there was an element of concern in his voice when he spoke again. "I hope you're not becoming emotionally involved with . . . a principal figure in the investigation."

Good Lord, I thought irritably, he's given up on me as a possible romantic interest, and now he wants to dispense advice, like Hank. "Why would I do that?"

He shrugged. "I've met Kostakos. He's intelligent, good-looking, personable, rich. I don't know why you *wouldn't* be attracted to him."

He meant well, but it really wasn't any of his business. I said, "He's also married. Don't forget that."

Jack relaxed slightly. "Just so long as you don't," he said.

16

Amy Barbour's apartment building wasn't really on my way across town to the Marina district, but I made an uphill detour so I could drive by there. I told myself I wouldn't bother to stop unless I spotted a convenient parking space; the police would have checked and rechecked the apartment, so chances were slim that Barbour was at home. When I reached the building, however, there was a vacant space almost in front of it. Destiny, I thought as I steered the MG to the curb.

The windows of the second-story bedrooms were dark; a Mercedes sports coupe stood in the driveway. The light in the vestibule showed that the metal security gate had been propped open, the way it might be if someone were carrying things in or out and didn't want to be bothered with unlocking it on every trip. Was Barbour moving in with Emmons tonight? If so, why hadn't the police located them here or at his place?

I went through the gate and up the stairs. The door to the apartment was slightly ajar, but I heard no voices, saw no lights. As I moved forward, the flesh along my backbone rippled slightly.

The interior was in shadow, but the draperies on the picture windows hung open, the glow from the farflung city lights silvering the room. It washed over the pale furniture and silhouetted the tall figure of a man who stood in front of the glass, looking out. When I pushed the door fully open and stepped over the threshold, he turned quickly, steel-rimmed glasses glinting. I fumbled for the light switch; one of the table lamps came on. The man was Rob Soriano, Larkey's partner.

In spite of his precise military bearing, Soriano seemed relaxed and not at all surprised to see me, as if he'd expected that sooner or later I'd turn up. He didn't speak, merely folded his arms across his chest and studied me. I returned his stare.

Tonight Soriano wore a gray business suit, lighter gray shirt, and muted striped tie. The monochromatic clothing, combined with the severe glasses and conservative cut of his hair, lent him a faceless quality, but even in flashier garb he would not be a man you would pick out of a crowd. His square-jawed face looked tired, as if he'd spent the day in wearisome negotiations; there were deep brackets from his nose to the corners of his mouth, which in no way could be termed laugh lines.

When it appeared he was waiting for me to speak, I said, "How are you, Mr. Soriano?"

"Fine, Ms. McCone. And you?"

"Fine also. May I ask what you're doing here?"

A small smile played around his thin lips. "I could ask you the same."

"I'm looking for Amy Barbour and Marc Emmons."

"Then we have a common purpose."

"Why do you want them?"

"Actually, I'm only interested in Marc. Our chubby comedian has failed to show up since Thursday night. Jay wants me to drag him down there so he can give him the axe."

Larkey seemed to rely on both of the Sorianos to run errands for him, I thought. But Rob didn't look or act like a gofer. "How did you get in here?" I asked.

"Same way you did. Both doors were open; it looks as if someone's been moving things out."

I glanced around the room. The furniture was undisturbed, but there were empty spaces in the record cabinet and on a bookcase. A half-packed box of kitchen equipment stood on the cluttered dining table. I moved down the hall to the bedrooms. The door to Tracy's was locked. Amy's bed had been stripped; the bureau drawers were empty, and only a few items of clothing hung in the closet. The bathroom was devoid of toiletries and towels.

Rob Soriano was sitting on the white leather sofa when I returned to the living room. He took out a pack of cigarettes, offered one to me, and when I shook my head, lit one for himself. "Where do you suppose our plump little birds have flown to?" he asked.

I sat down at the other end of the couch. "Amy was planning to move in with Emmons."

"Well, she must have gotten lost en route; there's no one at his place, either."

It occurred to me that the police might have picked them up in the last few hours; that would explain why Amy had interrupted her packing. I decided, however, to say nothing about that to Soriano. "How come you're out tracking down Emmons?" I asked. "You said your wife is the one who takes the active role in Café Comedie."

"Kathy's hardly the one to haul a large, protesting young man down there."

From what I'd seen of Kathy Soriano, I judged her to be more than a match for most people, but I didn't voice the opinion. "What about Larkey?"

"Jay's busy overseeing the operation of the club. Besides, he has . . . difficulty dealing with Marc."

"Why is that?"

Soriano blew a smoke ring and watched as it wafted through the air, its shape gradually becoming distorted. "Marc was the Kostakos girl's boyfriend," he finally said.

"So?"

"Jay was also her boyfriend—although that's not quite the term to apply to someone of his age."

I was silent, assimilating this new information.

Soriano noted my surprise and added, "It's a wonder no one's told you about that. Everyone knew."

"Larkey claims he was fond of Tracy as a father would be. And it never came out at the Foster trial."

"Well, I'm sure that at this late date Jay doesn't want to admit to being a middle-aged fool. And as for the trial, it simply wasn't relevant. Also, the prosecution tried to paint little Ms. Kostakos as the girl next door. If her relationship with Jay had come out, other things would have, too."

"Such as?"

"Tracy was a very busy girl. There was Marc, of course. I like to think of that as her last uncorrupt attachment. After Marc, there was Jay. She used him—to get an extended contract at the club, for an introduction to a talent agent, for spending money. Oddly enough, I think she genuinely cared for him; all the kids do, it's hard for them not to. But she *did* use him, and her behavior on the side would have distressed him, if he'd known."

"What do you mean by 'behavior on the side'?"

Soriano smiled bleakly. "Ms. Kostakos had a nasty habit of

worming her way into people's lives, taking what she could, and using it in her routines. She'd become close to a person, cast herself in a role; she wanted the whole experience, the whole flavor. There was the Foster kid—"

"You know about that?"

Now it was his turn to look surprised. "Yes. How did *you* find out?"

"He told me."

"Huh. I thought he'd never break his silence. Well, anyway, I don't think she ever got to put that material to use, and she certainly didn't in my case—"

"You?"

"No, I saw through her and put a stop to it. But in the case of Lisa McIntyre . . ."

"The lesbian waitress routine?"

"That's right. Tracy's portrayal of her had an undertone of viciousness. Lisa had no idea what her motives were when they had their brief . . . fling, and when she saw the routine, she was furious."

"God." All I could think of was George, how it would hurt him should all this come out. If it was humanly possible, I would make sure he never heard any of it. "Are you aware that I found what I thought was Tracy's body at a cottage up at the Napa River yesterday?" I asked.

He nodded. "My wife told me."

"Well, it turned out not to be hers."

"Oh?"

"The sheriff's department is comparing the remains with Lisa McIntyre's dental records."

He had been about to stub out his cigarette, but his hand stopped inches from the ashtray. For a moment he froze. "That's a curious turn of events. It's difficult not to draw a very distasteful conclusion."

"Yes, it is."

Soriano finished putting his cigarette out and stood, adjusting his suit jacket. His face was even more drawn now, and I thought I detected a trace of anger. "If the conclusion's correct, it'll put Jay through hell. He blames himself."

"For what?"

He shook his head. "That's his business. And frankly, I'm sick of sitting around here waiting for the Porky Pig of stand-up. That club has been nothing but a pain in the ass for me; from now on I'm confining myself to Atlas Development."

Atlas Development. Where had I . . . ? Of course! "The car that was stolen off the club's lot that night—the one that the prosecution claimed Foster used to kidnap Tracy—was registered to Atlas Development."

"That's right. It was the company car used by my executive assistant, Jim Fox. He'd dropped by the club for the first time that night, at my invitation. Met a lady and went home with her. When he went back for the Volvo, it was gone."

"Exactly when did he report it stolen?"

"Not until early the next evening. The lady dropped him at work, and I drove him to the club after we'd finished for the day."

So that was why the vehicle registration check that the highway patrol routinely makes when issuing citations hadn't shown the Volvo as stolen.

Soriano seemed to have lost interest in our conversation. He glanced at his watch and said, "Now I really do have to be going. If you see Marc, please don't tell him he's about to be canned. I'd hate to spoil the pleasure Jay will take in the act." Before I could reply, Soriano bowed curtly and left the apartment.

I remained where I was for a minute or so, digesting this latest information. The picture of Tracy that was emerging was an unsavory one, and my distaste created a sour sensation in my stomach. I'd never really regretted not having children, and now I was beginning to feel positively blessed. The pain these revelations would cause George—if I couldn't somehow suppress them—was incalculable, and I was selfish enough not to want to be the one who caused them to be aired.

After a moment I shoved my musings aside and went down the hall to the linen closet, where I searched for the probe that opened the locked door of Tracy's room. It wasn't in evidence. I felt in my bag for a suitable implement and came up with a long nail—a piece of the detritus that accompanies a homeowner in the throes of renovating. It took some maneuvering, but in thirty seconds the lock snapped open and I stepped through the door.

A strangled cry came from the darkness in front of me.

I flattened against the wall, one hand groping for the light switch, the other going reflexively to the side pocket of my bag, even though I wasn't armed. When the overhead flared, I saw Laura Kostakos.

She crouched on her knees between the bed and the armoire by the window. Her blue lounging pajamas were crumpled and looked as if she hadn't taken them off since I'd interviewed her the previous Thursday; her gray-blond hair was limp and disheveled. Her eyes worried me more than her grooming: they were wide with fright and curiously unfocused. She opened her mouth as if to cry out again, and I raised a hand in a calming gesture.

Laura slumped closer to the floor, her bowed head all but disappearing from my view. I hurried around the bed, murmuring soothing things, and grasped her arms to help her up. They were matchstick thin; the gardenia perfume smelled fetid, as of flowers that had fallen from the bush and rotted. Her body sagged against mine. I managed to prop her in the nearby rocker.

She leaned her head back, breathing raggedly. ". . . Frightened me."

"I'm sorry. I didn't know you were in here."

"A man came into the apartment. Strange man. I locked the door and hid."

"That was Jay Larkey's business partner. He's gone now."

She nodded wearily, closing her eyes and beginning to rock.

I sat on the edge of the waterbed; waves rippled inside, sloshing softly. "Mrs. Kostakos . . . Laura," I said, "what are you doing in here? It can't be good for you to keep coming here, waiting, dwelling on the past."

She continued to rock silently.

"If Tracy were to come back," I added, "it wouldn't be to this apartment. She probably doesn't even know you've kept it."

"She does."

"Why do you think so?"

"Because she told me to come here when she called me. Both times."

A chill touched my shoulder blades. "When was that?"

"New Year's Eve, in the afternoon. And again today, around five."

"Are you sure it was Tracy?"

"I know my own daughter's voice."

"Exactly what did she say?"

"The first time, just to come to the apartment, she'd meet me here. I waited all night, but she never arrived. Today she apologized, said she'd been detained, but that tonight she'd be here for sure. But then that man came, and now you. She's probably been frightened away."

Or was never coming to begin with, I thought. Had it really been

Tracy who had called, or someone perpetrating a cruel hoax? "Why do you think she would be frightened of Rob Soriano or me?"

No reply..

"Laura—*why?*"

She shook her head, rocking harder.

I watched her silently, taking my earlier line of reasoning to its inevitable conclusion. If Tracy had been involved—either directly or indirectly—in the killing at the Napa River, she would have good cause to fear being seen, particularly by Rob Soriano, who had known her. Had she given her mother any indication of what had happened that night, or in the intervening years? Or had she merely summoned her? And in either instance—why now? Because she had heard the case was being reopened? That presupposed her being in touch with someone who knew about my investigation.

"Laura," I said, "were Tracy's calls long distance?"

". . . I don't know where she was."

"But did they *sound* like long distance?"

". . . No. She couldn't have been too far away, not if she planned to meet me here in the evening."

I was silent again, assessing what she had told me. Tracy could really have called, or it could have been someone pretending to be her. Laura could be lying, or she could have imagined both episodes. I had no basis for determining which possibility was the truth.

Laura sat up straighter and opened her eyes, glaring defiantly at me. "I know what you're thinking," she said. "That I'm making it all up or hallucinating. You're just like George. You don't believe me."

At the mention of his name I felt a stab of guilt. I had slept with her husband the night before, would probably sleep with him again tonight. And in the meantime, this woman sat in a dark room waiting for a daughter who might never come to her. A daughter who, in any event, would never again be the child she had raised and loved.

"Just like George," she said again, and began to cough.

Alarmed, I asked, "What's wrong?"

She waved an arm at the door and choked out, "Water."

I hurried to the kitchen, found a glass among the welter of objects on the counter, and rinsed it. I was filling it when I heard a crash. Startled, I dropped the glass in the sink, shattering it, and ran toward the bedroom. But partway through the living room I realized the crash had been the front door slamming; Laura was gone.

I rushed outside and down the stairway. By the time I got to the sidewalk, Laura was climbing into the Mercedes sports coupe that was parked in the drive. I ran around to her side, but she had locked the door. She started the car and it hurtled backward, tires barely missing my toes. By some miracle, there was no oncoming traffic on Upper Market.

As I watched the Mercedes careen downhill and out of sight, I hoped Laura had enough control not to kill herself or someone else on her way back to Palo Alto.

17

George said, "I'll call a colleague of mine and ask him to look in on her. If she refuses to see him, though, there's not much I can do."

We were seated in the kitchen of his borrowed house, drinking wine. The promised pizza was on its way. He had gone ahead and ordered it, I thought, as a way of maintaining the illusion of normalcy, but my news about Tracy's purported telephone calls and Laura's behavior had shaken him badly.

"Maybe you should be the one to talk to her," I began tentatively.

He shook his head. "No, Sharon, I can't. It's over with Laura and me. Last night affirmed that." To my inquiring look, he replied, "No, you're not the first woman I've slept with since the separation. And I confess I wasn't always faithful to my wife. But you were the first woman since Laura with whom I've shared that essential connection that makes it the beginning of a relationship, rather than a casual affair. I can't encourage Laura to think there's still something between us, no matter how bad a shape she's in.

"Besides," he added, "Laura's a very perceptive woman, even when she's in a poor emotional state. She'd realize I was only coming round out of pity, and that would take away her pride. She'll need her pride if she's going to survive whatever's ahead."

I nodded, twirling my wineglass slowly between my fingers. "Just so long as someone looks in on her. But what about those phone calls, George? Do you think they actually were from Tracy?"

His eyes were clouded, their hazel tinged with green. "The phone calls . . . I just don't know. The whole thing's so clandestine, spooky—so unlike Tracy. And yet I have to remind myself that it was also unlike her to disappear and maintain a silence while

130

her friend was convicted of killing her. I just don't know, dammit!"

"Is it possible the calls are a figment of Laura's imagination?"

"Yes." He grimaced, then laughed bitterly. "You know, part of me wants to believe that, because I can't imagine what Tracy's become, that she would put us all through such an ordeal. But on the other hand, if Laura's imagining them, she's deteriorated drastically in the course of a week."

"Do people just suddenly . . . go like that?"

"Sometimes. It could have been accelerated by the holidays. She refused to do anything during them, even though some relatives had asked her to visit. *I* even tried to get her to go to dinner with me on Christmas Eve, but she wouldn't."

I felt a prickle of jealousy, even though I hadn't so much as known of George Kostakos's existence then.

He smiled and covered my hand with his. "I only did that because I felt sorry for her. I should have known better. She saw right through me, of course." He paused, studying my face, his candid gaze asking me to believe him. After a moment I lowered my own gaze to the tabletop, discomforted because he had seen through me as easily as Laura had seen through him.

He understood that, too, released my hand and rose briskly. "I'll call my colleague. You listen for the pizza delivery guy."

I remained at the table, sipping wine moodily and staring at a big bunch of dried red peppers that hung from a black iron pot rack. Strangely ambivalent feelings were welling up in me. On the one hand, I wanted George all to myself; on the other, I wanted him to do something to help Laura. The night before, I had not thought of him as a still-married man with a badly disturbed wife; tonight it was the only way I *could* think of him. Perhaps this relationship would prove to be more than I wanted to handle—

The doorbell rang. I picked up the money he'd left on the table and went down to meet the man from Domino's.

We spent the remainder of the evening in tacit agreement not to discuss either his wife or my investigation. After we ate, we built a fire and—in lieu of comfortable furniture—piled blankets and pillows on the floor in front of the hearth. For a while we stared at the flames and traded past histories and small confidences—the mortar that binds the bricks of physical desire and runaway emotion into a structure far stronger than either of those elements alone.

I learned that George had always lived in Palo Alto, except for the years he spent in college at Harvard and postgraduate work at the University of Michigan; that he'd turned his back on the family business—oil exploration and drilling—by entering the Ph.D. program, and thus became estranged from his father. He met and married Laura, who was also doing graduate work, in Ann Arbor; unlike many academic couples, they both managed to secure faculty positions at Stanford. After Tracy's birth, he and his father reconciled, and when his father died some dozen years ago, he found himself in possession of a small fortune.

"But the money never made a difference," he said. "It was nice to have it, and we lived well, but it just . . . didn't make a difference."

"How do you mean?"

"Things went along much as they always had. Life fell into a predictable routine, day to day, month to month, year to year—the way it does when you're building careers and raising a child. It wasn't unpleasant, but . . ." He fell silent, watching the fire for a moment.

"You know," he went on, "there's a whole period in my life that's gray. I really don't remember much about it. Little things stand out: a nice Christmas, Tracy's high school graduation, a good vacation. But it's as if they happened to someone else and were told to me. What I *do* remember are things from early on: winter mornings in Cambridge, when it was so cold you dressed inches from the electric heater and literally slid to class on ice-slicked snow; autumn days in Ann Arbor, when the whole Huron River Valley was hazed with leaf smoke that still didn't mute the fall color; a special evening with Laura shortly after we moved to Palo Alto, when we walked through the eucalyptus groves at Stanford after a rain, with that overpowering smell of the trees all around us and water dripping off them onto our bare heads. For a long time I thought maybe I'd lived all my real moments and that those scattered memories were all I ever would have."

"And then?"

"And then Tracy disappeared. The pain was searing, but it brought me out of it. Surprisingly, what I found wasn't totally bad. At least I was alive again. At least I could *feel*."

He turned to me, cupped my face in his hands, and conversation became superfluous. Making love seemed to have a catalytic effect on George's worry and pain, transforming it into a force that swept away whatever residual guilt and separateness I'd been feeling.

Afterward I lay suspended in a warm satiated state, perfectly secure, all but the most pleasant of senses dulled.

Sometime after midnight the phone rang. George took the call in the kitchen; when he came back, his step was lighter. "That was my colleague," he said. "He's talked with Laura, and she's agreed to see her therapist tomorrow."

I sat up, pushing my hair back off my face. "What about those phone calls—does she still claim she received them?"

He crawled under the comforter, pulled me down beside him. "My friend says yes."

"Then I'll proceed on the basis that Tracy is alive and has been trying to meet with her mother."

For a moment I felt tension creeping back into his lean body; then he turned me toward him. For a time we were able to ignore the fact that a world where death and pain and loneliness are the rule, rather than the exception, lurked just outside the circle of each other's arms.

At nine the next morning George had an appointment with someone from Living Victims, the support group for relatives and friends of murder victims, which he was assisting with grant writing. I asked if I might stay at the house for a while to view some of the videos of Tracy's performances; he pointed out the cabinet where they were stored and went off looking reasonably cheerful.

Before I sat down to watch, I phoned Stan Gurski. The news from officialdom was what I'd expected: Barbour and Emmons had not yet been picked up; Larkey had released McIntyre's dental records but declined to assist, due to a prior commitment. When I phoned Larkey at his home, however, he told me that he just hadn't been able to stomach viewing the remains a second time. I assured him I sympathized with him, and asked for the name and number of the talent agent he had introduced Tracy to. I didn't address the issue of Jay's affair with Tracy, merely set an appointment to talk face-to-face that afternoon.

The agent's name was Jane Stein. I called her office on Wilshire Boulevard in L.A., and when I mentioned Larkey, was put right through to her. Ms. Stein was confused when I asked if she had heard from Tracy Kostakos since her disappearance, and surprised when I said I was investigating the possibility she might be alive. Coincidentally, she was about to leave for the airport, to fly to San Francisco for a meeting with a client. Since she was going on to New York in the early afternoon, she said, she planned to have lunch with the client at SFO. Could I meet with her beforehand? She'd like to hear more about the situation, and perhaps she could offer some insight that might help me. I agreed to meet her in the main lobby bar at the United Airlines terminal at eleven-thirty.

That left me with only two hours to spare. I decided to watch only the tape containing the routine about the lesbian waitress, then go home, change, and drive to the airport. The tape was still in the machine. I rewound it and dragged over the least spine-punishing chair in the room.

The tape had been recorded on extended play; it held six hours of routines—thirty-some individual performances dating over the two-month period before Tracy's disappearance. I looked briefly at each, fast-forwarding through some, examining others with more interest. After a while I became aware of a pattern that hadn't been apparent from reading Tracy's sketchbook.

In most of the routines—the bewildered feminist, for example— it was obvious Tracy was fond of the character she had created. Her wit was sharp but affectionate; the fun she poked was gentle. But in others—notably the lesbian waitress—her humor became caustic and needling, as if she shared Larkey's opinion that comedy had to hurt to be funny. Her portrayal of Lisa McIntyre held particularly malicious undertones, and I could certainly understand why the waitress had been enraged. Not only had she been sexually used by Tracy, but then humiliated in front of the public and her coworkers. I suspected Tracy might have handled her material that way in angry reaction to her own guilt over what she'd done to Lisa, or perhaps because she blamed Lisa for allowing herself to be used. Lisa couldn't have known that, however, and I now wondered if her own rage had been strong enough to provoke a violent confrontation.

After a while Tracy's routines stopped being funny to me. Now that I knew how she had gone about creating them, they seemed trivial compared to the suffering they had undoubtedly brought many of the women they were patterned on. I shut off the VCR and stood at the front window for a bit, staring out at the misted lagoon across the street, then wrote a brief note to George—lover's nonsense that didn't really fit my mood—and went home to change.

There were five messages on my answering machine, four of them personal and one from the contractor, reminding me supplies were due to be delivered that afternoon so he could start work on the back porch the next morning. I swore softly, readjusting my mental schedule to make time for that. Watney waited for me in the kitchen, howling indignantly about my protracted absence. When I fed him, he turned up his nose at his favorite chicken-and-liver; I sent him outside, telling him to catch some mice, if he thought they were so much better.

For my meeting with a genuine Hollywood personage (and with the idea in the back of my mind that it might be novel for George to see me in a grownup person's outfit for a change), I put on a black knit skirt-and-tunic outfit and tied a colorful silk scarf around my neck. As I spiffed my hair, I examined the gray streak that had been in it since my teens, wondering if I ought to start dying it. Once it had looked exotic among the black, but I was old enough now that it merely seemed as if it was supposed to be there. Then I thought, Why should I dye it? Men consider their gray hair distinguished; I think mine is, too.

Cheered by the thought, I went off to the airport.

18

Jane Stein was a pleasant surprise. With the typical snobbery of northern Californians for Tinseltown, I'd been anticipating someone flashy, a trifle tacky, perhaps loud. The dark-haired, conservatively dressed woman seated at a window table in the airport bar was none of those. Her manner was reserved, her firm handshake and low voice were quietly confident, and she was even sipping coffee rather than the wicked dark drink that I'd imagined. She invited me to sit down and dispatched the waitress for my iced tea with a minimum of fuss, then leaned forward, regarding me with keen brown eyes.

"It's a pleasure to meet a real private investigator, rather than those cinematic horrors we're always creating down south," she said.

"I'm glad you feel the way I do. I can't watch those shows or films. I like most mystery novels, but the way we've been portrayed on the screen . . ."

Stein leaned back in her chair, seeming satisfied with the rapport we'd established. "Well now," she said, "tell me what this is about Tracy Kostakos being alive."

I outlined my case to date, leaving out the sleazier side of Tracy's behavior. Stein listened thoughtfully. When I concluded, she said, "It's quite bizarre, but I've seen enough things in this business that nothing truly surprises me. I assume it's the same for you."

I nodded, moving my arm so the waitress could set down my tea.

"You know, I wonder. . . ." Stein paused, her gaze on the other side of the room. "Let me tell you about my last meeting with Tracy."

"When was that?"

"Monday, two weeks before she died . . . disappeared, whatever. We were here in this very bar. I frequently meet with my San Francisco clients at the airport when I'm on my way to New York. There's enough time between connections for a couple of conferences, and it saves me an extra trip north." She smiled. "Most of my clients up here aren't at the point in their careers yet that they can easily afford to fly down to see me. Anyway, I'd met Tracy only twice before—once when I caught her act at Café Comedie, and again when she and Jay made a trip to L.A."

"You knew they were lovers?"

"Oh yes. Jay made that clear; he was proud of it, you see. He's had his rough times in recent years: his career waning, substantial financial losses. He needed a pretty young woman like Tracy in his life as much as she needed him." She shook her head. "What he *didn't* need was to lose her the way he did."

"Why did you meet with Tracy that last time?"

"She'd called me, said she needed to talk. It seemed she wanted to get away from San Francisco and hoped I could book her into a club in L.A. I had the impression things were going badly in her personal life. Perhaps she'd tired of Jay, or there was someone else, and she wanted to break it off. At any rate, she said she needed a change. I pointed out that she'd just signed a very lucrative contract with Jay; I doubted he would let her out of it, and I didn't feel it would be ethical to try to break it."

"How did she react to that?"

"Petulantly—but I'm used to that in my clients. We also talked about the possibility of film or TV work. I felt she wasn't ready for either yet and counseled her to be patient. She showed me a new approach she'd been working on for her routines, and I felt that with some more development and practice she might have a good thing there."

"What was it?"

Stein signaled for more coffee. "Very improvisational. She would take the daily newspaper and open it at random to a feature article—or ask a member of the audience to do so—then create a routine based on the piece. It's nothing that hasn't been done before, but you have to think extremely well on your feet to pull it off. I felt she had that ability."

"She actually demonstrated it to you?"

"Yes. When I said I was wondering about something . . . well, I'll lay it out for you, and you tell me if you think it's relevant." Stein waited until the waitress had poured her refill before continuing.

"I had that morning's L.A. *Times* with me. She turned to the feature section and did a very funny sketch about a woman who had built a twenty-thousand-dollar doghouse for her seven Dalmatians and was trying to persuade her neighbors not to take her to court for zoning violations. It was rough in spots, but I was quite impressed. Then an odd thing happened."

I waited as Stein sipped coffee before going on.

"Let's see if I can get this as accurately as possible," she said. "We talked some more, and I made some notes. While I was writing, Tracy paged through the newspaper. I looked up a few minutes later and . . . something wasn't right. Her face was very pale and—on later reflection, I decided—a little frightened. I asked her what was wrong, but she shrugged it off, said nothing, that she'd just gotten an idea."

"And she wouldn't elaborate on it?"

"No. We discussed a few other things—contractual matters—and then it was time for my New York flight."

"And that's it?"

"Except for one thing that didn't strike me until today. She asked me if she could have my copy of the *Times*. Given what you've told me, I can't help but wonder if it wasn't something she saw in the paper that frightened her. Something that has bearing on her disappearance."

"Did you notice which section she was looking at?"

"Sorry, no."

"But it was definitely that morning's paper?"

"Yes. Monday, February . . . whatever it was that year."

"And it was the edition for L.A. proper?"

She nodded.

I sipped iced tea and looked out at the runway where an L1011 was landing. What Stein had told me could mean a great deal—or absolutely nothing. Her recollections of the meeting were nearly two years old, and her perceptions were bound to have been colored by the intervening events.

"What do you think?" she asked.

"I'm glad you told me about it. I'll check that issue of the *Times*." I rested my forearms on the table, toying with my cocktail napkin as I phrased my next question. "Ms. Stein, would you mind giving me your personal impression of Tracy Kostakos?"

"I'll be glad to." She paused, considering. "She was . . . a type we frequently see in the business. Narcissistic in the extreme."

She was beginning to sound like George. Was everyone a psychologist these days? "Would you explain that?"

"Tracy had an overdeveloped ego. Naturally in show business a healthy ego is a necessity; there's no way to survive without one. But Tracy's wasn't healthy; she was a bundle of contradictions. On the one hand, she was very insecure and needed constant praise and reassurance; on the other, she felt superior and entitled to special treatment. She felt the rules simply didn't apply to her, and she was very insensitive to other people's feelings."

"No one's pointed out her insecurity before."

Stein smiled. "She did her best to hide it, but that sort of thing quickly becomes apparent to an agent. She was by no means the most poorly adjusted client I've had. I was willing to put up with her shortcomings because she was extremely gifted. She lived for her work. When she denied other people their rights or disregarded their feelings, it was usually because they came between her and her art."

Perhaps Stein was right, I thought, but she had viewed Tracy from a purely professional standpoint. There was another component of her character that had gradually communicated itself to me as I'd watched the videotape earlier. The way she moved, spoke, and interacted with the audience told me Tracy was a total sensualist, and not just in the sexual interpretation of the term. As Rob Soriano had commented, she wanted every experience, to taste the whole flavor of life. Her art gave her the opportunity to indulge her fascination with the inner workings of other people's lives, and so long as she'd only observed and recorded she'd been fine. But eventually she'd overstepped the boundary between observation and actual participation in life-styles that were foreign to her own: the woman who slept with black men, the lesbian. It was then— when her behavior had exceeded what was acceptable not only in the upper-class world where she'd been raised, but also in the subculture of the comedy clubs—that she'd gotten into trouble.

Actual participation in other people's lives. I was beginning to have an idea. . . .

Stein was watching me with interest. "Will you let me know what you find out?"

"Yes, of course."

"My evaluation of Tracy may have sounded pretty damning, but I really did like her. She was talented and dedicated; that combination is harder to find than you'd expect." She broke off, her gaze moving to the bar's entrance. "My client," she said.

I stood up. "Thank you for your time."

"Don't mention it." Already she was on her feet, attention turning from the lost promise of Tracy Kostakos to the future prospects of the curly-haired young man who approached the table.

I went to the bank of pay phones in the ticket lobby and placed a credit-card call to Detective Gurski. He'd told me earlier that he'd sent a man down to the city for McIntyre's dental records and that he was pushing the coroner's office to have the results of the comparison to him by noon. It took a long time for him to come on the line, but when he did, his tone was warmer than on the previous occasions we'd spoken.

"Your suggestion was a good one, Ms. McCone," he said. "We have a positive identification."

"The bones were Lisa McIntyre's."

"Yes. I guess you realize what this means. The new focus of our investigation will be very distressing to the Kostakos girl's family."

"I'm aware of that. May I have your permission to continue to work on the case, on behalf of Bobby Foster's attorney?"

"I've got no problem with that, so long as you report any developments to me."

I thanked him and hung up, then placed a second call to Rae at All Souls. "Anything on McIntyre yet?" I asked.

"Not a thing. The manager of her apartment building hasn't been there, and Kathy Soriano refuses to talk with me. I've just gotten started on the skip trace, and I suppose it'll take a while for people to get back to me."

"I doubt they'll have anything for you." I told her about the coroner's findings, then added, "I want you to keep going, though."

"Why, if the woman's dead?"

"Just an idea I have. I'll explain later. One thing you might do is contact unions for service workers, such as waitresses. I don't know how to reach any of them, or what you'd need to do to get information, but call Johnny's Kansas City Barbecue—that's that restaurant in the Fillmore that's been there forever and just got 'discovered'—and talk to Johnny Hart. He's an old friend of mine and may be able to help you."

"All right," Rae said, the dubious note in her voice telling me what she thought of the idea. "By the way," she added, "George Kostakos called. Said he'd try later."

"Oh, good. When he does, ask him if he can meet me at my house around four. I have to be there to take delivery on some Sheetrock."

"Don't mention Sheetrock to me."

"Sorry. Is the room finished?"

"I'm still painting. I'll probably be painting forever."

I wished her luck with it, then went to pay a king's ransom to the airport parking authority. As I drove back toward the city, dark clouds were massing ominously along the barren slopes of San Bruno Mountain.

19

The rainstorm hit full force as I was walking across South Park to Café Comedie from the small restaurant where I'd stopped for a burger. I sprinted through the benches and playground equipment, my boot heels sinking into the damp ground, to the shelter of the red-white-and-blue striped canopy. The club was closed, but Larkey had said he would be there for our two-o'clock appointment. I pounded on the door until he looked out, his brown hair curling riotously from the humidity.

"Good Christ," he said, peering past me to where the water cascaded off the canvas. "It's a fucking cloudburst. Did you get soaked?"

"No, I'm more chilly than wet." The interior of the club was almost as cold as outside. A maintenance man in a down jacket was vacuuming the carpet near the stage, and the bartender who had served me on Thursday night was unpacking a case of liquor with gloved hands.

"Sorry it's so cold in here," Larkey said. "We've been having trouble with the furnace—gas leak, and PG&E can't get it fixed right. Come on back to my office; I've got a space heater on. You want a drink?"

"One would help, thanks."

"Mike, would you make us a couple of hot toddies and bring them back to the office?" he asked the bartender. Then he motioned for me to follow him through the door that said Yes.

After the chill outside, the office seemed excessively warm, and even more disorderly than the first time I'd seen it. Several cardboard file boxes were stacked in the center of the floor, a wastebasket full of what looked to be receipts on top of them. Although Larkey was again clad in a sweat suit—a natty red and

142

yellow one this time—he obviously hadn't been using the exercise bike, since it was draped with a sport coat, a dress shirt, two ties, and a pair of pants. While I shed my trenchcoat, he looked around helplessly, then picked up a pile of newspapers and magazines from a chair and dumped them in a corner. I sat there, and he took his desk chair, propping his feet on the littered blotter.

"So," he said, "what's happening?"

"The Napa County coroner has made an ID on those bones. They're definitely Lisa McIntyre's."

He grimaced, as if experiencing sudden pain. "Poor kid. I'm sorry. What the hell was she doing up there, anyway?"

"I'm not sure. Do you have a picture of her—in her personnel file, perhaps?"

He started to shake his head, then took his feet off the desk and rummaged in a lower drawer. "The staff gave me a birthday party that year. Somebody took pictures. There might be . . . here's one—Lisa at the bar with Tracy."

I got up and took it from his extended hand. They sat on stools, half turned toward the camera. Tracy's expression was wary, perhaps because she was anticipating the glare of the flashbulb. Lisa smiled boldly. She had a heart-shaped face with a turned-up nose; her light brown hair fell smoothly from a center part, then belled out in soft curls that touched her shoulders. The shrewd, knowing expression in her eyes was strangely familiar; Tracy had caught it perfectly in her portrayal of Ginny the waitress.

I wasn't sure why I'd wanted to see a picture of the dead woman; perhaps I'd hoped to erase my mental image of that pitiful jumble of bones by seeing her in the flesh. I surprised myself further by asking, "Can I keep this?"

"Help yourself. I've got no use for it." As I tucked it in my bag, he added, "What gave you the idea it might be Lisa up there?"

"Just the timing of her disappearance."

"I wonder how she got there, or even knew where it was. It's isolated, and you've got to know which fork in the road to take—" Abruptly he broke off, realizing what he'd implied.

"Tracy had taken you there, then?"

He made a motion, as if to erase my question.

"Jay, I know you were having an affair with her. Apparently everyone knew at the time."

There was a knock at the door. Mike the bartender entered with our toddies. Larkey waited until he handed them around and departed before speaking. "Yeah, I guess everyone did know. I didn't bother to hide it."

"Why would you have reason to? Affairs between men in their prime and women of Tracy's age aren't uncommon."

"Especially in this business. Maybe that's why I don't want to own up to it now. It was such a trite situation. Older man clinging to the fringes of the business and needing reassurance. Young woman on her way up, thinking he can help her. An old, old story."

"I'm sure Tracy didn't see it that way. From what I hear, she genuinely cared for you."

His mouth twitched, and he quickly drank some of his toddy. "No," he said, "she didn't. But that's got nothing to do with . . . anything."

"Can I ask you another personal question?"

"About Tracy?"

"Yes."

"Go ahead."

"Did you ever give her money?"

"You mean besides what I paid her to perform here? Yeah, I did."

"Why?"

"On my part that should be obvious. I thought if I gave her money I wouldn't lose her. But it was more than that; the kid was needy." To my surprised look he added, "Not in a monetary sense. Her family's rich. But she was angry with her parents on a very deep level and badly wanted to be independent."

"And she couldn't get by on what she earned? Jane Stein told me her contract with you was 'lucrative.'"

"She could have gotten by if she hadn't been so . . . needy is the only way I can describe it. Tracy had to buy things—clothes, possessions. They filled an emotional gap. It was the same way with applause from the audience. But when she got either, the applause or the things, it was never enough. Fifteen minutes later, its affect would have dulled, the way the affect of a fix does for a junkie. Then she'd start needing all over again. There sure as hell must have been something missing in her childhood, to make her that way."

I thought of the first character in the sketchbook, whom I'd suspected might be Tracy herself. The mother had never hugged her; the father had barely seemed alive. And I thought of George's description of all the years of Tracy's upbringing—those gray years that he scarcely remembered. A desolate feeling welled under my breastbone: for Laura, who was incapable of expressing her love;

for George, who hadn't been able to feel; for Tracy, who had starved emotionally.

Larkey was watching me curiously. I pushed the thoughts aside and asked, "Did she take you up to the river often?"

"Only twice. It was someplace she liked to get away to, and her roommate let her use it whenever she wanted. I hated it; it was too rustic for me. But I went along . . . well, for the same reason I gave her money."

"Do you suppose she took other people there?"

He ran his sharp little teeth over his lower lip. "Why do you ask that?"

"As you pointed out, Lisa would have had to know how to find it. Unless she went with Tracy that night."

"There's no way she would have," he said flatly, shaking his head.

I studied his face, trying to gauge what he knew about Lisa and Tracy. Probably not the whole story, I thought. It was hardly something Tracy would have confided in him—nor Lisa, for that matter.

After a moment he added, "Besides, the logistics aren't right. Tracy left here right after her last performance—that was established at Foster's trial. Lisa worked until closing at two. I can confirm that."

"So she drove up there after her shift ended—"

"No. She didn't own a car."

"Are you sure of that?"

He nodded. "A lot of times I drove her to her bus stop after work. That night it was raining, and normally I would have driven her, but I was . . . tied up here. So the Sorianos took her instead, drove her all the way home, since her apartment was on their way to the Golden Gate Bridge."

"You're certain about that?"

He nodded.

"Lisa could have borrowed a car after she got home. Or the next day. The time of her death can't be established."

He frowned, apparently realizing the direction in which my questions were leading. "You're not implying that Tracy . . . ?"

"It's a possibility."

"I refuse to believe that!"

"I don't want to, myself. But I don't know what else *to* think."

Larkey stood up and began to move restlessly around the office, snatching up the clothing from the exercise bike and wadding it together, then dropping it on the floor. He turned around, banged into the stack of file boxes. The wastebasket of receipts teetered; he grabbed for it, and it fell to the floor, scattering bits of paper like snow on the carpet.

"Shit!" For a moment I thought he would get down on his knees and begin gathering them up, but instead he kicked furiously at them. "Goddamn things, what's the use, anyway?"

"I'm sorry?"

He flung out a hand at the littered floor. "Stuff for a meeting with Rob and my tax man tomorrow afternoon. I don't know why I even bother. The losses alone'll save me from forking over."

"The club's losing that much money?"

"The club? Christ, no. It's the fucking real estate business that's killing me."

"Atlas Development? I talked with Rob Soriano and got the exact opposite impression."

"Ah, that's just hype. Rob probably thinks you've got some bucks to invest. Truth is, we're up to our asses in loans we can't pay off; we're stuck with property we can't give away, much less rent. People are holding off on buying or renting in SoMa until the Planning Commission comes up with guidelines for its development. Rob and I are barely treading water these days."

"But he seems so confident—"

"That's just his way, but don't let it fool you. He and Kath are up to the limits on all their credit cards, their house is triple-mortgaged, and the lenders are closing in on them. We've still got the club, but if he had his way, that'd be mortgaged up to the hilt, too. I'm not all that worried, though; Rob's led a charmed life. He's one of that kind that always land on their feet."

"You've known him a long time?"

"Awhile. I met him when I was playing Vegas, on my way down. We hit it off, maybe because he didn't give me the bullshit celebrity treatment. He knew I was on my way out, and he let me in on a couple of land deals he had going there. They worked out. He'd been a developer other places—Florida, Texas—and knew what he was doing. I cleared enough to buy this club."

"And he went into partnership with you?"

Larkey shook his head, sitting down on the edge of the desk, one foot scuffing rhythmically at the scattered receipts. "For the first couple of years this place was my baby. But things weren't going so good. This was a rougher neighborhood then, people didn't want to come down here. I was about to lose everything when Rob showed up—with his new wife, the toothsome Kathy—and bailed me out again. When things got going here, we formed Atlas."

There was something about his tone when he spoke of Kathy. . . . I thought of Tracy's description of Soriano's wife in the sketchbook, how she indulged in affairs as petty revenge against her husband. "You and Rob have had your ups and downs," I said. "Are you close friends?"

"Not friends, but—until recently—we did good business together."

"What about Kathy? Is she a friend?"

He looked surprised, then flashed his foxy little grin. "You're a nosy one, Ms. McCone. I suppose it goes with the territory. Yes, she's a friend. He doesn't care. I don't care. And it makes the lady feel better. Now, I think that's enough of personal questions."

"About Tracy—"

"I said enough. I don't want to talk about her, and I especially don't want to hear any more about what you suspect her of doing."

I picked up my untouched toddy. It was still warm. "Okay," I said. "I really don't have anything else to ask, anyway. But while I'm drinking this, would you humor me and do my favorite routine of yours—the one about Jake and Edna's Rottweiler farm?"

As I'd suspected, the request pleased him. When I left Café Comedie, my sides ached, and my eyes were damp from tears of laughter.

The storm had blown out to sea by the time I reached my house around four. The truck with the Sheetrock had already arrived, and George sat on the front steps talking with the driver. As I approached, I had to smile, remembering how in awe I'd been of my professors when I started at U.C. Berkeley. What would that young woman have thought of this learned gentleman in the Stanford sweatshirt, faded jeans, and well-worn athletic shoes who was earnestly discussing the Giants's chances in the upcoming season with a truck driver whose use of the word "fuckin'" was only surpassed by that of the phrase "shit, man"?

I unlocked the side gate so the Sheetrock could be taken in through the rear, then led George inside the house. He looked around with interest, complimenting me on the front parlor—by far the nicest room, but seldom used. After owning the house for a few years, I'd finally concluded that I like to do my living as close to the kitchen as possible, and had bought a comfortable sofa and moved the TV to the dining room—formerly a repository for paint and building supplies.

When we reached the kitchen at the rear of the house, I sat George down with a beer and sorted through the stacks of files on the table for the slim volume on creating a new identity that Amy Barbour claimed she'd found in Tracy's bedroom bookcase. I thumbed through it to the page about establishing a mail drop and studied the notation in the margin. Then I handed it to George and said, "Is this Tracy's handwriting?"

He examined it at length and finally shook his head. "I can't honestly say. It looks to be, but it's been a long time since I've seen anything she's written." He turned the book over, looked at its cover. "What is this, anyway?"

"Amy Barbour says she found it in Tracy's room. But if she did, it was planted there." I removed Tracy's sketchbook from the bottom of one of the piles and flipped it open, studying the handwriting. It varied from entry to entry, as most people's will do, and there was a gradual change from beginning to end, presumably because the pages had been penned over a long period of time, but its style was distinctive and the individual letters remained fairly consistent. I sat down at the table, drew the sketchbook closer, and took the other book from George. As I flipped through it, I found a series of notations.

After several minutes of study, I said, "I don't think Tracy made any of the notes in this book." I went around the table and laid the two open in front of him. "The capital *L* in Los Angeles is consistent with the way Tracy made hers. See this big upward loop, and the way the tail of the bottom one trails downward?"

"Uh-huh."

"But the capital *A*—it's not how she made hers, although it *is* how she made her lowercase *A*s."

"Meaning?"

"These notations could have been copied from a sample of her handwriting. Say someone had a letter from her, and it was signed 'Love, Tracy.' They would be able to get the *L* right. But if there weren't any capital *A*s in the letter, an inexperienced forger might just assume that she made them the way she made her lowercase *A*s, only larger. An experienced forger wouldn't make that assumption."

"So what you've got is someone on the amateurish side who marked this up to make it appear Tracy had used it to plan her own disappearance. Why?"

"I don't know. It doesn't make a whole lot of sense. My reopening the investigation must have been what prompted it, though, because the book wasn't where Barbour says she found it when I searched last Thursday evening. Between then and when she gave it to me on Monday morning, I'd conducted a number of interviews; a lot of people knew about that."

"But what did the person who planted this book hope to accomplish?"

"That's what I don't understand. Finding this—if I'd accepted it as genuine—would only have convinced me I was onto something and made me work harder. So whoever put the book in Tracy's room can't have wanted me to drop the investigation. On the other hand, since I was already on the case, a person who wanted Tracy found wouldn't have needed to go to such lengths."

"Unless whoever it was knows where she is, and there's some clue in the notes in the margins."

It was a farfetched idea, but at that point I was willing to consider anything. I took the book back around the table and made a list of the notations on a legal pad. After looking it over and arranging them in various sequences, I shrugged and passed the pad over to George. "If there's a clue here," I said, "it's damned obscure. I think these are nothing more than what the person who marked the book thought a reader who had studied it carefully might note."

He looked the pad over, did some rearranging of his own, and finally nodded in agreement.

"Another thing to consider," I said, "is who had opportunity to plant it there. Who had access to that apartment? Amy Barbour. Marc Emmons. Any number of people who may have visited there. And Laura."

"I can't imagine her doing such a thing. My wife is disturbed, but not irrational."

"Even if she were, this sort of thing doesn't strike me as her style. My guess is that it was either Amy or Marc. She came forward with the book. He became quite angry when I suggested he'd planted it. They're the logical ones to suspect, except . . . You know, I keep thinking of how Bobby Foster's notebook—the one with the misspellings that matched those in the ransom note—turned up conveniently, too."

"The notebook actually belonged to Foster, though."

"That's true." Discouraged, I went to the refrigerator for a glass of wine, then slumped in my chair, frowning down at the table. When I looked up, I saw that George was reading the first entry in the sketchbook. My impulse was to snatch it away from him, but I resisted and merely waited.

When he finished, he closed his eyes and rubbed his hand across them. "This is herself she's describing, isn't it?"

"I think so. She only did that once—as her first entry." The lie came out easily; there was no way I was going to let him read that final entry. I reached for the book, but he held on to it with both hands.

"'The beloved father, for all his academic knowledge, was little better. Vague, fondly absent. Sometimes she thought him only half alive.' Jesus, what did I do to my daughter? And to Laura? No wonder she was cold—she had a husband who wasn't really there."

I didn't speak for a moment, because I wanted to phrase what I was about to say very carefully. I knew that how I said it, even more than the actual sense of it, would be crucial to the future of our relationship.

"You can only offer what you have at a given time," I finally said. "I know that sounds simplistic, but you can only do and feel whatever your current capability is. And the situation, the flaws in it, are never wholly of your own making. Perhaps there was something in Laura and Tracy—in who and what they were and how they responded to you—that made you unable to act as a so-called proper husband and father should."

He considered that, then nodded and reached across the table for my hand. "It's true. People change, depending on the situation and the others involved in it. I'm not like that any longer—vague or fondly absent. I won't be that way in the future, either. That much I can promise you."

I entwined my fingers with his, leaned forward for his kiss. And the phone rang.

It was Stan Gurski. "I have some information that I thought might interest you," he said. "By way of a repay for your tip on McIntyre."

"Oh?" I glanced at George. He was paging through the sketchbook.

"McIntyre was shot. Bullet was lodged in the ribcage, a .38. Makes it look premeditated."

"Why?"

"When I called the owner of the cottage in Mexico Monday morning—easier to get his permission to enter and search the premises than to get a warrant—I routinely asked if any weapons were kept there. He said no; he's strictly a fisherman. So we can assume whoever shot her brought the gun with them. Gun like that means business, too."

I was well aware of that. I own a .38 and consider it a necessary precaution for a woman whose job requires her to go into dangerous places and situations. But I don't take the responsibility lightly, and I never carry it unless I'm fully prepared to use it.

"Another thing," Gurski said. "She was shot in the car."

"What?"

"Uh-huh." There was thinly veiled pride in his voice now. "When the ME reported the probable cause of death, I called SFPD. They still have the car impounded—capital case, appeals coming up. I asked them to look for other bullets. There was one, lodged in the door panel on the side where the bloodstains were. Our preliminary comparison shows it's from the same gun as the one lodged in the remains. San Francisco's finest sure screwed up on this one."

They had, in more than one way, and it unnerved me to think how close to the gas chamber that combination of mistakes had taken my client. I said, "Well, this completely invalidates Foster's confession. I'll pass the information along to his attorney."

The delivery-truck driver came through the door from the back porch, invoice in hand, looking for a check. I thanked Gurski for calling and terminated the conversation, then paid for the Sheetrock and went out to lock the side gate.

When I came back to the kitchen, George had Tracy's sketchbook open to the last page. He was staring into space, his face rigid with pain. My breath caught, and I stopped in the doorway.

Slowly he turned his head toward me and said, "Why did you lie?"

Perhaps he'd known his daughter better than he thought. Had I been in his place, I would not have recognized her—would not have *wanted* to recognize her—in that brief paragraph.

I said, "I hoped you'd never have to know."

"But *you* know. And we can't allow a secret of that magnitude to come between us."

I nodded and went to sit at the table.

"I think," he added, "that you'd better tell me everything you know about my daughter."

20

Wednesday dawned clear and cold—one of those mornings following a rainstorm when everything looks hard edged, vivid, and clean. My mood didn't fit the weather, however. By eleven I had swiveled away from my desk and was scowling out the bay window at the flat sprawl of the Outer Mission, wondering what right such a dingy neighborhood had to look so good in the sunlight. The desk behind me was stacked with papers and folders. Our holiday slowdown had ended, and our clients were once more suing and being sued, divorcing and getting arrested and appealing sentences. I no longer would have the luxury of pursuing the Foster/Kostakos investigation full-time; I'd give it until Monday morning, then juggle it with my other duties.

I had to acknowledge that a good part of the reason for my low mood was the way George and I had left things the afternoon before. As he'd asked, I'd been frank with him about Tracy, and what I'd had to relate disturbed and depressed him. He left around six, saying he needed some time alone. That was the last thing *I* needed, so after microwaving a couple of burritos (or "nuking" them, as my nephew Andrew calls it), I left the house and embarked on what I knew would probably be a fruitless tour around the city: to the public library to look for the copy of the L.A. *Times* that Jane Stein had mentioned, where I found the microfilm room closed; to Amy Barbour and Marc Emmons's buildings, in case they'd slipped past the police patrols; to Lisa McIntyre's building, in the vain hope its manager might be home; to Café Comedie, to see if Larkey had heard from Emmons.

While I was at the club, I ran into Kathy Soriano and asked if I might speak with her about Lisa and Tracy. She pleaded lack of time, vanished through the door marked Yes, and never came back.

I asked Larkey if he would intercede and arrange an appointment for me with Kathy. He said he didn't know how strong his influence was in those quarters lately, but he'd try.

Eventually I ended up at the Remedy, kicking around my ideas on the case with Jack and Rae. All that did was leave me several dollars poorer (Rae was so broke Jack and I had to take turns paying for her beers) and as confused as before. When I went home, my bed seemed too cold, large, and lonely. I was a long time getting to sleep, and when the contractor arrived to start work at eight the next morning, I was barely coherent. Not a good start to the day.

And now I'd had no word from George all morning. Larkey hadn't phoned about the appointment with Kathy Soriano. Rae had received no response to any of her inquiries. My spirits were sagging so fast that I calculated they'd be about ankle level by noon.

When the phone buzzed, I snatched up the receiver and growled something that sounded like one of those syllables in the crossword puzzle that correspond to the clue "kennel sound."

Larkey said, "What's the matter—you caught a cold?"

"Oh, Jay, hi. No—just a frog in my throat."

"They do better in ponds. Listen, I talked to Kathy, and she's willing to see you if you can get to her house in Tiburon by noon."

"Tiburon by noon. No problem. What's the address?" I scribbled it down, thanked him for arranging things, and left the office buoyed by the relief of a kid going out for recess.

Kathy Soriano didn't look very good that day. Her makeup was freshly applied, but there was a pallor under the tan base; her expensive suede shirt had a grease spot on it, and her leather boots bore scuff marks. Her hands shook as if she might have a hangover, and her greeting was subdued.

I found myself feeling sorry for her, even though she had a Jaguar sedan in the drive of the redwood-and-glass house set high above the bay. Her windows might overlook Angel Island and pine-studded hillsides, her living room might be filled with bronze sculptures and Imari porcelain, but I remembered what Larkey had said about the creditors closing in on the Sorianos. And I remembered Tracy's brutally frank description of Kathy as a woman who jumped when those in power snapped their fingers, and who felt compelled to betray her steely eyed husband. Kathy moved and spoke like a nervous, unhappy woman and seemed pathetically alone in the big house. And because of the attitude I had sensed in her toward others of her gender, she probably didn't even have a woman friend whose shoulder she could cry on.

She seated me facing a glass wall that overlooked a veritable forest and offered me a glass of wine, which I accepted. When she returned from the wet bar, I noticed her own drink looked to be something far more potent than wine. She drank half of it straight off, and gradually her color improved.

"I'm sorry I ran out on you so abruptly last night," she said in the tones of a little girl whose parents have told her to apologize. "I wasn't feeling well, and I needed to get home."

"That's too bad. I hope it's nothing serious."

She shrugged and looked away. The little girl had told her polite social lie but didn't want to be bothered with elaborating on it.

"Thank you for seeing me," I added. "I suppose Jay's already told you that the body I thought was Tracy Kostakos's is actually Lisa McIntyre's?"

She nodded.

"I'm trying to find out when Lisa went up to the Napa River, and why. Jay tells me you and Rob drove her home the last night that any of you saw her."

"Yes, we did. It was raining pretty hard by then, so we took her right to her apartment building."

"I also understand that you went around to her apartment at Jay's request the next week, and the manager told you she'd moved out."

"Skipped out is how she put it. Lisa didn't give any notice, and she left a lot of her stuff there. She was also behind on her rent."

"What's the manager's name?"

". . . I don't remember."

"I've been trying to contact her, but there's never anyone home."

"I'm sorry I can't help you, but it was a long time ago."

"No matter. Let's go back to that Thursday night. Your husband's executive assistant, Jim Fox, had come around to the club. The next day he found that his company car had been stolen off the lot."

"Yes, by Bobby Foster."

"I've recently found out that Tracy was the one who took it—"

"That's ridiculous!" She finished her drink quickly and went to the bar for another. "Tracy wouldn't have done that. She was a nice girl. Everybody liked her. I even liked her, and let me tell you, I'm not too keen on women. She wouldn't have ripped off one of our cars. She wouldn't have needed to, with all her family's money."

"Nevertheless, it appears she did. Would you go over the sequence of events that night for me?"

"I'm not sure I understand. About the car or about Lisa?"

"Both. Why don't you start with when you arrived at the club."

"I was there from about ten o'clock on. Around closing Rob wanted to go over some papers about the real estate business with Jay. The place was practically empty by then, so Lisa changed out of her uniform and waited with me at the bar."

"How did she seem?"

Kathy turned, drink in hand, bracing herself against the edge of the counter with her elbows. "You mean how did she act? Quiet. Lisa was always quiet around me, probably on account of me being an owner's wife. And frankly, I didn't encourage her. She was just a waitress, and not a very good one at that. She'd been closeted with Jay in his office for a while before Rob went back there, and Jay had probably chewed her out about something, as usual."

"All right, you waited together at the bar. What time did Jim Fox leave with the woman he met?"

"The . . . I guess while we were sitting there. I'm not sure."

"He wasn't involved in going over the papers with Rob and Jay?"

". . . I don't think so."

"How long were Rob and Jay together in the office?"

"Not long. Maybe fifteen minutes."

"And what time did you drop Lisa at her apartment?"

"Two-thirty or so. I know we were home by three."

I had run out of questions. Suddenly I wondered why I had even requested this interview. I cast about to make sure I had asked everything I needed to. "Did you see Tracy leave the club that night?"

For some reason that bothered her. She turned back to the bar and began removing a cork from the corkscrew. "I watched her routine, of course."

"A number of people said she wasn't at her best that night."

Kathy shrugged.

"She also made a phone call before she left. Do you know anything about that?"

". . . No. All I remember is watching her routine from our usual table in the last row."

"And after that?"

"After that she was gone. And that was it." The words were firm and flat, but her body language told me she was lying.

Kathy came away from the bar, set her glass on a coaster on the coffee table, but remained standing. "If that's all," she said, "I need to get ready for an appointment that I have in the city."

As she showed me out of her big, heavily mortgaged house, her step was lighter, as if she'd performed a difficult task and felt she'd acquitted herself well.

I hadn't eaten lunch, so I stopped at Sam's on the Tiburon waterfront. The clear weather had enticed a few diners onto the outdoor deck, and I joined them, snuggling deep inside my heavy pea jacket. As I waited for my crab sandwich, I thought about Kathy Soriano's evasiveness.

She'd been relatively candid and forthcoming early in the interview, possibly because the questions I asked were more or less what she'd expected to hear. Then my revelation that it was Tracy, rather than Bobby Foster, who had stolen the company car had shaken her composure. And my question about whether she'd seen Tracy leave the club that night had led to her curtailing our conversation. I wondered about Kathy's relationship with Tracy; she'd admitted to liking her, even though she wasn't "too keen on women." Was it possible they'd been friends? That Kathy knew more about what had happened than I'd initially suspected? Perhaps Larkey could shed some light on that.

After I finished eating I called the club. Larkey was there, dealing with yet another representative of PG&E about the persistent gas leak. He told me he would be in a meeting with Rob Soriano and his tax accountant until three; why didn't I come by at three-thirty? I said I would, and started back to the city. I wanted to stop once again at McIntyre's former building; Kathy's report of what the manager had told her about Lisa's departure wasn't particularly enlightening. Then I'd check the microfilm room at the library for the copy of the L.A. *Times* before keeping my appointment with Larkey.

I was buzzed in as soon as I rang the manager's apartment at the building on Pacific Avenue. The smell of baking bread from the store downstairs wafted up as I climbed to the second floor. It would be hell, I thought, to live over a bakery. The instant they took their wares from the oven in the morning, I'd be down there, my nose pressed to the glass, waiting for them to open.

The manager looked as if she'd never so much as glanced at a croissant. She was extremely thin, clad in black jeans and a turtleneck that emphasized the spareness of her frame, and had milky white skin that pulled so tight over her cheekbones that it seemed nearly translucent. Her youthful clothing and long hairstyle belonged on a woman in her twenties or thirties; her eyes hinted at at least two more decades of experience. She came into the hallway rather than admit me to her apartment. As we spoke, she pulled off the browned and shriveled fronds of a half-dead Boston fern that hung from a skylight at the top of the stairs.

Her name was Ms. Wilson, she said, and yes, she had been manager when Lisa McIntyre had lived there. No, she didn't remember the woman from the comedy club who had come looking for Lisa after she'd moved out. That had been a bad year, and it was possible she had forgotten the visit. I braced myself for the story of the bad year—strangers have a way of confiding their tales of woe in me—but none was forthcoming. Ms. Wilson, it turned out, was a woman of few words.

I said, "The woman who was looking for Lisa claims you said she 'skipped out' without giving notice and left a lot of her things behind."

The manager frowned. "I said no such thing—if I spoke to this person at all. Lisa didn't give notice, but she left me a note saying to keep the security deposit to make up for the lost rent. The apartment was furnished; she took what was hers, left what belonged there. I wouldn't call that skipping out, would you?"

"No, certainly not. Did you keep the note?"

"There was no need to."

"Did she leave a forwarding address for her mail?"

"No."

"Didn't that strike you as odd?"

She permitted herself a small smile; it seemed to cost her a fair amount of effort. "Most of what the tenants do strikes me as odd."

"Did Ms. McIntyre have many visitors while she lived here?"

"I don't know. I keep to myself and hope the tenants do the same."

"Did you see her move out, perhaps see someone helping her?"

"No."

"And no one has inquired after her?"

"No."

"Is it possible you've forgotten, seeing as it was a bad year?"

She closed her left hand over the dead fronds she held, crushing them to dust. Her fingers were bony, their skin as pale and stretched as that of her face. "It wasn't *that* bad a year. Now that I've had a few minutes to reflect on it, I'm sure no one came looking for her. That woman who says she did, whoever she is, is lying to you."

Someone sure was.

There was a pay phone in the bakery downstairs, so I stopped and checked in with Rae at All Souls. When she came on the line, her voice was high-pitched with excitement.

"Where the hell have you been?" she demanded. "I have this news for you, and you never call in!"

"What is it?"

"Your friend Johnny Hart got me the information you wanted on McIntyre from the food service workers' union. Sharon, you were right! Listen to this: The Great American Laugh-in, 27333 Reseda Boulevard, Reseda. I've already checked; there's no residential listing for her down there."

It was another comedy club; she hadn't been able to stay away from them. Not Lisa McIntyre—Tracy Kostakos hiding behind Lisa's identity.

I rummaged for my pad and pencil. "Reseda. That's—"

"L.A. area, in the San Fernando Valley. From the airport, you take the 405 freeway north, then swing west on 101. Reseda Boulevard intersects it."

"Great. Call—"

"USAir."

"And find out—"

"They have flights leaving for LAX almost every hour. You've got a reservation on the three o'clock one, open return."

"I'll need a—"

"Car. It's reserved. National."

"One more thing: I've got an appointment with Jay Larkey in half an hour. Cancel it, and tell him I'll be in touch later."

"Will do."

"Rae, thanks. I'll check back with you . . . whenever."

21

Early rush-hour traffic crawled north from L.A. airport on Interstate 405, past industrial areas and old tracts of small, lookalike houses. After about ten miles the freeway began to climb into the hills, and names made fabled in the days when motion pictures were still a glamour industry began to appear: Sunset Boulevard, Mulholland Drive.

I'd traveled this road many times before, en route from my parents' home in San Diego to San Francisco and, earlier, Berkeley. Nothing much had changed over the years except the swelling number of cars. I kept wary eyes on the bumper of the van in front of me and tried to control my mounting tension.

It now seemed that the theory I'd first dismissed as very shaky had at least some basis in reality. Tracy had gone to the cottage on the Napa River. Lisa had later joined her there. Perhaps the two of them had been alone, perhaps there had been a third party. But the end results had been Lisa's death by gunshot and Tracy's flight and assumption of Lisa's identity.

She'd come to the Los Angeles area, a good place for a young woman to lose herself. Since she had been a waitress before Larkey gave her her chance at performing, it had been easy for her also to assume Lisa's occupation. But she'd made the mistake that most people who attempt to disappear do: she hadn't totally disassociated herself from her prior life. She hadn't been able to keep away from the comedy clubs.

I was satisfied with those simple facts, but there were others that still didn't fit. The stolen car. The premeditated nature of Lisa's murder. The faked kidnapping. Tracy allowing her friend Bobby to be convicted of a crime he didn't commit. The phone calls to her mother, after nearly two years' silence. And the motive for it all . . .

I would find that out soon, and when I did—

The brake lights on the van in front of me flared. I jammed my foot down hard on the pedal. The car—a low-budget Japanese import—shuddered to a stop inches from the van's bumper. I restarted it and crept up the grade in pace with the rest of the traffic.

At the point in a case when assorted facts start to form a more or less understandable pattern, I usually feel a thrill of excitement. But now I felt only a strung-out tension and queasiness in my stomach—a dread of what I would find out. A dread of what additional horrors I would have to offer up to George.

He didn't deserve for his daughter to be embroiled in such a mess. Neither did Laura. True, George had been a "fondly absent" father; true, Laura had been a cold mother. But they had loved Tracy. Whatever I was about to find out was guaranteed to be bad, perhaps more than even George could bear, and certainly enough to topple Laura's precariously balanced sanity.

And bad for you, too, my all-too-truthful inner voice told me. Disastrous for this new relationship—the first that's promised to matter in a long time—for you to be the one who blows it all wide open. *You* don't deserve that.

But Bobby Foster didn't deserve to die, either.

My stomach spasmed. I gripped the steering wheel harder, forcing down the queasiness.

Near Sherman Oaks the interstate dipped down into the San Fernando Valley and crossed the Ventura Freeway. Traffic slowed close to a standstill on the westbound access ramp, then speeded up after it completed the merge. The exit for Reseda Boulevard, according to my map, was only about four miles beyond the interchange. As I drove, I squinted into the glare of the setting sun, its red and orange and gold smeared across the car's windshield, all but obscuring what lay ahead of me. By the time I coasted off the freeway and turned north, my eyes had begun to smart.

The boulevard was a wide one, lined at first with stores and restaurants and gas stations. Farther on, I came upon a vast area of apartment buildings: two- and three-storied stucco with the obligatory tiny lawns and palm trees, arranged around courtyards containing the obligatory tiny swimming pool and more palm trees. Many of their balconies overlooked the boulevard; they were furnished with lounge chairs from which tenants could view the passing cars, and potted plants that had somehow adapted to breathing exhaust fumes. Weber barbecues and hibachis stood as mute testimony to the good life.

Farther on, in Reseda proper, business establishments regained prominence. I checked the address Rae had given me and began watching for The Great American Laugh-in. It appeared on the left, between a Mexican restaurant and a shoe store. Parking was plentiful; I pulled into a metered space directly across the street.

Like Café Comedie, the club had a colorful facade—yellow, green, and orange—but it gave off a less sophisticated aura, as if its relative proximity to Disneyland had caused it to be exposed to too strong a dose of sunny, cloying fun. A former storefront, its blacked-out windows were painted with a barrage of balloonlike happy faces. As I crossed the street, I saw that twin clowns on either panel of the double entry pointed jovially at the doorhandles. I made a sour face at the clown on the left as I stepped into the dimly lit lobby.

Plywood cutouts of more clowns greeted me: one pointed the way to the checkroom, another to a door marked RESTROOMS; a third had a mechanical arm that semaphored toward the club proper. I went that way, feeling the breeze from the arm's whirling. The large room's arrangement was also similar to that at Café Comedie, except the bar ran along the right-hand wall.

A woman's husky voice said, "We don't open until six, ma'am."

It was only a little after five now. "Then what's he doing on the job so early?" I motioned at the clown.

The woman laughed. She was perched on a stool at the end of the bar, a calculator and stack of order forms in front of her, and wore a costume that made her resemble Ronald McDonald. "Switch is broken. Son of a bitch never stops flailing around. Like a lot of men I know."

I smiled companionably and took a seat two stools down from her. "I've known a few of those, too."

"Seems all some of them can do these days. I've got one at home—can't keep a job, can't cook, won't dirty his hands house-cleaning. I ask you—why do I keep him?"

"Well . . ."

"Yeah. That's exactly why I keep him. Look, I don't mean to be rude, but I really can't serve you until six."

"I'm not a customer." I never knew how to play situations like that until I saw who I'd be dealing with. This woman appeared hardheaded and fairly streetwise, so I decided to play it straight—up to a point.

When I placed my identification on the bar beside her, her eyes became knowing and wary. "Private cop, huh? What's Bart done now?"

"It's not Bart I'm looking for—whoever he is. It's Lisa McIntyre."

"What's *she* done?"

"Nothing so bad." The trick was to give her an acceptable story—certainly not the old ploy about a long-lost relative leaving a fortune—that would compel her to reveal "Lisa's" whereabouts. I bided my time until I could get a better handle on what would work with this woman. "Your name is . . . ?"

"Annette Dowdall. I'm manager and bartender."

"Does Lisa still work here?"

"Who says she ever did?"

"Her records with the union. And you asked what she's done, so you must know her."

Ms. Dowdall digested that, nodded slightly.

"You happy with Lisa's work?" I asked.

She shrugged. "She's kind of a ditz. Forgets to return change, spills drinks, breaks glasses. But the customers like her. I like her."

"You wouldn't want to lose her, then."

"No, of course not. Look—what's *with* Lisa?"

"As I said before, nothing so bad. She skipped out owing back rent on her apartment in San Francisco a couple of years ago. Somebody from the building saw her down here and told the management. They had me run a check."

"So what do they want—just the rent?"

"That and the storage costs on all the stuff she left behind."

"She left her stuff there? That's something!"

"What do you mean?"

"The poor kid can't get it together to buy *anything*. Not that it would fit in that studio—" She got up abruptly and went around the bar. "Look, you want a drink or something?"

"I thought you couldn't serve me until six."

She grinned. "I can't serve *customers* until six."

"In that case, white wine, please."

She poured the wine and a Bud for herself, then came back around the bar. "Look," she said, "Lisa's a nice kid. She doesn't have much money, certainly not enough for that rent and storage. Can't you just tell them you couldn't find her?"

I shook my head. "There's no point in that. They'd only hire somebody else, who might not be as pleasant with her as I would."

Ms. Dowdall still looked doubtful.

"I won't be rough on Lisa," I added. "And frankly, I think my client will arrange for her to pay the debt in installments. I suspect he's really more interested in getting her things out of storage than anything else. If I take him Lisa's check for part of the storage fee and her written permission to dispose of what she left, I think he'll probably forgive the rent."

She thought about that while I sipped my wine. Finally she said, "I'd just hate to see the kid get in trouble."

"You seem fond of her."

She shrugged and poured the rest of the bottle of beer into her glass. "It's more I feel sorry for her. Lisa's kind of pathetic, if you know what I mean."

"Not exactly."

"Well, she doesn't have any friends that I know of, and she never even tries to make some. She just comes to work and then runs home to her wretched little studio—I know it is, because I drove her home one time when she wasn't feeling so good, and I guess she thought she had to ask me in. Sometimes she hangs around here on her nights off and watches the stand-up acts, kind of wistfullike. I think it's that she wants to be a comedian, but she knows she hasn't got what it takes, so she just sort of hovers on the fringes."

What made her wistful, I thought, was that she knew she was good and could never perform again.

Annette Dowdall frowned, picking at the label on the empty beer bottle. "There's something not right about Lisa."

"How so?"

"It's not that she's a loner. She's *lonely*. And every now and then I get the feeling she's scared."

"Of what, do you think?"

"I'm not sure. Sometimes she seems to be . . . watching. Like she thinks somebody's going to show up and . . . I don't know. Not somebody like you, looking for back rent. Something more serious than that."

"Something bad in her past, perhaps. What do you know about her?"

"Not much, other than her employment record, and I didn't actually check it out. Her union card was in order, and waitresses in a place like this, they come and go, no big deal. But there was one thing. . . ." She hesitated, still picking at the label.

I took a sip of wine, giving her time to decide whether to trust me. My restraint paid off. She said, "There was this one day last August. She came on shift at six. We don't do much business until later, so she was sitting here at the bar. The TV was on to the national news. I wasn't watching it, I was doing paperwork. But she was, and all of a sudden she got very upset—gasped, went pale. I asked her what was wrong, but she wouldn't tell me. And for the rest of her shift she acted like this was a funeral parlor, not a comedy club. I finally told her to go home early."

"You don't recall anything about the newscast?"

"No, when I'm working with figures, I more or less blank everything else out."

August was when Bobby Foster had been convicted and sentenced to die for Tracy's so-called murder. The case had received national publicity because it was a no-body conviction. It sounded to me as if Tracy had heard about it on the news, been distressed, yet still not come forward.

"Is . . . Lisa scheduled to work tonight?" I asked.

Annette Dowdall shook her head.

"Will you give me her address and phone number, then?"

She hesitated a bit longer, then said, "She doesn't have a phone—something about owing back bills and they won't give her one till she pays up. But I guess it would be okay for you to go over there. You see how she lives, you'll know it's only right to ask them to go easy on her." She took a cocktail napkin off a nearby stack and scribbled on it. "That's right down the street—the Tropic Palms."

"Thanks." I took the napkin. "Let me pay for my drink."

"No," she said, "it's on the house."

I thanked her again, said I was sure something could be worked out with Lisa, and went out into the gathering darkness.

The Tropic Palms was one of the older and shabbier buildings in the residential strip I'd noticed earlier: two storied, fake Spanish, on the same side of the boulevard as the comedy club. Mailboxes honeycombed one wall of the entryway; a number of them appeared to have been broken into. A heavy wrought-iron lamp on a massive chain was suspended from the arched ceiling; its bulbs had burned out. The building had no buzzer system or security gate.

I went through the archway into the courtyard. The lighted swimming pool lay in its center—a murky jade pebble. Floodlights illuminated the various tropical plantings; their brittle leaves shivered in the cold wind that gusted about the enclosed space.

Rusted lounge furniture stood around the pool, skeletal in its wintertime abandonment.

The apartment number written on the cocktail napkin was 209. There was a central staircase to the rear of the courtyard. I skirted the pool and climbed it. A sign at its top indicated that apartments 201–221 were to the left. I turned that way, the dread I'd felt on my drive to the valley worsening. By the time I arrived at 209 and pressed the doorbell, my heart was pounding.

After a few seconds a voice called out for me to hang on. It was flat, dull—not much like the vibrant tones I remembered from Tracy's videotapes. Of course she would have changed. . . .

The door opened and I came face to face with her.

The woman before me was painfully thin. The bone structure of her heart-shaped face was more prominent than two years before, her cheeks hollowed. Her curly light-brown hair seemed to drag under its own lifeless weight. When she saw me, a stranger, she blinked and jerked her chin up.

This was not Tracy Kostakos.

It actually was Lisa McIntyre.

22

For a moment I just stared at her, my mouth agape. She frowned and took a step back, partially shielding her body with the door. I found my voice and said, "Lisa McIntyre?"

She nodded warily.

I reached into my bag for my identification, trying to fit this development into my previously conceived notions. And failing. Lisa was here, alive. But the Napa County coroner had skeletal remains that matched her dental records. Since those bones couldn't be Lisa's . . .

I introduced myself and handed her my identification. She studied it as if it were in a foreign language, then thrust it back at me. "What's this about?" she asked. Aside from a faint twang left over from her early years in Oklahoma, her voice was curiously without inflection.

"Ms. Dowdall at the club gave me your address—" I began.

"You saw Annette? Why would she . . . what do you want? I haven't done anything."

The questions I'd rehearsed on the plane were no longer applicable; the scene I'd envisioned had failed to materialize. I said, "I'm working on the Bobby Foster case, for his attorney."

She stiffened. "Bobby . . . they sentenced him to death."

"There's going to be an appeal. We've found evidence that proves he made a false confession. I'm talking to everyone who was at Café Comedie that night, so we can put together what really happened to Tracy Kostakos."

"I . . . I don't know anything about that."

"You may know more than you realize. May I come in and talk with you?"

She looked as if she would like nothing more than to slam the

166

door, but then she shrugged and motioned for me to come inside. There was a listlessness in the gesture and a resignation in her brown eyes that told me that, given an unpleasant situation, Lisa would usually opt for the path of least resistance.

The apartment was fully as dismal as Annette Dowdall had said. The room was not more than twelve by twelve; most of the floor space was taken up by an open and rumpled hide-a-bed. A kitchenette ran along one wall, its counter cluttered with an accumulation of dirty cups and glasses and frozen food trays; the half-open door to the bathroom revealed a litter of castoff clothing and towels. The tiny balcony overlooked its counterpart in the next building. A black-and-white TV with a snowy picture was tuned to a game show. Lisa went over and shut it off.

I looked around for a place to sit, overwhelmed by the air of hopelessness trapped in the confined space. A rattan chair with a basket of dirty laundry on it stood next to the balcony door. Lisa said, "Just move that stuff off of there," and went to close the door to the bathroom.

I set the clothes basket on the floor and sat. Lisa faced me, her posture defensive, as if she expected me to remark on the apartment's chaotic state. When I didn't speak, she said, "I could make some coffee."

"I don't want to put you to the trouble."

She nodded, clearly relieved. I suspected that to her, most things would be too much trouble. When she sat down on the edge of the unmade bed, she slumped forward, fingers splayed on her denim covered thighs. For a moment I wondered if her apathy was genuine, or if she'd assumed it in an effort to appear unconcerned about the matter at hand. Then I decided that wasn't important; a few questions would shake her out of it.

I began innocuously enough. "You worked at Café Comedie how long?"

"Six months, maybe."

"You like it there?"

"It was okay."

"Was Jay Larkey a good boss to work for?"

That got a reaction: a mere flicker of her eyelids, but the mention of his name had touched a nerve. ". . . He was okay."

"What about the other people who worked there?"

"What about them?"

"Did you enjoy working with them?"

"Yeah. Sure."

"You knew Bobby Foster?"

"Pretty well."

"Marc Emmons?"

"Yeah. He's a nice guy."

"Tracy Kostakos?"

She drew her hands together and pushed the fingers down between her knees. "I didn't know her well at all. She was one of the . . . stars there. You know."

"I'm not sure I understand. From what I've seen, it's a small club, and the comedians mingle with the other employees. Besides, Tracy was a waitress like you before Jay let her try her hand at stand-up."

Lisa's mouth twisted bitterly. "Tracy was *never* just a waitress. I could tell that the first time I laid eyes on her."

"I see. Let's go back to the night she vanished. Tell me everything you can remember about it."

She ran her tongue over her lower lip. "Is this really going to help Bobby?"

"Yes, it is."

"I *want* to help him. It's just that . . . I don't *know* anything about what happened. I went to work, waited tables like usual, and went home. It was just a normal night."

"I don't think so, Lisa."

She looked down at her hands. "What's that supposed to mean?"

"For one thing, you and Jay had a confrontation in his office around closing time."

"Who told you that?"

"Kathy Soriano."

"God. Well, it wasn't anything, not really. He was mad at me for screwing up some drink orders. He used to yell at me a lot. As far as I was concerned, that was a normal night."

"Except that Tracy disappeared. And after that night you never went back to the club, not even to pick up your paycheck."

She was silent, still looking down at where her fingers were trapped between her knees.

"Lisa," I said, "you left San Francisco because of something that happened at Café Comedie that night. Will you please tell me about it?"

"That's not true. I left town because I . . . wanted to. It didn't have anything to do with . . . anything. Tracy got killed, and I'm sorry, but there's nothing I can do about it."

"I don't think you're sorry she got killed."

Now she raised her head, lips parted.

I added, "I know about the character she based on you—Ginny the waitress. And I know how upset you were about it. And what went on between you and Tracy before that."

She compressed her lips and closed her eyes. It was a moment before she said, "Okay, I hated Tracy. She used me and made me feel . . . like some lab animal she'd experimented on. But that doesn't mean I killed her."

"I'm not trying to say you did. But I think you know more about that night than you're admitting. And the knowledge is scaring you."

She shook her head vehemently, eyes still closed.

"Lisa, a skeleton has turned up in a remote place where Tracy used to go in Napa County. They've had some difficulty identifying it, but I think it will turn out to be Tracy's." Strange, I thought, that I felt a wrenching as I spoke the words. I supposed that in the back of my mind I'd harbored the unrealistic hope that I'd find George's daughter and somehow things would work out—in spite of all evidence to the contrary.

"Someone shot her," I went on. "But it wasn't Bobby. That means the person who killed her is still at large—and a danger to anyone who has the slightest knowledge of her murder. For your own sake, as well as Bobby's, help me!"

She squeezed her eyes more tightly shut, and tears slid down either cheek, forming symmetrical tracks. I remained silent. After a moment she leaned forward and rooted around on the floor for a Kleenex box, wiped her face with a tissue.

"Okay," she said heavily. "I guess I knew it would catch up with me someday. So I'll tell you. But first you have to promise you won't let him find out it was me that told."

"Who?"

She shook her head. "Just promise."

"I do."

"Okay. The way it was, Bobby and I were friends, sort of. We talked a lot. That night I ran into him on my break, about eight-thirty. There's a room in back where the employees put their stuff and hang out. Bobby was there. I could tell he was high—he'd been doing crack—and really upset. I asked him what was wrong, and he told me about . . . him and Tracy. Do you know about that?"

"Yes."

"Well, he didn't seem to realize why she'd done it, but I could guess she'd used him, just like me. It made me furious. She'd done this horrible thing to both of us. And everybody knew she was fucking Jay for what he could do for her career. And then there was Marc: she'd broken off with him, but whenever she wanted anything, all she had to do was whistle. Anyway, Bobby went back to work, and I sat there getting madder and madder. And then there was Tracy, the star, breezing in to do her routine."

"Did you confront her?"

"Damned right I did! I told her what a cunt she was, and that I was really on to her now. And I said I was going to tell everybody—including Jay." Lisa paused, head cocked to one side. "You know, I thought she was a tough one, but that really threw her. She started to cry. And that only made me more furious. Why should she cry, when she had everything? I stormed out of there and waited for the chance to talk to Jay."

"And did you?"

"Not right away. He was busy. The Sorianos came in, first Kathy and then Rob. They met some people, investors in the real estate business, I think. I didn't get to talk to Jay until nearly closing, in his office."

"And that was why you seemed upset to Kathy later on, when you were sitting at the bar."

"Upset? That's mild. Jay totally freaked out." Lisa's voice grew hushed, the memory cowing her even now. "He demanded to know all sorts of things—when, how many times, you know. And then he started hurling stuff around the office. I was terrified, all I could think was, *What if this guy just grabs me and rips me apart?* I mean, my father used to beat me when I was a kid, and a couple of the guys I was with before I turned off men were pretty violent, but Jay—I never knew he had it in him."

I hadn't suspected that, either.

Lisa was watching me with worried eyes. "You see why you can't tell him it was me that told. After I heard Tracy had disappeared, and about the kidnapping, I was so scared I couldn't go back to the club. Because he knew that I knew—"

I held up my hand to slow her down. "You think it was Jay who killed Tracy?"

"Who else? He was so furious, so violent. And he knew where she was going that night."

"He knew she was going up to the Napa River?"

"Uh-huh. The way it went, Kathy and I were sitting at the bar around closing, waiting for Rob. I guess she told you that. She'd offered me a ride home, since it was pouring. Jay came out of the office to get something from behind the bar and asked Kathy what she was still doing there. She told him she was waiting for Rob because she'd loaned her car to Tracy so she could go to the cottage. And right away Jay said, 'The cottage on the river?' So I know he knew—"

"Wait a minute! Kathy *loaned* Tracy *her* car?"

Lisa looked blank, the shock in my voice stemming her gush of words. ". . . Well, sure. Kathy said Tracy'd already called Marc and tried to borrow his car, but he'd said he needed it the next day."

"Let me get this straight. Kathy told me Rob's assistant in the real estate business was with them that night, and that it was his car that was stolen off the lot that night. He testified to that at Bobby's trial."

"I don't know anything about any stolen car or any assistant. I'm just telling you what I heard."

"You didn't follow the news stories on the case, hear about the stolen car that eventually turned up in the mountains with blood-stains inside it?"

"I didn't follow it at all. I didn't want to *know* anything about it. It was only by chance that the TV at the club was on the day they sentenced Bobby, or I wouldn't have known about that."

"What kind of a car did Kathy drive, do you recall?"

"A Volvo, blue. I rode in it quite a few times, to the bus stop or home."

I didn't know whether to believe her or not. It made no sense for Kathy to loan Tracy her car, then turn around and have Jim Fox report it stolen. I said, "Wasn't loaning her car out of character for Kathy? She doesn't strike me as a particularly generous woman."

Lisa shrugged. "Kathy liked Tracy. And I think she knew Tracy was going to make it big; when she did, Kathy wanted for them to be friends." She paused, thoughtful. "Actually, Kathy's not so bad. She came around to see me that week when I was afraid to go back to the club. I told her I wanted to get out of town and why. She said it was a good idea, on account of Jay not being too stable. And you know what? She gave me money. A thousand dollars and a plane ticket, so I could get started down here. She even drove me to the airport."

I considered that for a moment, balancing it against what Kathy had told me. Of the two, I tended to believe Lisa. I said, "What kind of car was she driving when she took you to the airport?"

Lisa frowned. "Not the Volvo. Another foreign model, more

expensive. It was the one Rob was driving when they took me home from the club that last night."

Probably the Jaguar I'd seen parked in their driveway earlier today. I asked, "Did you ever see a gun in Jay's possession?"

"He kept one behind the bar. Marc used to complain about it, because he doesn't like guns. But Jay said it had to be there for protection."

"Do you know anything about guns?"

"Yeah. My old man was a cop."

"What kind was the one at the club?"

"A handgun, thirty-eight."

Same as the bullets found in the remains and in the Volvo.

I stared at the blank TV screen for a minute, thinking of the dental records that had been used to identify those remains as Lisa's. Thinking of how Marc Emmons, who presumably had known where Tracy had been bound that night, had suddenly become one of the "stars" at Café Comedie in the aftermath of her disappearance. And wondering about Jay Larkey and Kathy Soriano, off-and-on lovers because, according to him, "it makes the lady feel better."

Or did it make the gentleman feel more secure?

Lisa said, "What if he finds out I told you?"

"He won't. He has no idea where you are. As long as you stay right here, you'll be safe."

I would call Stan Gurski as soon as I left her, tell him what I'd found out. He would want to question her, probably would have her taken into custody, but Lisa didn't need to know that yet. I suspected that the policeman father who had beaten her had left her with a deeply ingrained aversion to the authorities.

I wanted to say something reassuring to her, but I could think of nothing to offer. Finally I repeated my statement that she would be all right if she stayed at home, and took my leave of her.

23

After I called Stan Gurski and relayed the information about McIntyre (and ruined his evening by dashing his previous conceptions about the case), I gave some thought to hunting up a copy of the two-year-old L. A. *Times* that I needed. A call to the nearest branch of the public library proved it to be closed—by budget cuts, I supposed, similar to those that kept San Francisco's libraries on shortened hours. The best place to try would be the *Times* itself, but first I decided to make my reservation for a return flight north.

As it turned out, USAir's departures were less frequent at night; there was only one seat available on the nine o'clock flight, and after that I'd have to take my chances on standby. Since the *Times* was located downtown, there was a distinct possibility that I'd miss all the flights and end up spending the night in L.A. I hesitated for only a moment, decided it was more important to be at the focus of my investigation, and reserved the last seat at nine.

On the return flight I sipped an unaccustomed bourbon and water and tried to reconstruct what had happened to Tracy on that rainy winter night, based on yet another set of new facts.

She'd arrived at the club and had the confrontation with Lisa. Uncharacteristically upset, she'd broken down and cried. Prior to that she'd worried about no longer being a good person; now she saw her world coming apart as a result of her shabby treatment of others. If Lisa told Jay everything, at the very least he'd break off their affair. He might even attempt to have her contract with the club invalidated. But worse than that, she'd be exposed as an unfeeling opportunist. Her impulse was to flee—to a place where she often went for solitude and contemplation.

But to do that she needed a car. At first she turned to Marc, but he'd refused, saying he needed his the next day. Next she

173

approached Kathy. Kathy had driven to the club separately from her husband, so she agreed to let Tracy borrow the Volvo. Tracy had probably taken the keys from the valet parking box when she left after her performance, but then she'd had her second confrontation of the evening, with Bobby Foster.

Why, if she was so upset and shamed by Lisa's threat of exposure, had she blurted out to Bobby the truth about her motive for sleeping with him? Possibly she assumed he'd find out soon, anyway. Maybe because she was hurting, she wanted to lash out and hurt someone else. Or because she was in a hurry, she said the first thing she thought of that would make him let her go. At any rate, she retrieved the Volvo from the lot and drove to Napa County. The two "sightings" of Tracy that the police had investigated most thoroughly were probably genuine; she would have had to travel via the Bay Bridge, where the former classmate claimed to have seen her, and could very well have stopped for groceries at the convenience store outside of Berkeley.

But that wasn't quite right. It left too much time unaccounted for. What had she done between ten o'clock and twelve-thirty A.M., when she'd supposedly driven across the bridge? Gone home for the keys to the cottage. And gone to Emmons's apartment, as she'd told Bobby she intended to do? No way of knowing.

Then what?

If I followed what Lisa had told me to a logical conclusion, in his rage Larkey had taken the gun from behind the bar, driven to the river, shot Tracy, and concealed her body. The shooting had taken place in the Volvo—perhaps she'd been trying to escape—and after Jay told Kathy what had happened, she'd decided it was less of a risk to leave the car at the cottage temporarily than to reclaim it and attempt to clean the bloodstains. I was sure Kathy had had no difficulty convincing Jim Fox, Rob's assistant, to report it stolen. But how had she explained that to her husband? Wouldn't she have had to tell him who was using the Volvo when they'd driven home from the club together the night before?

I thought about the relationship between the Sorianos. The one time I'd seen them together, they'd seemed to be in different worlds. She prattled on, he barely listened. Given that type of interaction, she also would have had no difficulty convincing him he'd misheard, that she'd actually loaned the car to Fox.

All right, I thought, at that point it's safe to assume that Kathy became an accessory. She aided Jay in fabricating the so-called kidnapping. And it would have required two people to move the

Volvo from the cottage to the isolated ravine in the Santa Cruz Mountains. Later, when police attention focused seriously on Foster, she made sure the notebook he'd used for his GED studies—and she and Jay had used as a blueprint for the ransom note—was passed on to them. After I discovered Tracy's remains, Jay switched her dental records with those of a frightened young woman whom Kathy had given money to leave town for good. Their reasoning, undoubtedly, was that lacking a positive identification of those remains, the conviction against Foster would stand.

I even had an idea about the phone calls to Laura from "Tracy." The first time I'd met Kathy, she mimicked Tracy's voice, repeating the punch line from the bewildered feminist routine. Later, when I viewed the videotape, the punchline had sounded familiar because Kathy's imitation had been a good one.

All of it—the switched dental records, the calls, the book on creating a new identity that they'd somehow placed in the apartment on Upper Market—had been designed to keep a true identification of Tracy's remains from ever being made.

So there it was: a more or less logical scenario. Except I couldn't quite buy it, not as it currently stood.

The problem was the motive. I simply couldn't imagine Larkey—no matter how enraged—driving up to the cottage with the intent to kill. I couldn't imagine him creating an elaborate frame of Bobby Foster, a young man he professed to like, much less standing mutely by while Bobby went to his death. It was not that I didn't believe Larkey was capable of such actions; I'd long ago learned that most people are capable of anything, given sufficient reason. But if Larkey had done those things, he would have had a much more compelling motive than mere anger. He would have had much more than his masculine pride at stake.

I stared distractedly at my reflection in the black airplane window. The bright cabin lights made me look washed out and sickly; my thoughts made me looked worried and frustrated. Quickly I glanced away.

What exactly was it that Tracy had said to her mother at their last Friday lunch? The things about not being a good person anymore, but something besides that. Something about a sin of omission. That, coupled with whatever she had seen in Jane Stein's copy of the *Times*, might give me an inkling of that motive. But where the hell was I going to lay my hands on a copy of an L.A. paper at this hour of the night in San Francisco? Perhaps I'd made a mistake in not staying over—

The flight attendants were passing along the aisles, collecting things. I finished my drink, handed the plastic tumbler over, and raised my tray table, as instructed, to an upright position.

I found the nearest bank of phones on the concourse and called All Souls. Jack wasn't there; Rae was on another line. I waited impatiently, tapping my fingers on the aluminum shelf. When she finally came on, she said, "Shar, thank God you're back. There's a woman on the other line who needs to talk to you. She's been calling off and on all afternoon."

"Who?"

"She won't give her name, but she says it's important."

"Get her number, tell her I'll call her back."

Rae put me on hold, came back about fifteen seconds later. "Shar, she still won't tell me anything. Just said she'll call again."

"Dammit! It's probably about this case."

"If she calls again, I'll make her give me a number somehow, or I'll tell her to come here. What happened in L.A.?"

Briefly I explained to her about finding McIntyre, and what that probably meant.

When I finished, Rae said, "You know, it's funny, but I think Larkey suspected something like that."

"Larkey? What's he got to do with it?"

"When I called him to cancel your appointment, he sounded kind of down, so I told him you'd gone to L.A. to locate Tracy. I thought it would cheer him up—you'd said he cared for her—but it didn't. He asked me to have you let him know how it turned out. Said that if it wasn't Tracy down there, he wanted to drive up to Napa tomorrow and check out those dental records again. Seems he'd been thinking about them, and something odd had occurred to him."

"What?"

"He couldn't go into it; he was in a meeting."

What had occurred to him, I thought, was that he'd better cover up switching the X rays and falsely claiming the remains weren't Tracy's. Perhaps he intended to go to Napa, take another look at them, and identify them correctly, in order to deflect suspicion from himself. I said, "I'll talk with him later. Any other messages?"

"George Kostakos. He's at home."

"What about Jack—where's he?"

"Had to go to Sacramento on another case."

"If you see him before I do, fill him in on what's happened. But right now I need you to do something for me. I'm not even sure it's within the realm of the possible, but I need a copy of the L.A. *Times*, metropolitan edition, for February second, the year Kostakos disappeared."

"I'll check the library."

"I doubt it's still open."

"This is a tough one." Rae sounded glum, then rallied. "Maybe Hank will have some idea."

"Hank. Is he still staying there on the couch?"

"As of this morning."

That was another thing I wanted to deal with—but not until this case was wrapped up. "Well, ask him."

"Will do. By the way, I went by your place earlier to feed the cat. The contractor was there; he said not to worry about locking up after him, because you'd given him a key to the side gate."

"Yes—he's bonded, and I couldn't let myself get tied down to his schedule. Thanks for looking out for Wat."

"Don't mention it. Where can I reach you?"

"I'm not sure. I'll check in."

I broke the connection and called George at his borrowed house. I wanted to break the news to him about finding McIntyre alive—and to break it in person, because it meant that his daughter really was dead. But I only reached the machine.

In a way it was good, I thought, because after breaking that kind of news, it would be very hard to leave him. And where I needed to go as soon as possible was Café Comedie.

24

On Bryant near Fourth Street, roughly two blocks from South Park, I ran into a monumental traffic jam. Odd, I thought, for close to ten-thirty at night.

I tapped my fingers on the steering wheel, staring at the sea of red taillights in front of me. Then I switched the radio on, to see if I could find out what was causing this. Out of old habit, I punched the button for KSUN, an AM station with an exuberant hard-rock format, where my former lover, disc jockey Don Del Boccio, now held court in the prestigious late-evening slot. (If, as Don was fond of saying, having the ear of half a million teenagers whose combined IQ was probably in the low seventies could be considered prestige.)

I was so irritated at the jam-up that I didn't even feel a rush of nostalgia when I heard Don's voice extolling the talents of a group called Matt and the Mercenaries, and I turned down their atonal screeching (perhaps they really *were* in a war zone?) so far that I almost missed it when minutes later Don said, ". . . traffic advisory." I turned the radio up again, expecting him to report an overturned big rig or some such thing on the bridge approach several blocks ahead.

". . . and also a news bulletin," he added. "We have a five-alarm fire that's backing up traffic on Bryant Street and nearby access routes to the Bay Bridge in San Francisco. Emergency vehicles are blocking Bryant at Second and Third, and while police are attempting to reroute traffic, it's pretty much at a standstill. So if you're traveling to the East Bay or South of Market tonight, it's best to avoid the main arteries. The fire is on South Park, between Second and Third streets, Bryant and Brannan. Fire crews and ambulances are on the scene, and police are asking that people keep

178

away from the area if at all possible. That's all we've got on it now, but we'll be keeping you posted."

South Park!

I clutched the wheel, my stomach knotting. Now that I knew about the fire I became aware of sirens, of an orange-red glow in the sky. A sickening feeling filled me. Was it possible this disaster was somehow related to my case? Was it Café Comedie . . . ?

I needed to get there and find out what had happened, but there were no side streets or alleys intersecting this part of the block. There were parking spaces along the curb, and I was in the far right lane, but the one next to me, as well as those in front of and behind it, were taken. Two cars ahead there *was* a vacant space, but now traffic was at a total standstill; hours could pass before I reached it.

Everywhere people were hanging out their windows, trying to see what had caused the holdup. Some got out and stood in the street; the driver of the pickup that was stopped next to the parking space I coveted climbed up in the truck's bed and looked around. If this continued, Bryant Street would soon look like a used-car lot on inventory liquidation day. I fumed and grumbled aloud, experiencing that feeling of impotence in the face of impersonal forces that is easily one of the worst aspects of urban life. If traffic didn't move soon, tempers would flare, and the street scene could turn ugly.

The guy in the bed of the pickup was the first to snap: he yelled, "Fuck it!" and jumped down onto the pavement. Then he climbed into the truck and started it. It lurched forward, into the bumper of the car in front of it, then back into the one behind. Its wheels turned sharply to the right; the pickup slewed through the empty parking space beside it and onto the sidewalk.

The car behind it barely hesitated before it followed suit. The two vehicles fishtailed down the sidewalk next to the logjam in the street. A woman two cars over leaned out her window and shouted, "Assholes!"

I agreed with her, but the lunatics had shown me the way out. I was about to execute the same maneuver when a siren whooped somewhere behind me. A motorcycle cop, obviously on his way to attempt to reroute traffic, raced down the sidewalk after the truck and car. A ticket and the ensuing delay was something I didn't need, so I settled for pulling into the empty parking space. Then I jumped out of the MG and ran toward South Park.

As I got closer, the air reeked of smoke; it clogged my nostrils and windpipe and made my breath come short. There were flashing lights ahead: red, blue, amber. The sky overhead glowed like an inverted red-orange globe. People were shouting. Radios in the emergency vehicles squawked and crackled.

When I turned onto Third Street itself, I saw the entrance to South Park was blocked by a police barricade. A great crowd milled about, resisting the officers' efforts to clear a path for an arriving ambulance. I could hear the flames now: a roar that sounded as if whole buildings were being sucked into a vacuum. The smoke-filled air was warm as a spring day.

The crowd acted as a solid mass, shifting this way or that, but providing no opening. I wriggled between two men, pushed a third aside, elbowed a woman so she stepped back. To my left a police officer shouted for people to move; he spread his arms wide, and one of his hands caught me hard on the shoulder. The lights of the ambulance washed over the tight press of humanity. As it crept forward, the driver hit the siren. That accomplished what no amount of police commands could: the crowd parted and the ambulance drove toward the barricade. I slipped under the officer's arm and darted in its wake.

As the ambulance sped through the barricade, a hand grabbed my arm. "That's far enough, lady."

I didn't reply, transfixed by the scene in front of me. Fire trucks clogged the parkway itself. Ambulances were pulled onto the grassy oval. People lay on stretchers, white-coated paramedics attending to them. At the picnic tables and on the ground, others—many in evening attire—sat or lay. Their faces and hands were smoke blackened, their clothing torn and disheveled.

Beyond the ring of barren sycamore trees, the facade of Café Comedie was enveloped in what looked to be a solid wall of flame. The wrought-iron fence in front of it had been flattened by the hook-and-ladders. The buildings on either side were afire, too. Great torrents of water arched through the air; smoke billowed. The swiftly moving figures of the firemen were mere sooty silhouettes. And over it all spread the consuming brilliance of the flames.

If they couldn't control this inferno soon, it would engulf all of South Park. Perhaps several surrounding blocks.

"Lady, move before you get hurt," the officer said, tugging at my arm.

"Do you know how it started?"

"Somebody said something about an explosion."

I stared at the wall of fire, remembered the gas leak Larkey had mentioned—the one PG&E couldn't fix properly. "Was anybody trapped in there?"

"Don't know. Now—move!"

I moved, but only a few yards away. I couldn't take my eyes off the flames. In spite of the efforts to quell them, they shot upward, as if to consume the sky itself.

A woman near me was having hysterics. She kept sobbing, "He promised! He promised!" I looked her way, saw she was bent over, a man clutching at her leather-jacketed shoulders. The man was Mike, the bartender from the club. As I drew closer, I realized the woman was Kathy Soriano.

Mike looked relieved when he saw me. He said, "I can't do anything for her."

"Let me try." I took hold of Kathy, dragged her down to a sitting position on the pavement. She hunched over, arms wrapped around her midsection, hands over her face, sobbing raggedly.

Mike squatted beside us. I asked him, "Is she hurt?"

He shook his head. "She was just handing her keys over to one of the valets when the explosion happened. I'd stepped out for some air on my break. I grabbed her, and we ran down here." He looked toward the flames. "My God," he added in awed tones, as if only now realizing what might have happened to him had he stayed inside.

Kathy was rocking back and forth now. "Jay," she sobbed. "Jay. He promised."

I put my arms around her. She buried her head under my chin. Over her rumpled curls I said to Mike, "Jay? Rob?"

He shook his head slightly—in the negative. "The explosion was back by the office, from what I could tell."

"Jesus."

Kathy began to sob louder. "The bastard! He promised!"

"Who, Kathy?"

"Jay, oh, Jay . . ."

"What did he promise?"

She jerked her head, and it connected violently with my chin. I shoved it back down, and the shriek she'd been about to let fly was muffled against my jacket. "She needs medical attention," I said to Mike.

"So do all of them." He motioned at the people in the park. "There aren't enough medics to go around."

He was right, of course. "Do you know who her doctor is?"

"Most of us go to the Potrero Clinic, but I don't suppose she—"

"No, but her doctor's probably in Marin, anyway. The clinic'll do in an emergency. Help me get her up."

The two of us hauled Kathy to her feet. She stumbled and swayed between us, hysteria spent now. I said to Mike, "My car's a couple of blocks away. Will you walk down there with us?"

He nodded, and we began making our way through the crowd. The same people who hadn't wanted to let the ambulance through gave Kathy sympathetic looks and cleared a path for us.

Traffic was moving slowly on Bryant Street now, rerouted down Fourth toward China Basin. Beyond Townsend Street there was an entrance to the 280 freeway, the quickest way to Potrero Hill. With any luck at all, I could have Kathy to the clinic within half an hour. Mike and I loaded her into the passenger seat of the MG, and then he loped off toward South Park to see if he could help some of the others.

Kathy slumped silently beside me, her head drooping forward. As I eased the car into the creeping stream of traffic, she gave a tremulous sigh, as a child that has spent itself crying will do. I glanced at her, wondering if she had blocked the knowledge of her husband's and lover's probable deaths. For her sake, I hoped so.

Fortunately I knew where the clinic was—on Arkansas Street near the Potrero Hill playground. I pulled to the white curb in front, went around the car, and hoisted Kathy out. She was a dead weight now; I staggered under the burden. A white-coated young man came bustling out with a wheelchair. Efficiently he got Kathy into it and trundled her inside.

The clinic was like many other low-budget, low-cost operations I'd seen: old, minimally furnished, but spruced up with a cheerful paint job and colorful posters. The young man wheeled Kathy to a counter, where a sign read ADMITTING. I was relieved to see Leora Whitsun sitting behind it. She stood up when she saw us, her face furrowing in concern.

Briefly I explained what had happened. "I couldn't think of where else to take her," I added. "She's in no shape to tell me who her doctor is."

"That's all right; we don't discriminate." Leora allowed herself a small ironic smile, then picked up the phone receiver, buzzed someone, and spoke quietly into it. "Room A," she told the young man. To me, she added, "You just go sit over there, Sharon. There're magazines, coffee in that urn in the corner. Be a little while." Then she picked up a clipboard and followed the wheelchair.

I sat on one of the two yellow vinyl couches, opposite a young Hispanic couple, who huddled together as if for warmth. The woman's face was crumpled and streaked with tears; the man was all of twenty, yet his bleak eyes suggested there was nothing he hadn't seen. He kept smoothing the woman's hair and murmuring the endearment "*querida.*" To avoid intruding, I grabbed a year-old copy of *Field and Stream* and kept my gaze fixed on an ad for rifles. After a while a doctor came through the door and ushered the young couple back the way Kathy had been taken. I set down the magazine and looked around for a pay phone, thinking to call All Souls.

I was about to borrow the phone on the admitting desk when Leora returned. "The doctor wants to keep her overnight," she said, "till we can find out about her husband. Are you sure he died in the fire?"

"There's no way of knowing yet."

"What about Jay? Did he . . . ?"

"Probably."

She touched her hand to her forehead, closed her eyes. "Poor man. I'll pray for him." When she took her hand away, she looked old and tired, as if the added weight of this latest tragedy had finally made her burdens more than she could bear.

I would have liked to say something encouraging about her son's case, but at the moment I couldn't think of anything that would make sense. Besides, my major suspect was probably dead, and I doubted Kathy would ever admit her own complicity. Instead, I patted Leora's arm, thanked her, and said I'd call later to check on Kathy. But halfway to the door I thought of something I needed to ask her.

"Leora," I said, "when Jay took Tracy Kostakos's dental records up to Napa County the other day, did he spend much time here beforehand?"

She shook her head. "None at all. He called, asked me to pull the file and envelope it. When he came by, he left his car in the white zone, just ran in and grabbed it."

Of course that didn't mean anything; he probably had switched the X rays a long time before that, on the chance that one day the body would be discovered. And yet . . .

I said to Leora, "You mentioned that Kathy came looking for him here on New Year's Day."

"That's right."

"Did she say why she thought he might be here?"

"No, just that she wanted to break the news about the Kostakos girl to him personally."

"What about Tracy's dental records—did she mention that the Napa sheriff's department needed them?"

Leora frowned. "You know, she did. She even offered to take them up there herself, since Jay would be upset by the news and might not want to deal with them. I told her he'd have to authorize their release before I could give them to her."

"What did she do then?"

". . . I'm not sure. We had a patient with a stab wound—family fight, what else?—and he was bleeding all over the place. There were other emergencies, too. I kind of lost track of her."

"Is it possible Kathy could have gone into the records room without you noticing her?"

"It's possible. And she would have had enough time to, because I saw her leaving more than fifteen minutes later. But why would she . . . ?"

Why, indeed? That, like many aspects of this case, made no sense whatsoever.

25

On the way to Bernal Heights I tuned to KSUN again, to see if they had an update on the fire. A news broadcast was in progress. The fire, the announcer said, was now under control; at least five people had died, and damage was estimated in the millions. When the broadcast ended, the deejay who held the midnight-to-six slot came on. I looked at my watch and was surprised to see it was twelve-ten.

I snapped off the radio and drove in silence, deeply discouraged and saddened. Tonight's tragedy eclipsed my earlier sense of urgency about wrapping up the case. I knew that if Larkey was dead, there was a good chance I would never find out exactly what had happened the night Tracy died, but somehow I just didn't care.

To tell the truth, I was fed up with the case. What had begun as a compelling search into the past had turned into an arduous sifting of sordid and depressing facts. I was sick of digging into the life of a young woman whose chief occupation had been getting what she wanted at the expense of everyone else. I was sick of people like Amy Barbour and Marc Emmons, who did shabby things and then tried to justify them, even to themselves. The users of the world had always disgusted me, but no more so than tonight. I'd lost sympathy for almost everyone involved in my investigation.

As I searched for a parking space near the co-op, I wondered about that loss of sympathy: what if it was indicative of something worse? What if I was also losing empathy—a quality, I'd often been told, that made others willing to open up to me, and thus made me a good detective? What if—worse yet—I was losing my enthusiasm for the work itself?

I thought of Rae, of the energy she applied to the most menial of investigative tasks, of her elation when a lead turned out to be a

185

solid one. Day after day she maintained that enthusiasm, while toiling for a salary that wasn't enough so that she could rent a decent apartment, and receiving little credit for her efforts, save my own (often infrequent) thanks. How did she do it?

Well, for one thing, Rae hadn't seen all that I had. She hadn't spent year after year experiencing what amounted to living nightmares. She hadn't spent over a decade uncovering secrets of people's lives that literally made one's flesh creep, hadn't repeatedly dealt with the havoc and destruction caused by human greed, carelessness, and stupidity.

So what I was really asking was what had happened to me, that I couldn't sustain the enthusiasm. And there was my answer.

Wait a few years, Rae, I thought. Just wait.

It was a fate I wouldn't wish upon her but couldn't warn her away from. Because—as Larkey had said of Tracy—she wouldn't listen to me, any more than I would have at her age.

I'd driven around the triangular park in front of the co-op twice and still hadn't found a space. Both of the driveway spots were occupied. For a moment I considered leaving the MG by a fireplug, but recent experience and a glance at the tinderbox buildings lining the street made me think better of the idea. I finally wedged the car into a semilegal space at the corner and hurried up the hill.

There were no lights in the parlor or any of the offices opening off the first floor hallway, but a glow came from the kitchen at the rear. I went back there and found Hank sitting at the table with Amy Barbour. He appeared to be sober for a change; she was eating a bowl of cereal.

I stopped in the doorway. Amy's presence was so unexpected, the scene before me so homey and normal in contrast to what I'd witnessed in the past two hours, that I was at a total loss for words. Hank glanced at me and said, "There you are. You have a visitor. She arrived about an hour ago—hungry."

Tonight Amy looked very much the waif who needed to be taken in and fed. Her artichoke-leaf hair drooped limply; her face was sallow, eyes underscored with dark smudges. She wore a stained Garfield T-shirt, rumpled jeans, and mud-splattered rain boots. I suspected she could use a bath. She'd started getting twitchy as soon as she saw me; now she set down her spoon and nervously licked a drop of milk from the corner of her mouth.

I nodded to her, then said to Hank, "Have you seen either Jack or Rae?"

"Not tonight. You had a phone call a few minutes ago. From a man, asking if you were back from L.A. When I said no, he asked if Amy had been in touch with you. I said she was right here, and he hung up."

"That's strange."

Hank shrugged and stood up. "I gather you and Amy have a lot to talk about, so I'll be going."

"Are you staying here tonight?"

"No." Without elaborating, he left the room.

I watched him go, wondering briefly if this meant he and Anne-Marie had reconciled, then turned my attention to Amy. "Go on with your cereal," I said, sitting down.

She looked around, a trifle furtively. "If you don't mind, I don't think I'll finish it. This whole-grain stuff is pretty disgusting, and there isn't even any sugar."

"There's usually a bowl of it—"

"No, there isn't. Hank said that one of the other lawyers threw out all the impure stuff right after New Year's."

I knew who she meant; we had a health nut on staff who conducted periodic purges of the refrigerator. But this was going too far. I made up my mind to speak to him about literally cramming his New Year's resolutions down everybody else's throats.

Amy said, "I wouldn't even have eaten what I did, but I hadn't had anything since a Wendy's around eleven this morning."

"Where have you been?"

"My . . . the apartment."

"Since when?"

"About noon. I called you as soon as I got to town. You weren't here, so I just holed up at the apartment and kept trying. Finally, at about ten tonight, your assistant said you wanted me to come here and wait for you. Nobody was around but Hank. He . . . he's nice."

"Yes, he is," I said absently. So Amy was my first mysterious caller. "Where have you been since Monday?"

"The cottage."

"Up at the river?"

She nodded. "It was the one place we figured nobody would look for us. We watched it for a few hours to make sure the cops were done there, then snuck in and hid."

"Marc was with you?"

"Uh-huh."

"Where is he now?"

"Still there. I drove his car in to talk with you. He figured if it was just me I'd be less recognizable. The police are looking for a couple."

What I figured was that Emmons preferred risking Amy's hide to his own. "How do you know the police are looking for you?"

"Marc's building manager stopped us while we were moving some of my stuff in on Monday and said a cop had been asking for him. Later on, one showed up at my place, but we didn't answer the door. That afternoon we went up to the river."

"And stayed there the whole time?"

"Uh-huh. At first it wasn't so bad, like camping. Marc even dug out some of my father's old fishing stuff and tried to catch us dinner. But then he got all depressed and nervous about . . . our situation. Obviously we can't stay there forever, so he said I should talk with you and see if you can help us make a deal."

"A deal."

"Yeah. What you really care about is finding out who killed Trace, right? I mean, you don't really want to turn us in to the cops for . . . What was it you called it?"

"Obstruction of justice."

"Yeah, that. So if we tell you what we know, you can go to the cops and get them to agree not to arrest us, in exchange for the information."

"You mean you want a guarantee of immunity from prosecution."

"Whatever."

"Why didn't you just go directly to the police? Or get a lawyer?"

"We're afraid of the police, and we don't know any lawyers—or have any money for one. Marc's parents were giving him an allowance, but they cut it off as of the first of the year. That's the reason he's letting me move in with him, to help with the rent."

"So you thought I'd work for free."

She hung her head. "Please."

"All right—tell me what you know."

"Do we have a deal?"

"I don't know what the police will do, but you and I have a deal."

She hesitated.

"Amy, I'm in no mood to play games! I've just come from South Park, where there was an explosion at the club. At least five people are dead—"

"The *club* exploded?"

"There was an explosion and fire, at about ten tonight."

She leaned forward, elbows on the table, running her fingers through her limp hair. "Oh God oh God! Marc *said* he was afraid something awful was going to happen. Oh God!"

I didn't see the connection between an explosion caused by a gas leak and whatever it was Emmons knew—or claimed to know. But since she'd obviously linked them in her mind, I used it to my advantage. "You see? You'd better tell me all of it."

"I would, but I don't *know* much. Marc only told me certain things. He said it was too dangerous for me to know everything."

I took a deep breath, tried to keep exasperation out of my voice. "Okay, tell me what he *did* tell you."

She raised her head and looked around. "Do you think I could have a drink? Some wine, maybe?"

I quelled a desire to take her by the shoulders and shake her, and went to look for some. There was a jug of dangerously cheap red under the sink that the health nut had apparently missed. I looked dubiously at it, shrugged, and poured a glass. When I returned to the table, Amy seized it eagerly.

"Okay," she said after taking a gulp, "I'll tell you what Marc told me. About two weeks before she died, Trace found out something really bad about somebody at the club. It upset her, and she didn't know what to do about it. A 'moral dilemma' she called it. Trust Trace to make it into a big deal like that. Anyway, she never said anything about it to me. She wouldn't. But she told Marc. And he said she ought to just forget it."

"And you have no idea what it was? Or how she found out?"

"No. Only that it was bad. It really bothered her. She wouldn't turn loose of it. And Marc . . . well, this sounds awful, but he saw some advantage in it for him."

"How do you mean?"

She hung her head and said in a low voice. "He went to the person involved and told them. He promised to keep Trace from doing whatever it was she wanted to do about it."

"In exchange for what?"

She looked up quickly. Her eyes were moist. I could tell she wanted to deny the obvious, but that wasn't possible. "Money, maybe. I don't know," she said miserably.

"Go on."

"Well, he had her pretty much convinced. But then, the night she disappeared, Trace came over to Marc's. She was really upset; something terrible had happened at the club. She said that at first she'd decided to go up to the river and sort things out. But then she'd realized that maybe she could salvage the situation—those were her exact words, 'salvage the situation'—by using the information she had. Marc tried to talk her out of it for a couple of hours, and she finally promised him she'd think it over up at the river for a day or so before doing anything. But he already knew what she'd decide. And then she left, and he never saw her again."

And he'd allowed Bobby Foster to be condemned to death while he kept his silence and reaped its profits. Damn the Marc Emmonses of this world!

"And that's it?" I asked harshly.

Amy licked her dry lips and took another gulp of wine. "Not exactly. This is the bad part. It makes Marc feel responsible for her dying. After she left his place, he made a phone call."

"To?"

"The person Trace had something on."

"Did he tell this person where she'd gone?"

"I guess. He wouldn't say." But her expression told me she suspected he had.

"The son of a bitch traded Tracy's life for money."

Now Amy looked frightened. "He wouldn't have!"

Right, I thought. Trying to keep my voice level, I asked, "Do you have any idea who this person is?"

"No."

"Not even if it was a man or a woman?"

She shook her head.

Well, there it was: the motive stronger than either male pride or anger that I'd needed to make my scenario work, with Jay Larkey cast as Tracy's murderer. She'd found out something damning about him—possibly from the copy of the L.A. *Times* that Jane Stein had had at the airport—and decided to blackmail him with it.

Blackmail, I thought. A vicious and stupid crime.

Tracy had exhibited nastiness previously, but it had been of a petty variety, not really what one could term vicious. And she hadn't been stupid. But she had been young. You do stupid things at that age. You dramatize yourself, think you're invincible. You're sure you can match your largely untried wits with those of the wiliest of the older generation. And it is that naïveté that makes you such easy prey. . . .

I said, "You're sure that's all Marc told you?"

"Yes."

"And you haven't told anyone else about this?"

"Well . . ." She wriggled around on the chair, picked at her dirty, ragged fingernails. "I called Jay this afternoon."

"You . . . why?"

"I was afraid for Marc. Being a comedian means more than anything else in the world to him; it's all he's ever wanted to do. I thought if I explained to Jay about the cops being after Marc, and how he'd had to hide out, Jay would forgive him for not showing up for work and not fire him. But I didn't tell him everything, just that we were staying at the cottage and would be back soon."

"What did he say?"

"That Marc should clear things up with the cops, and then they'd talk. I said I was going to get you and take you up there, so you could help us cut a deal."

"Did Marc know you planned to call Jay?"

"I didn't *plan* anything. It just occurred to me while I was sitting around the apartment waiting for you to get back."

"What time did you make the call?"

"I guess sometime after two."

If Larkey had interpreted what Amy told him to mean Marc planned to trade what he knew about Tracy's death for immunity from prosecution, he might have decided to drive to the river and attempt to dissuade him—either verbally or with force. There would have been ample time for that between her call and when the club opened. Stifling my alarm, I said, "Why don't we drive up there and talk with Marc?"

"Sure. Can I use the bathroom first?"

"Of course," I said, trying not to sound impatient. "Upstairs, on the right."

While she was up there, I went out to Ted's desk and checked the chalkboard on the wall next to it for a message from Rae. There was none. Was she still trying to get hold of the copy of the *Times?* I wondered.

The phone on the desk rang, startling in the postmidnight silence. I picked it up. "All Souls Legal Cooperative."

"Sharon?" George's voice.

"Hi. I tried to call you at home earlier, but you'd gone out."

"Sorry—my mistake. When I said home in my message, I meant Palo Alto, not the city."

Of course he would still consider the Palo Alto house home, and yet . . . "Is everything all right?"

"Not really." Now I recognized an undertone of despondency in his words. "Apparently the woman whose body they thought you found is still alive. The Napa sheriff's department called to see if we could tell them how to locate Tracy's earlier dental records. Unfortunately, they contacted Laura rather than me."

A chill crept across my shoulder blades. I should have called him from L.A., I thought, even though it meant breaking the news to him on the phone. And I should have repeated my warning about Laura being emotionally unstable to Gurski when I told him about finding McIntyre.

"Oh, George, I'm sorry! How is she?"

"Not good. She didn't know anything about a body turning up; I'd kept it all from her. When she realized . . . well, it was a confrontation with reality that she didn't need just now. She called me, and I got hold of her therapist and drove down here. They're probably going to admit her for observation at the med center."

"This is my fault. I should have warned Gurski again—"

"You knew about it?"

"I flew to L.A. this afternoon, thinking I'd located Tracy. Only it was actually Lisa McIntyre. I was planning to tell you in person."

There was a long silence.

Thoughts crowded my mind, each one jostling the previous one aside: what a terrible thing for him to go through . . . a terrible thing for Laura . . . he'll blame me . . . *I* blame myself . . . this will ruin what we have between us . . . every time he looks at me, he'll see the woman whose carelessness caused this. . . .

"Sharon? It's okay. None of this is your fault."

"I feel responsible."

"Don't." In spite of his weariness and depression, the flatness of his voice was leavened by warmth. "I've got to go now, the therapist wants to talk with me. But I'll call you as soon as I can."

The connection broke, and I was left clutching a silent receiver. As I heard Amy coming down the stairs, I thought, I want to believe you, George, I really do.

But why, *why* did you have to call Palo Alto "home"?

26

When Amy and I stepped through the front door, Rae was getting out of her old Rambler American, which she'd parked so it was blocking the driveway. She waved vigorously, her ratty brown coat billowing open, blue and gold scarf trailing to the ground on one side.

"Got it!" she called.

"The paper?"

"Right." She loped up the steps, obviously wired. "From a friend of Hank's. Calls himself an archivist. What *I* call him is a pack rat. Weirdest-ass house you ever saw. Out in the Avenues, big place. The upstairs is full of reference books and two of the fattest, ugliest dogs in creation. I'm certain they're descended from pigs. Downstairs is like the Catacombs, only the rooms are filled with newspapers, rather than bones. Before he let me take this, he practically made me swear on the heads of my unborn children to return it in good condition. So guard it with your life, or we're all in deep shit."

She thrust the paper at me. I took it and said, "You're a genius!"

Amy was staring at Rae as if she found her fascinating. I made introductions and explained where we were bound, omitting my concern for Emmons's safety.

"You want me to go along?" Rae asked.

"Is there room for three in your car?" I asked Amy.

"I was kind of hoping we could take yours. Marc's isn't too reliable; it was acting up on the way down here."

"And neither is mine," Rae said, "so that lets me out." She paused, then added, "Awful about the fire at Café Comedie, huh? I heard about it on the radio. Did Jay Larkey . . . ?"

"Probably." But I had begun to wonder about that. The bartender had said the explosion was in back near Larkey's office, but he hadn't actually placed his boss on the scene at the time. And there was also the matter of the male phone caller who had hung up on Hank after asking if I was back from Los Angeles and if Amy had contacted me yet. That combination of facts was one which only Larkey had possessed. "Are you going to be up for a while?" I asked Rae.

"For hours. I'm too wired to sleep."

"If anyone calls for me, will you tell him I'm still in L.A.? And if he asks about Amy, say she's still here but asleep."

"Sure." Her eyes were curious.

Quickly I motioned to Amy and we went down the hill. I wanted her to drive so I could look through the *Times*, but she said she couldn't handle a stick shift. I considered checking the features section right then and there, but my worry about Emmons was strong enough that I decided not to waste any more time in getting to the river. Whatever Tracy had seen in the paper might not hold any significance for me; better to wait and let Emmons tell me his story—if he was in any condition to.

There was little traffic on the freeway, and we made good time, passing Richmond by one-thirty. Flame billowed from a remote tower at the refinery on the shore; the faintly illuminated storage tanks hulked on the dark hillsides. Amy was uncharacteristically silent, her head turned away from me as she stared out the side window.

At the other end of the bridge over the Carquinez Strait, the toll taker yawned as she accepted my dollar bill. The neon of the frontage-road businesses in Vallejo was softened by a light mist. Amy stirred and pointed to a twenty-four-hour coffee shop. "Can we stop? I need to use the bathroom."

What *was* it with her and bathrooms? I thought irritably. Probably nervous, or maybe she wants to do some coke. Nothing would surprise me anymore.

I pulled off the freeway, drove to the coffee shop, and parked in front. "Don't take too long."

"Aren't you coming in?"

"I'll wait here." As she got out, I took the copy of the *Times* from where I'd set it on the rear carrying seat and switched on the car's dome light.

The features sections was called "View." I turned to it first. The piece Tracy had used to demonstrate her new comedy technique— about the woman who built the twenty-thousand-dollar doghouse—dominated the front page. To its left was what looked to be a regular entertainment column; below it was an article on the spring fashions. I turned to the inside: a personality sketch of a New York–based cartoonist, with ads below the fold. Similar arrangement on the facing page, with a horoscope and Dear Abby.

Of course Tracy might not have been looking at the View section when she saw whatever it was that had given her such a turn. Perhaps it was a straight news item.

Page four contained a continuation of the entertainment column and a cartoon strip, but a piece on page five caught my eye. Titled "Unsolved Crime of the Week," it appeared to be a regular syndicated feature describing an open police file and asking readers to contact their newspaper should they have knowledge of the perpetrator. That week's crime was a five-year-old arson-murder in Fort Meyers, Florida, on the Gulf Coast.

I skimmed the article quickly. The arson had occurred at a shopping-and-entertainment complex in the affluent resort area, at three in the morning during the height of the winter tourist season. There was no question that the fire had been set: traces of a liquid accelerant—gasoline—were found in a crawl space below the level of the blaze.

Due to the lateness of the hour, only one person had been killed. The charred remains were initially thought to be those of the complex's developer, Warren S. Howard, but a positive identification could not be made. And in the weeks that followed the fire, a number of little-known facts about Howard came to light: he was dangerously overextended and deeply in debt; several of the stores and restaurants in the complex had failed to renew their leases; he'd tried to raise capital by selling off a tract of land he owned near the Fort Meyers airport, but the growth rate in that area had not been as projected, and there were no takers; various liens against his property and lawsuits had been filed.

A real estate developer on the brink of bankruptcy. A fire.

The police began to suspect that Howard had set fire to the complex in order to fake his own death and escape his creditors. The body found in the ashes, they theorized, could have been a derelict or other person who would not be missed, whom Howard had lured inside and knocked unconscious or perhaps drugged. The theory was given further credence when Howard's wife, Melinda, who had been trying unsuccessfully to collect on his personal and business insurance, suddenly disappeared from the area. And it was confirmed when the charred remains were identified as those of an old man who had run away from a nursing home in nearby Cape Coral the previous December.

I let out my breath in a long sigh, my fingers dampening the newsprint where I grasped it.

Warren and Melinda Howard sounded like two people I knew. But how had Tracy recognized them from this account? I had tonight's fire at Café Comedie to lead me to make the connection. What had told her . . .?

And then I noticed that the piece was continued on the following page. I flipped it over, found a plea for information and a photograph of the Howards.

Melinda Howard was at least fifty: short, plump, with frizzily permed blond hair and glasses. Warren Howard looked older: his hair was white, the flesh under his eyes deeply pouched. He could have stood to lose fifty or sixty pounds.

People I'd never seen before.

I wanted to scream in frustration. It fit: a real estate developer and his wife, a near bankruptcy, a fire. It was perfect.

And all wrong.

Inside the coffee shop I could see Amy, chatting with the cashier, a take-out container in hand. My irritation level rose to the boiling point. Why was she buying something to drink when I'd told her to hurry? I leaned on the horn.

Amy looked my way, exchanged a few more pleasantries with the cashier, then came toward the door. She walked slowly, juggling her purse with the paper cup and fishing around inside it. Before she got to the car, she took out a stick of gum, unwrapped it, stuffed it into her mouth, and dropped the wrapper on the ground.

"Sorry I took so long," she said.

I gritted my teeth. Amy closed the car door, snapping her gum.

"What's that?" she asked, motioning at the paper with her cup and spilling cola on her hand.

I wanted to crumple the *Times* and hurl it behind the seat. In the interests of Rae's unborn children, I restrained myself.

Amy leaned over, snapping her gum again and breathing wintergreen on me. If she was going to make sounds like a ruminant all the way to the cottage, I'd probably throttle her.

"Hey, that's funny," she said.

"What's funny?" I elbowed her back onto her own side of the car.

"That old guy." Her finger stabbed at the photo in the paper. "He looks like he could be Rob Soriano's father."

I knocked her hand away and scrutinized the picture. Now I saw what Tracy—who had spent a great deal of time observing others—had discerned instantly. The only thing that surprised me was that Amy had caught it before I did.

The man's stiff military bearing was the same as Soriano's, as were the deep lines that bracketed his mouth. The wavy white hair could easily have been clipped short and dyed a uniform brown. The pouches under the eyes, upon closer examination, looked to be the product of heredity rather than age; such things were surgically correctable, and any irregularities could be masked by glasses. Weight could be lost, muscles toned. And Melinda, who in no way resembled Kathy? A wife who had died or been discarded.

Warren Howard *was* Rob Soriano.

Rob Soriano, not Jay Larkey, had murdered Tracy.

I folded the paper and put it back on the carrying seat. As I flicked off the dome light and started the car, I said to Amy, "I want you to watch for cops, so we don't get stopped. We need to get to the cottage in a hurry."

27

There were no cars parked in front of the Barbour place or in the turnaround where the road ended, and only one tucked into the trees by the driveway of the farthest house. Lights showed over there, but the Barbour cottage was dark. I pulled the MG next to the vine-covered fence and shut off the engine.

I said to Amy, "Are you sure Marc said he'd wait for us?"

"Where would he—oh, you mean because there're no lights. The shutters keep them from showing. We were pretty sure the cops wouldn't come by, but we left them closed just in case."

I got out of the car, motioning for her to do the same. The night was crisp, a strong wind blowing off the river. A full moon hung overhead; in its rays the vast plain belonging to the salt company looked glacial. I stood still for a moment, listening to the muted rippling of the water and rustling of vegetation. In the distance a dog howled mournfully.

Amy came up beside me; I could smell her wintergreen gum. She said, "I'm scared."

"Of what? There's no reason." But I knew why: there was a wrongness about the place, because of the evil thing that had happened here. I myself felt a chill along my backbone.

She took out a key and unlocked the padlock on the hasp, removed it, and pushed open the side of the gate whose hinges had not given way. It swung all the way back and rested against a pyracantha bush. Amy shoved it closed again and started through the thicket.

The bright moonlight helped us find our way. On the other side of the bushes I made out thin lines of light where there were gaps around the shutters on the windows overlooking the cottage's front porch. Its sagging roof was outlined against the sky, chimney slightly atilt. On the porch the dilapidated wicker furniture hunched in the shadows; the glider moved fitfully in the wind, bumping the wall behind it.

The sense of wrongness was stronger here. Reflexively I patted my shoulder bag, wishing I had my gun. In the past I'd owned two, kept one at home and the other in the glovebox of the car, which I'd had fitted with a special lock. But a few months ago, someone had broken into the MG and gotten the compartment open. Later I'd decided against replacing the gun. Now I wondered if that had been a wise decision.

Amy seemed to have banished whatever fears she'd felt, however. She hurried up the sagging steps, fitted another key into the door lock, and pushed it open. I put out a hand to restrain her, to urge caution, but she stepped inside.

Directly ahead I saw a dark brick fireplace, with a huge stuffed fish that certainly had never swum in these waters mounted on a plaque above it. A fishing rod—the old-fashioned varnished-wood kind with big metal guides for the line—leaned against the mantel, an open tackle box on the floor next to it. The ceilings were low and beamed; the floors were hardwood, covered by brown rag rugs; around the hearth stood a grouping of the sort of knotty pine and chintz-cushioned chairs often found in summer houses. A pair of floor lamps equipped with low-wattage bulbs and yellowed shades illuminated the semicircle.

Marc Emmons sat to the right of the fireplace. Amy said, "We're here!" and trotted over to him, leaving me to shut the door. When I came all the way into the room, she was standing beside his chair in a stiff, defensive posture, eyes fixed on the man who sat in the shadows across from him.

It was Rob Soriano, aka Warren S. Howard. He perched tensely on the edge of the low chair. In his right hand was a .32 revolver.

Belatedly I realized that the car I'd seen pulled under the trees farther down the road was parked at an inconvenient distance from the lighted house, but not really all that far from this cottage.

Soriano nodded at me, steel-rimmed glasses glinting. Behind them his eyes were jumpy. When he said, "Ms. McCone, I thought you'd never get here," his voice was higher pitched than usual.

I placed my hands on the back of the chair in front of me. "Have you been waiting long?"

"Less than an hour. Marc here has been trying to convince me you wouldn't show up at all, but since I'd found out that Amy was waiting for you at All Souls, I knew it would be only a matter of time."

So that had been Soriano on the phone. I'd figured the right motive for the call but the wrong caller.

I glanced at Emmons. His face was pasty and sheened with sweat, in spite of the chill in the room. He licked dry lips and said thickly, "He found out from Jay where we were and that you were going to bring her here. Why the hell'd you have to call him, Ame?"

Amy didn't reply. She was still staring at Soriano.

Oddly enough, I wasn't afraid, even though I now knew Soriano had somehow rigged the explosion at the club and probably intended to kill all of us, too. Dead calm settled over me. I dropped my shoulder bag onto the chair and thought, I'll take this slowly. Very slowly.

Emmons said to me, "Rob was there in Jay's office when your assistant called and said you'd gone to L.A. looking for Tracy. You found Lisa instead, didn't you?"

"The lead in L.A. didn't pan out," I lied. Since he'd been there, Soriano also had overheard Larkey tell Rae he'd realized there was something odd about Tracy's dental records. Blowing up a crowded nightclub seemed an extreme measure to take to prevent Jay from passing on his suspicions to the authorities, but Soriano had committed murder and arson before—maybe more than once. He couldn't be aware that I knew about his past, however. . . .

I cast a pointed look at the gun in Soriano's hand and said, "What is this, anyway? I came up here because Amy and Marc want me to help them deal with the sheriff about a minor obstruction-of-justice charge. I don't understand why you're here."

Soriano said, "I wasn't aware you were an attorney."

"I'm not. Seems they're too cheap to hire one."

He didn't respond. I glanced at Amy and Emmons, to see if they understood how I wanted to play this. Comprehension was dawning in Emmons's eyes; Amy merely flashed me a reproachful look.

Emmons said to her, "Is that what you told her, Ame? I *said* I'd be glad to pay. Why didn't you just bring one of the lawyers, honey?"

Even now nothing registered with her. She glared down at him. "That wasn't the plan—"

"Honey, it was too." To me he added, "I'm sorry she dragged you up here. Why don't you just go back to the city? We'll settle our problem with Rob and get in touch with one of the lawyers in the morning."

"Marc! I'm not staying here with him—"

"Then you go with Sharon, honey. The problem's really between Rob and me."

Soriano was observing the exchange with grim amusement. "Not too bright, is she?" he said. His meaning was clear; he saw through our charade.

Amy whirled on him, face suddenly twisted in fury. "*I'm* not too bright! Look who's talking!"

Emmons reached for her arm in a panic, but she slapped his hand away. My God, I thought, she's going to tell him off while he's got that gun in his hand!

The smile faded from Soriano's lips. "What's that supposed to mean?"

"Well, just look at you. You're dead broke—oh yeah, Marc told me all about that—and then you go and burn the club down with all those people inside, including Jay. I suppose you think you can collect on the insurance."

Soriano half rose from his chair. His face was ashen now, and his lips writhed, seemingly incapable of forming words. In that instant I realized that this was a man on the brink of coming apart. Rigging the explosion had been an act of madness, without regard to the consequences. Silencing Emmons—which undoubtedly had been his next intention—had grown complicated, now included silencing both Amy and me. He had no way of knowing what we'd told others, who else might know enough to turn suspicion on him. Soriano's world was collapsing around him, in spite of frantic efforts to shore it up.

"See how stupid you've been?" Amy said triumphantly.

Shut up, I thought. *Shut up!*

"So now who's not too bright? You should have learned from the last time."

He got himself under control, said hoarsely, "The last time?"

"Yeah, in Florida." She looked at me. "That arsonist in the newspaper picture was old Rob, all right. I always suspected his hair was dyed. He was just porkier then, and needed a facelift—"

Soriano took a step toward her. Amy retreated behind Emmons's chair. Emmons sat very still, gripping the wide armrests with whitened fingers.

Soriano said to me, "You've seen the newspaper article."

"I don't know what she's talking—"

"Don't give me that! If you hadn't seen it, the first thing you'd have mentioned when you arrived here was the fire at the club."

I didn't reply. Thanks to Amy, there was no more need for pretense.

"And I suppose," he added, "you want to turn the information over to the police—just like Tracy Kostakos."

"Was that what she planned to do?"

"You suspected blackmail instead?"

"She had her ways of getting what she wanted."

"Blackmail wasn't one of them. The girl had an incongruous moral streak when it came to crime. Marc had been trying to persuade her not to do anything for over a week before she died. But that last night she thought Jay had turned on her. She saw going to the police as a noble protective gesture toward Jay—one that might make him forgive her rather rampant promiscuity."

I watched Soriano silently. His eyes darted about the room, resting first on me, then Emmons, then Amy. A tic had developed in one of the lines that bracketed his mouth; it fluttered, was still, fluttered again. When I glanced at Emmons, he seemed frozen. Amy had finally figured the situation out; her eyes were wide with terror, and she was backing up against an old upright piano on the wall behind Marc's chair.

The peculiar calm still infused me. I stared intently into Soriano's eyes, trying to divine what his next move would be. They showed nothing but panicky purpose; there was not a trace of remorse, or distaste for what he intended to do.

I thought, This is the most evil person I have ever known. I refuse to die by this man's hand.

I said, "You haven't asked about your wife. Whether she was one of the people killed at the club."

"Was she?" He spoke almost absently.

"Yes."

I'd hoped to elicit some sort of reaction with the lie. Soriano merely said, "Too bad."

Those cold, cold words accomplished what his obvious insanity and the implied threat of death hadn't: my calm shattered. An equally icy rage rose in its place.

I waited until I could speak in a deceptively level voice. "She meant that little to you?"

"The woman was a fool. Like that one over there." He jerked his chin toward Amy. "Like the other fool in the chair. He's a prize, Marc is. I'm glad I won't have to rectify his blunders any longer. The idiot couldn't even keep from getting blood all over Kathy's car when he dumped the Kostakos girl's body. I had to lay out damn good money to convince my assistant to report it stolen from him."

At first I thought I'd heard him wrong. But I hadn't. I narrowed my eyes until my vision blurred. When I widened them, everything was clear.

I looked at Emmons. "*You* killed her."

He merely sat there, his mouth partially open.

Soriano said, "You thought *I* did?"

"Not anymore." He hadn't known that she'd been shot in the car. Or that Emmons couldn't have taken her body by car to the boat where he'd hidden it. Soriano had no reason to lie about that—not with all the other deaths he had caused. "How much did he tell you about the murder?" I asked.

"He wasn't making much sense when he came to our house afterwards. He may have discussed the details with Kathy at some point, but I didn't want to know any more than I had to."

Emmons continued to sit still. His breath wheezed faintly through his open lips. Amy stood rigid in front of the piano, her hands jammed over her mouth.

"Why?" I asked him. "Why?"

After a moment he shook his head, as if awakening from a trance. He looked at me, then at the gun in Soriano's hand. Finally he let out a sigh that was very nearly a whine. "She wouldn't agree not to go to the cops. When I called Rob at the club after she left my place that night, he promised me an immediate slot on the program if I would shut her up. So I came here and tried talking to her again, but she wouldn't listen. She tried to run out on me, so . . . ."

"Where did you get the gun?"

"I had it at home."

"Was it the one from the club?"

"Yes. I took it a week or two before."

"Why?"

He shrugged.

"You planned to kill her, didn't you?"

He rose unsteadily from his chair, big body swaying. Shook his head again. "I . . . at first I planned to kill myself. She'd left me for Jay, and I'd heard rumors about . . . others. But when this thing about Rob came up and I thought I'd have a chance at what I'd always wanted . . . well, all that was standing between me and it was Tracy."

Behind him, Amy closed her eyes and screamed, "You *bastard!*"

His clown's face twisted. "You don't understand, Ame," he said. "I *hated* her. Hated her for what she'd done to me—and what she was going to do to me. It was my life, and she was just going to crumple it up and toss it away."

Amy began to sob, slumping against the piano's keyboard. Chords crashed dissonantly.

Emmons took a step toward her, stumbled and lurched back toward Soriano. Soriano brought the gun up.

Emmons slewed around, saw it, lost his head, and lunged. I darted inside the semicircle of chairs, intent on getting my hands on the .32.

Soriano shoved Emmons away. His big body crashed into mine, knocking me toward the fireplace. He fell back against his chair.

As he lay there panting, Soriano shot him in the head.

28

Emmons's left eye became a ragged, bloody hole. He slumped back in the chair, limbs twitching.

Amy screamed and ran toward the door.

My rage flashed from cold to white hot. As Soriano raised the .32 at Amy's fleeing form, I grabbed the fishing pole that leaned against the mantel. Swung it up and slashed it down on his gun hand.

He howled and dropped the .32. Whirled. Lunged at me.

I swung the pole again. It caught him a glancing blow on the temple. The metal line guide left a bleeding track on his cheek.

I whipped the pole back, brought it down on his shoulder. He staggered, bent over, looking for the gun.

I whacked him on the small of the back. He gave a high-pitched scream. Then he bolted for the door. I went after him. He got the door open before I could hit him again, and ran outside. By the time I reached the porch, he had disappeared into the pyracantha thicket.

Behind me Amy sobbed hysterically. I turned, saw she was lying on the floor in a fetal position, arms wrapped around her knees. Ignoring her, I dropped the pole and hurried back to the semicircle of chairs to check on Emmons. He was dead.

I felt none of the things that I'd come to expect when confronted with violent death—nothing but the rage, burning dangerously high now. Dropping to all fours, I located the gun under the chair Soriano had sat in. Then I ran back outside.

The branches of the pyracanthas had stopped rustling. I listened, but heard no footfall, no car engine. Cautiously I made my way to the gate; it was closed, as Amy had left it. I looked down the road. The car was still parked under the trees. I could make out its shape now: it looked to be the Jaguar that I'd seen parked in the Sorianos' driveway the previous noon.

Why was it still here? Soriano had had ample time to get to the car and drive away. Then I thought, No, he doesn't want to leave witnesses to his murder of Emmons. I suspected he was hiding nearby, recovering from the blows I'd dealt him, waiting for another chance at Amy and me.

I wanted to go hunting him, but I couldn't leave Amy alone; that would be inviting him to kill her or take her hostage. And I couldn't summon help; the cottage had no phone. But there was another way. . . .

I hurried back to the cottage. Amy was still lying on the floor, her sobs diminished to whimpers now. I knelt and placed a gentle hand on her shoulder.

She thrashed around in sudden panic, making a protesting sound. "Amy," I said, "it's me. Soriano's gone."

After a few seconds she opened her eyes and peered at me from under her drooping petals of hair. "Gone?"

"Yes. He can't hurt you."

She unwrapped her arms from her knees and struggled to sit up. "Marc?"

"He's—" I hesitated. "We need to get help."

"Marc killed Trace. He *killed* her!"

"Don't think about that now."

"That's why he sent me for you. He was going to confess, wasn't he?"

"Probably. Everything was closing in on him." I went to where my bag sat on the chair, rummaged around until I found my Swiss Army knife, and jammed it into the pocket of my coat. Then I got her to her feet, turning her so she couldn't see his body. "Let's go."

She looked down, saw the gun in my hand, and shuddered. I said, "It's okay. He's unarmed. I'll protect us."

Slowly she nodded. I put my arm around her shoulders and led her to the door, gripping the .32 in my other hand.

When we reached the gate, I peered through it; the Jaguar was still there. I stood for a minute, looking up and down the road, debating which way to go. There were no lights in the houses in the row that extended back toward the railroad bridge, but through the trees at the far end of the turnaround, the lights I'd glimpsed earlier were still on. I guided Amy through the gate, and we set off, straight down the middle of the road, where we couldn't be ambushed from the shrubbery.

Moonlight fell on the rutted pavement and the plain belonging to the salt company; once again I was reminded of an ice floe on the barren terrain. The air was chill, and a strong wind whipped tree branches about; their soughing was punctuated by snaps and thumps in the underbrush. Warped phantom shapes darted through the shadows to the side of the road, vanishing as quickly as they appeared. My gaze pursued the fleeting images, but they eluded it in the dark.

I kept my arm firmly around Amy's shoulders, the gun ready, and led her along.

We had almost reached the turnaround when there was a loud tearing sound. Amy cried out as a jagged tree limb crashed to the pavement inches from us. I spun, bringing the gun up, peering into the underbrush. Nothing but shifting lines and shadows.

I reached for Amy, grasped her elbow. Whispered, "Just the wind, that's all."

"I'm scared."

"It's only a little farther."

We kept on, to where Soriano's car was parked. Now my own tension heightened, and I searched the darkness to see if he might be lurking close to his means of escape. I saw no one, heard nothing.

Beyond the car was a narrow dirt track leading through a grove of trees toward the lighted house. Amy and I turned in there. The underbrush was close on either side now. The shifting, sighing branches created a babble that would mask all but the loudest of sounds. When I looked around, the phantom-shapes danced and leaped, playing tricks on my eyes.

I said to Amy, "Let's walk faster now," and hurried her along.

When the track emerged from the grove, it meandered across a large area of cleared land. The house was perhaps fifty yards away. I waited until we were well in the open before stopping, then scanned the terrain on all sides of us. No one was in sight. Over by the house a dog began barking; it must have been chained up, because it didn't come running out to see who was there.

Amy stood beside me, silent and motionless. I looked at her and realized she was no longer afraid. The slickness of her mouth and the sluggish way she moved her eyes told me she was operating automatically now, her emotions shut down. She didn't question why we'd stopped, just waited quietly.

I studied her face, pallid in the moonlight, wondering if she was enough in touch with her surroundings to do what I had in mind for her. Finally I decided that her trancelike state might work to my advantage.

I said, "Amy, I need your help now."

She nodded.

"He's out here somewhere. He may get away if I don't find him. I need you to go on to that house alone."

She looked over at the lights as if measuring the distance to them.

"I'll be right here," I added. "With the gun. He won't come near you anyway, not with other people so close."

After a moment she nodded again.

"When you get to the house, tell the people to call nine-eleven."

"Nine-eleven."

"Tell them there's been a homicide, we need the sheriff's department."

"Homicide. The sheriff."

"Then just stay there."

She looked toward the lights again. Took a deep breath and squared her shoulders.

"Can you do that?" I asked.

"I can do it." She hesitated a few seconds longer, then took off at a run.

I watched her go, gun raised, should Soriano suddenly appear. She ran awkwardly, arms flailing, but she didn't falter. When she reached the house, she pounded on the door. After it opened and she disappeared inside, I turned away.

Then I went after him.

I crouched by the right front tire of the Jaguar and stabbed at it with the Swiss Army knife's largest blade. I'd never slashed a tire before; it was more difficult than I'd imagined. But after working at it for half a minute, I made a slit. The air hissed out, and the car began to settle onto the wheel rim.

Soriano wasn't going anywhere now.

I stood, jamming the knife back into my pocket. He was still somewhere close by, of that I was certain.

But where?

Not beyond the turnaround; I'd have spotted him if he was. Not on the property belonging to the salt company; it was fenced in barbed wire, possibly patrolled. He wouldn't have gone down the road, either; the houses were too numerous, packed too close together.

So he had to be somewhere behind the Barbour cottage.

I gripped the gun and started off, intent on searching every inch of ground between here and the river.

I stood at the edge of the grove of pepper trees behind the cottage. The rush of the river's water was louder here. I strained to hear other sounds through the sighing of the trees; there were only typical night noises.

Between the grove and the levee the land was barren and moon washed. If Soriano was hiding somewhere out there, he would spot me easily when I crossed it. But if he broke cover and tried to run, I'd have the advantage.

I ran across the ground and up to the top of the levee.

Moonlight sheened the water. The river moved swiftly, swollen by the recent rain. The falling-down dock shivered with the strong current. The wind blew steadily, tossing the branches of the willow tree that sheltered the derelict fishing boat. I stared at it. Saw a movement in the shadows. A different sort of movement than that of the tree's drooping limbs.

Soriano had found Tracy's gravesite.

I stopped close to the willow, stood with my feet apart, gun braced. It had taken minutes to make my approach, shielded by the hump of the levee. Another minute to slip down here. By now he knew I'd found him.

"Soriano!" I shouted. "Come on out."

Silence. Then a faint, unidentifiable sound from the boat.

"Soriano!"

He was waiting for me to try to take him.

I stayed where I was, listening for sirens. Nothing. More than half an hour now since I'd left Amy. How much longer would it take?

A scraping sound from the boat. A thump.

It was probably a ploy to get me onto the boat, into close quarters with him. Perhaps he underestimated me, thought I didn't know how to use the gun properly. That was a common fault of men like Soriano—to underestimate others, particularly women.

Slowly I started toward the boat.

A few of the planks had been tossed on the ground by the lab crew that removed Tracy's remains, but otherwise it looked the same as when I'd first seen it. I climbed carefully onto its side.

"Soriano, save us both a lot of trouble and give up."

No reply. No more telltale sounds.

I moved forward toward the collapsed pilot house, testing my footing with each step. The hatch cover was back over the opening in the rotten planking. I was certain the lab crew would not have replaced it.

I went closer. Studied it. Extended my right foot and nudged it. It didn't budge.

I braced myself against one of the pilot house's support beams, worked the toe of my boot under the cover's edge. Kicked upward.

The cover fell back with a crash. The musty odor of the grave rose to my nostrils.

Extending the gun at the opening, I leaned forward. Looked down at Rob Soriano.

He looked back at me, unspeaking. Something seemed wrong with one of his eyes; then I realized the lens of his glasses was cracked. Blood trickled from the gash in his cheek. His mouth twisted violently, and he recoiled.

I'd expected Soriano to crack eventually, and he had. Now he was terrified.

As I stared down at him, I felt nothing but the rage—cold and steady again.

I could shoot him point-blank, I thought. The way he shot Emmons. *Should* shoot him. No sense in letting this evil man live. No sense in going through the motions of arrest, trial, imprisonment, even execution, because it won't make any difference.

He moved a fraction of an inch. My hands tensed on the .32. I'd claim self-defense.

I could hear the sirens now, distant but clear in the still night. Dogs began to howl in imitation of them.

Soriano moved again, farther back into the boat's hull. Moonlight filtered through the wind-whipped branches of the willow, rays glinting coldly off the cracked lens of his glasses.

Self-defense, I thought again.

The sirens came closer.

Give me a reason to pull this trigger. Any reason.

Sirens down near the railroad bridge now. Screaming along the row of cottages. I moved closer to the opening in the planking, gun extended.

Sirens cutting off, back at the Barbour cottage. Men's voices shouting.

Soriano moved frantically, slipped on the exposed ribwork.

I raised the gun and fired a single shot.

Into the air, so they'd know where to find us.

29

The visiting area at San Quentin seemed more cheerful on a Saturday. Perhaps it was the fact that so many children were there; dressed in go-see-Daddy finery, with freshly scrubbed faces, they imparted an air of normalcy and hope. Or perhaps it had something to do with knowing this would be my last trip here—for a long time, if not ever. It certainly had a lot to do with the joy on Leora Whitsun's face as we waited to see Bobby.

I hadn't wanted to come; I didn't want to hear thanks, and I didn't want to answer questions. But Leora had insisted, and there I was.

This time there wasn't much of a wait, and the desk officer actually smiled at us when we identified ourselves. The guard who led us to the small, spare visiting room said to me, "Nice going." The case had been featured prominently in both local and national news; anonymity would be in short supply for a while.

After the guard locked us in, Leora sighed and looked around. "How many more times do I have to sit here and stare at these four walls?"

"Not many. Maybe none. There are legal formalities, but Jack's set them in motion. There's been too much media attention for anyone to drag his feet."

"It'll be good having my boy home again." She sat, smoothed her denim skirt. "Home won't be the projects, either."

"No?"

"Nope. I found me an apartment. Near the clinic. Not much of an apartment, but it'll be *home*." She nodded emphatically, gold earrings bouncing to reinforce her words.

The door on the other side of the grille opened. Bobby entered.

211

212 / MARCIA MULLER

His stiff, defensive posture was gone, replaced by a long, loose stride. He was free—almost.

"Sharon," he said, "I'm so happy Mama talked you into coming. I got to thank you for everything you done." He came up to the table that bisected the room and placed the palms of his hands flat against the grille.

I leaned forward and placed my hands on my side of it, so we could touch. "You don't have to thank me."

"Well, I do."

He sat in his wooden chair, and I sat in mine.

For a moment there was an awkward silence. Bobby's eyes clouded and he said, "That motherfucker Emmons killed her."

Beside me, Leora clicked her tongue in disapproval.

"Right name for him, Mama."

"Maybe so. I got no call to correct you, anyway. You went in here a child, you're coming out a man."

He nodded brusque thanks at her, trying not to show how much her words pleased him.

I said, "Emmons killed her, I think, because he had really envied and hated her for some time. She had everything he wanted: talent and the ability to make her own opportunities."

"That what you call what she did to me and Lisa and Jay—makin' her own opportunities?"

I'd thought a good bit about Tracy over the past day and a half. Now I said, "She was young and greedy, and she used very poor judgment. That's a reason, Bobby, not an excuse."

"Ain't they the same thing?"

"I don't think so, not really. An excuse removes blame; you realize a person's not guilty of wrongdoing, and you forgive them. A reason just tells you why they did what they did; then you have to work at forgiving."

"Never thought about it that way." He stared at the scarred tabletop for a moment. "Guess I do forgive her. I had a lot of time to work on it in here."

There was a silence. I sensed all three of us were entertaining private thoughts about Tracy Kostakos, about what was forgivable and what wasn't. Finally Leora said, "What about Rob Soriano? Jack Stuart says there's no way to prove he set that fire and killed Jay and all those other people."

The death toll from the fire had climbed to seven; Larkey was among them. The arson squad had found fragments of what might have been a simple, timed incendiary device in the club, placed in such a position as to take advantage of the persistent gas leak from the furnace line. Soriano had probably counted on the blast destroying the apparatus completely, and that had nearly happened. There was not enough left to reconstruct it, and no evidence as yet that the fragments had ever been in Soriano's possession. Had his past in Florida not come to light, he would possibly have escaped suspicion; too many people were aware of the gas leak and PG&E's seeming inability to repair it properly.

Soriano, of course, had admitted nothing.

I said, "It's a long shot. And the Florida arson can't be used as evidence, because other charges pending against a defendant aren't admissible. They could allow extradition to Florida, but the case there isn't all that strong, either. But they've got him for murdering Marc Emmons. Amy Barbour and I are eyewitnesses."

"What about his wife?" Bobby asked. "She know anything?"

"Quite a lot. Kathy's willing to testify to him being an accessory after the fact to Tracy's murder, in exchange for immunity from prosecution."

I'd visited Kathy that morning at the clinic where her personal physician had had her admitted—more to satisfy my curiosity about certain things than out of charitable impulse. She'd already spoken with the district attorney and talked freely to me about how she and Rob had helped Emmons fake the kidnapping in exchange for his silence.

At first, Kathy said, they had only intended to create confusion around Tracy's disappearance, patterning the ransom note on the wording in Bobby's notebook to make it seem the kidnappers were poorly educated. The idea of framing him occurred to Rob the next week when Kathy relayed what Lisa McIntyre knew about Tracy's relationship with Bobby. But Lisa's knowledge also had the potential to cause all sorts of complications, so they decided it was best to pay her way out of town.

Kathy also admitted to helping Emmons move the Volvo from the cottage to the mountains about two weeks after the killing. Her switch of the dental records on New Year's Day, the bogus phone calls to Laura, the marked-up book that Emmons planted in the apartment—all of those things were last-ditch ploys to preserve the fiction that Tracy had disappeared of her own volition.

Leora said, "How could that woman have married such scum? She must be as bad as he is."

"She's pretty bad. But she claims she wasn't aware of his past until Emmons showed up after killing Tracy and blurted out about

214 / MARCIA MULLER

the newspaper article. I tend to believe her; it's turned out that Soriano established an elaborate phony background for himself and took measures to ensure he wouldn't have to appear at public functions or get his picture in the papers."

"Still, she'd have to be pretty dumb or pretty evil not to go to the cops once she knew. Didn't she realize he'd probably kill somebody else? Or set another fire?"

"She says Rob promised her nothing like that would ever happen again." I didn't know if she was telling the truth or not, but the memory of her repetition of the words "he promised" during her crippling hysterics at the scene of the fire made me lean toward accepting what she claimed.

"Well, in my book she was stupid to believe the man. And him—for somebody who's supposed to be such a smart high-roller, he's really kind of stupid, too."

"I think what he is is shrewd, but with an overblown idea of his own capabilities. His kind often conceive grandiose schemes, but then they get tripped up by details. That's what happened in Florida. This time, though, he won't be able to disappear and start over somewhere else."

Bobby bared his teeth in something that didn't even pretend to be a smile. "Never thought I'd say it, but I'm glad they got the death penalty in this state."

I remembered my primitive, near murderous rage as I'd stood over Soriano on the derelict fishing boat, gun in hand. "I know what you mean," I said.

Late that afternoon I stopped by All Souls to put my desk in order. A bunch of people were sitting around the living room eating pizza: Rae, Jack, Ted, Hank, Anne-Marie. Even the health nut was there; his purge of the kitchen must be over, because he was sucking on a beer. They all wore grubby work clothes and seemed in a festive mood.

Rae waved at me. "Come join our moving party!"

I went only as far as the archway. "Who moved?"

"Well, first Hank did. Then we picked up some furniture I bought at Junk Emporium and dragged it up to my new room."

I looked at Hank in confusion. He was sitting on the couch with Anne-Marie, his arm around her shoulders.

Anne-Marie said, "Don't panic; it's not a big deal. The Andersons vacated our upstairs flat three weeks early. Hank and I talked it over and decided we can't live together but don't want to live apart. So he moved upstairs, I'm staying down. We're extending one another liberal visiting privileges, of course."

"Of course." Although it sounded somewhat bizarre on the surface, it struck me as a sensible arrangement.

"Why don't you have some pizza?" Ted said. "There's plenty—even anchovy."

"Sorry—I have a dinner date, and I'm running behind schedule."

Rae smiled knowingly; she'd suspected all along that something was developing between George and me. Jack looked glum and reached for another slice of pizza. I grabbed a beer out of one of the six-packs on the table and went up to my office.

When I arrived home, there was a note from the contractor taped to my front door. He'd finished work on the new bedroom, it said, and had locked up. He'd be by the next afternoon with the extra keys, to pick up the final payment on our contract.

I hurried inside and inspected his work. It looked great. All I needed to do now was paint, lay carpet, and install miniblinds. Then, I decided, I'd invite the All Souls's moving crew over to help me haul my bedroom furniture back there. Afterward I'd feed them spaghetti, or maybe lasagna.

But right now I needed to get ready for my date with George. I wanted to look particularly good, because I felt apprehensive about it. Too many things had been left unsaid between us over the last few days. Tonight we would have to say them all.

30

It was a drizzly night in February, nearly two years to the day since Tracy Kostakos died. South Park was shrouded in mist; it hazed the street lamps and softened the ragged outlines of the burnt-out ruin that once had been Café Comedie. A casual passerby, new to this place, might not even notice it, much less guess at the tragedy that had been played out here.

I'd come, as I often did these days, to walk in the park. The ground still bore scars where the ambulances had driven, but frequent rains had begun to heal them, bringing fresh blades of grass. Soon other reminders would go; eventually there would be none at all.

I walked with my head bent forward, hands thrust in my pockets, barely noticing the damp. The park was familiar territory now; I came here so often that the old black men who congregated on the benches on nice days were starting to think of me as a regular. One of them had waved to me the other afternoon.

If anyone had asked me why I kept returning to this place, I would have been hard pressed to give an answer. It had something to do with trying to make sense of it all, but I didn't expect anyone else to understand that—because I didn't really understand it myself.

Trying to make sense of Tracy Kostakos, whose greed for everything the world has to offer had destroyed both her talent and her life.

Trying to make sense of Marc Emmons, who had allowed himself to be used until love turned to hatred, hatred to violence.

Trying to make sense of the evil at the core of Rob Soriano, and the primitive rage it had triggered in me.

There was senselessness, too, in the fact that Bobby Foster, although innocent, was still incarcerated, due to the ponderously slow machinations of our criminal justice system.

Senselessness in the fact that George wasn't with me.

That Saturday night he'd sat across from me in a North Beach restaurant, candlelight showing new lines of pain etched into his rough-hewn face. Held my hand as he told me he was moving back to the Palo Alto house, to be near Laura while she remained in the psychiatric clinic and, later, to support her when she was discharged as an outpatient.

"It won't be forever," he'd said, "but it's something I have to do. I owe it to her. To myself. In a way, to you."

I shook my head, unable to comprehend.

"I know I can't ask you to wait for me," he added. "I don't see why you would. But when it's all over, when she's on her feet again, I'll come to you, see if you'll still have me."

"We could just—"

"I know what you're going to say. I can't do that to either of us. You shouldn't have to share a burden that's really mine alone; I couldn't stand to always be leaving you with the knowledge that I'd be going home to another woman."

"So what . . .?"

"When I've worked this out, we'll see if you want to start again. I know I will."

He was an honorable man, George Kostakos. But sometimes on cold, lonely nights, I cursed him for that honor. And when I was feeling particularly low, I wondered if his scruples would have remained intact had I not been the one who exposed the sad truth about his daughter's life and death.

The drizzle was turning to real rain now. I ignored it, turned up my collar, kept walking. South Park was silent, deserted. A pall had settled over it these days, thick as the pall of the smoke from the fire. I wondered if it would ever come alive again. If I would.

A car turned in from Third Street. Its headlights blinded me. I shielded my eyes, waiting for it to pass.

It pulled to the curb a couple of yards away from me. A voice said, "Hey, lady, want a ride?"

Rae, in her old Rambler American.

I went over and leaned down, looking through the window at her. "What are you doing here?"

"Detective work. I followed you. I've followed you here several times now. Don't you think you ought to give it up?"

"Give what up?"

She gestured out the window at the park. "All of this. The past. Get on with your life."

Normally I would have been furious at such interference. But suddenly I knew that this was the one person who did understand. At least as much as I did.

"What we're going to do," she went on, "is go get some Thai food. I found a great new restaurant. Cheap, too."

"Rae—"

"Then there's this little club, way out by the beach. Jazz. I'm friends with the drummer. The piano player's interesting; you'll like him."

"Rae, no fix-ups."

"It's not a fix-up. We'll just stop in, have a few drinks. I usually get them on the house. If we stay till closing, they'll take us out for burgers—Clown Alley's open twenty-four hours—and Jim—that's the piano player—knows of this ferry service that runs bay cruises all night long, even in the rain."

I started to say no. Hesitated. Looked back over my shoulder at the park, cold and sodden in the darkness. Straightened and looked over the roof of the car at the deeply shadowed ruins of Café Comedie.

"Why the hell not?" I said.

Rae was right: it was time to get on with it.